To [illegible]

MADDOX...

By Eva Carmichael

Best Wishes

Eva Carmichael

First Edition

Nitere Publishing: ISBN 978-1-9998113-4-1

Also Available on Kindle: ISBN 978-1-9998113-5-8

Cover Design by Chris Hart

1EDCHAMZ2408

Acknowledgements

Once more, grateful thanks to Chris and Tracey for their help and guidance in publishing this book. They've both worked tirelessly and have done a fantastic job. Thank you.

Jane provided input into the book as my beta reader this time. Her suggestions and advice have been invaluable. Thank you.

As always, Billy and Judy have gone out of their way to enable me to promote my work on Redcar Market. Also, Jackie and Helen at The Gypsy Rover have been brilliant selling the books on my behalf in the pub. Sincere thanks to all of you.

A big thank you also to my husband, Derek, who's still providing the tea, coffee and occasional wine, and thank you also to my family for their continued encouragement.

Last, but by no means least, I would like to thank the people of Redcar and surrounding area who have bought my books over the last few years. The wonderful comments of support I have received make all the hard work worthwhile.

Sincerest thanks to all of you.

PROLOGUE

Karl,

Hope you and Paul are both keeping well and managing to keep out of trouble. It's been almost a year since you fucked off to god knows where. I still think you're being over cautious having me forward my letters through my brother-in-law, Henri in Paris. Still, you can't be too careful I suppose.

Everything here in Leeds is going like clockwork, just like you said it would. That bastard policeman who was chasing you has been taken care of thanks to Spud's handiwork. I'll tell you about that when we meet. You'll piss yourself laughing!

Geoffrey Lawrence died in a fire at his house three weeks after you left. Everything was destroyed, including his computer, so there's no trace left of that damned book he was writing.

By the way, Cupid's Angels is continuing to expand. The money's rolling in. Molly and Julia are running the day-to-day business, still based at the same place as before. We've got girls in twelve cities now. All the money has been put in your overseas account, just like you asked.

So you see, there's no reason you can't get your arse back to Leeds. A warrant was never issued for your arrest, and even if it had been, there's no evidence to link you to anything. That's all been taken care of as well.

Lenny and Danny send their best. By the way, I know this is going to sound crazy, but those two are actually a couple now. Can you believe it? I never knew Lenny was into blokes.

Come home, boss. It's safe, you have my word. We all miss you being around. Things just aren't the same.

Your loyal friend,

Simon

1

Karl read and re-read the letter.

"That from Si?" Paul asked as he drained the last of his beer from the glass.

Karl remained silent, staring at the sheet of paper in his hand.

"Is everything alright? Not bad news, is it?"

Karl stood up, passed the letter to Paul and strode purposefully to the window. Looking out at the breathtaking view of the Caribbean, even the cool turquoise sea could not soothe his restlessness.

He sighed deeply. "I think it's time to go home. I don't know about you but I'm getting bored with Playa El Yaque."

Paul scowled as he studied the letter. "I'm not. I like it here."

Karl strode over to the drinks cabinet and poured himself a large whisky. "What you mean is you like the endless totty."

Paul laughed. "Well, yeah, there is that I suppose, but I'm getting a taste for the soft life. Nothing to do but soak up the sun, eat, drink and then hit the nightlife."

Karl sipped at the whisky and slowly shook his head. "Suit yourself," he said. "I'm giving Roger a call to make arrangements. I've still got the house. You could stay with me until you find a place of your own. There's plenty of room."

Paul sat bolt upright. "Karl, you're not serious about going back? You'll be risking getting banged up for years."

"You've read Simon's letter. Everything's been taken care of."

"Fuck Simon's letter. You're wanted for murder, don't forget. They'll come after you as soon as you step off the plane."

"Not without evidence they won't. Simon says the copper's been taken care of."

"I think you've had too much sun. It's affected your brain. Besides, what about Patrick Flynn. He's still out there."

"He's hiding out here just like we are."

"Except he's had the good sense to have his face changed. He's barely recognisable now."

"You and I know what he looks like. That's all that matters."

"What do you think he's up to? He's backwards and forwards like a yo-yo. Where do you think he goes?"

"How the fuck do I know? He's obviously up to something, that's for sure."

"So you're just going to leave it at that?"

"Patrick Flynn has been hauled up less than ten miles away for the past year. He hasn't clocked we're here and that's fine by me."

"Flynn's dangerous. Once you stick your head over the parapet he'll come after you. You know he will."

"If he does, I'll be ready. You worry too much, Paul. Anyway, we'll be back in England soon."

“I still think you’re mad going back. What about Joe? He saw what you did to that tart. He spilt his guts out to the police, remember?”

“Let me worry about Joe. Now, make your mind up. Are you staying here or should I ask Roger to make arrangements for two?”

2

Simon was in the lounge when the two women wearing blue and white tabards entered the room.

"Everything's done," said the older of the two women. "We've made up the beds and put clean towels in the bathroom."

"Did you stock the fridge like I asked?"

"I went to Tesco this morning," the younger woman said. "I got everything you asked for."

Simon handed each woman a brown envelope. "Good. Here's the money we agreed. I've put a little extra in for your discretion."

The older woman frowned. "Discretion? I don't understand."

"It's for keeping your mouth shut. You were never here. Understand?"

"Come on Liz," the younger woman said, tugging at her companion's coat. "Let's go."

Liz sniffed and putting the envelope in her coat pocket, turned to leave. "We can come back again next week if you want," she said. "We have Wednesday free."

"That won't be necessary. I can take it from here."

"Alright, if you're sure, but it's no trouble." She opened her bag and took out a card, handing it to Simon. "If you change your mind, give us a call." Simon took the card and walked towards the lounge door, followed by the women.

"It's alright, love. We can see ourselves out."

Both women hurried through the hall and out onto the herringbone tiled drive.

"What do you think that was about, Sue?" Liz said, once they were out on the street. "That bloke looks a bit shifty to me. Who do you think he's expecting? The Queen Mother?"

Sue giggled. "I don't think he's shifty, I think he's sexy."

"You think every man's sexy."

"Only the good-looking ones, and you've got to admit, Simon is good-looking."

"I still think there's something dodgy. That place hadn't been lived in for months."

"You do know who the house belongs to?"

"No. Who?"

"Karl Maddox."

"What, the bloke who owned all the clubs? I thought he was dead."

"No, of course he isn't. My sister used to work at The Emerald before Karl sold it."

"Do you think he's on his way back to Leeds?"

Sue huffed. "Who knows? Kelly said you don't mess with a bloke like Karl Maddox. He's dangerous."

Liz turned her head, looking back at the house. "If that bloke doesn't want anyone to know about Karl coming back, you can bet they're up to no good."

"That's none of our business, Liz. Now hurry up or we'll miss the bus into town."

3

It was ten o'clock that night when the Mercedes, driven by Simon, pulled up in front of the house. Karl Maddox was in the front passenger seat and Paul Borowicz was sat in the back.

"Well, here we are," Simon said smiling. "Home, sweet home."

Paul yawned his indifference as, getting out of the car, he joined Simon and Karl in the front porch.

Simon opened the front door. "I've had the house thoroughly cleaned and the fridge has been stocked."

Karl sniffed. "I hope you've got plenty of Macallan."

"Don't worry, boss. There's a full case."

"Good man," Karl strode through the hall into the lounge, followed by his two companions.

"It's good to have you back," Simon said, once they had settled into the luxurious lounge suite. "You too, Paul. The place just hasn't been the same."

Karl scoffed. "So you keep saying, in fact I think that's probably the fourth time since you picked us up at the docks."

Simon grinned. "Sorry boss, it's just... well, it's just good to have you back." He got up and hurried over to the drinks cabinet. "I bet you're ready for a decent drink, eh, Karl?"

Karl nodded. "You bet." Then you can tell me everything that's been going on whilst we've been away."

Simon busied himself with the drinks, handing one to Karl and then Paul, before pouring one for himself.

Karl lit a cigar and settled back into the couch, giving a satisfied sigh as the aroma from the cigar filled the air. "Did you arrange for a meeting with Beauchamp like I asked?"

"Ah, there's a problem there I'm afraid. Jeramiah Beauchamp retired six months ago."

Karl snorted. "Retired? Why has he done that? He's only a couple of years older than me."

Simon supressed a smile. "From what I've heard, he's living in the Isle of Wight and spends most of his time sailing."

"The man's an idiot. Retirement will kill him. You'll see. I bet he's dead within five years."

Simon shrugged. "Beauchamp did recommend his niece, Gina. She's taken over from him at the firm. I've made you an appointment with her at two o'clock the day after tomorrow."

"Is she any good?"

"Beauchamp assures me Gina is excellent at her job. She was the solicitor who got Alex his divorce."

"Oh, so Alex has finally got rid of that bitch, has he? Have you been keeping an eye on him like I asked?"

"Yes, of course. Your boy's doing alright for himself. He completed his retraining and is working at the Leeds General Infirmary in A&E."

"That's something I suppose."

"You know Christina is in Australia with Matthew? They had a baby, a little boy five months ago. They've called him Andrew."

Paul began to chuckle. "Congratulations, grandad."

Karl ignored his remark. "What about Lisa? I take it she's still living with them?"

"Yeah. She lives in the spare room."

Karl sighed. "I don't understand why Matthew went to Australia in the first place. They had a good life here."

"I think he decided to go after his mother died."

"Lydia's dead?"

"About a month after you left. She had another breakdown and got sent to the looney bin again. Rumour is she overdosed on pills, but officially it was a heart attack."

Karl snorted. "It was that bitch that caused all the trouble. If she hadn't started raking up the past with Geoffrey Lawrence..."

"Well you can forget about all that business. Lawrence is dead. There was a fire at his house. Everything was destroyed, including his computer, so that's the end of his damned book."

"How did the fire start?"

Simon shrugged. "Who knows? A discarded cigarette, an electrical fault?"

Karl arched an eyebrow. "Or somebody pouring petrol through the letterbox?"

"Nothing so crude. It's been officially recorded as accidental."

“Let’s hope so. I don’t want that shit at my door.”

“Stop worrying. The guy knew what he was doing. And look on the bright side, the problem has been solved. That’s what you wanted, wasn’t it?”

Paul got to his feet. “I’m whacked,” he said, suppressing a yawn. “I haven’t had a decent kip in nearly a week.”

“Yeah, me too. I think we’ll continue this later.”

“Okay, boss,” Simon said, walking towards the hallway. “I’ll call in tomorrow with Danny and Lenny. They can fill you in with everything else that’s been happening.”

“Goodnight, Si, and thanks for everything.”

“Goodnight, boss. See you tomorrow.”

4

Karl awoke at eight o'clock the following morning. The sky was grey with low hanging clouds threatening to rupture at any minute. A howling wind gave testament that winter was on its way. Looking through the window he scowled. "Welcome to England," he muttered.

He quickly showered and dressed before going down to the kitchen. Paul was already at the table with a plate of bacon and eggs in front of him.

"'Morning, Karl," he said cheerily. "Sleep well?"

Karl responded with a grunt as he poured himself a coffee from the cafetiere.

"Your breakfast's in the microwave," Paul said, biting into a slice of toast.

"No thanks. I'll just have coffee."

The two men remained silent for a few minutes. It was Karl who spoke first.

"I've got Laverick coming over later."

Paul put down his toast. "What for? You're not planning any more trips, are you?"

"No, nothing like that." Karl encircled the coffee cup with both hands. "I've decided to get The Emerald back."

"Why? You don't need to work. You can afford to live here like a king."

Karl banged his fist on the table. "I didn't come back to sit on my arse," he ranted. "I was forced out by that bastard Lawrence and that damned policeman sticking their noses into my business. Well, their noses have now been cut off now, so I'm free to carry on. I want The Emerald and I mean to get it."

Before Paul could respond the doorbell rang.

"That'll be Si and the guys," He got up from the table and hurried towards the front door. A minute later he returned followed by Simon, Danny and Lenny.

Danny rushed over to Karl and threw his arms around him in a man hug. "Good to have you back, Karl," he beamed. "You're looking great."

"Yeah, yeah," Karl said as he wriggled free. "Hope you lot have been keeping out of trouble while I've been away."

Danny gave a mischievous wink. "Of course I have. By the way, Karl, you'll never guess what. Me and Lenny have bought a pub over in Elland."

"Oh?"

"It's a... it's a gentlemen's club."

Simon grinned, shaking his head. "It's a gay bar. They've called it Bar Dalziel."

"D and L?"

"No, not D and L. It's Dalziel, like the cop show. Dalziel and Pascoe."

Karl raised an eyebrow. "You've called your pub after a cop? I don't believe it."

Lenny poured himself a coffee. "Are you back for good now, boss?"

"That's the idea," he said, "Now, I need to know everything that's been happening whilst I've been gone."

Lenny took a deep breath. "Well, for a start The Emerald has been closed down by the cops. They got a tipoff that drugs were being dealt in there. They couldn't believe their luck with what they found."

Danny began to chuckle. "That Laverick bloke didn't have a clue. I couldn't believe how easy it was to plant the drugs."

"Did you know Laverick has changed the name of the club?" Danny asked. "He's called it 'The Empire Club."

Karl scowled. "The Empire Club? What sort of a name is that?"

"That's not all. The Sapphire is now The Imperial Club."

Karl turned to Simon. "Did you stay on working in Sheffield like I asked?"

"Yeah, I'd no choice. There's not much work about."

"The good news is you can pack in working there. I'll have something for you very soon."

"That would be great. Laverick's a proper twat to work for. He doesn't have a clue about running a club."

"What about the Topaz? What's Laverick done to that?"

"The Topaz has been turned into a restaurant. It's called 'Roger's Bar & Grill'."

"And the Amathyst?"

"Laverick sold that and the casino to some Russian bloke soon after you left. Made a pile, so I heard."

Lenny sipped his coffee. "The best thing though was when Spud planted hardcore kiddy porn in

Inspector Wilson's computer. He's got sent down for it."

"Wilson's in jail?"

Lenny began to chuckle. "Yeah. He got eight years. Spud did a great job with the computer and I managed to get into his flat and hide hardcore videos and magazines. By the time we'd finished the poor bastard didn't have a leg to stand on."

The doorbell rang.

"I'll get it," Lenny said, hurrying into the hall. "It'll probably be Spud."

The door opened and a smiling Lenny came into the kitchen, followed by a petite young woman dressed from head to foot in black. Her short, spikey hair was a vibrant shade of purple and her pale, oval face bore several silver piercings.

"This is my cousin," he said proudly, placing his arm affectionately around her slender shoulders. "Spud, this is Karl Maddox."

Spud gave a slight nod of acknowledgement but remained silent.

Lenny pushed her forward slightly. "Tell Karl how you fixed that copper, Spud. Go on, tell him."

"I understand I owe you a debt of gratitude, young lady," Karl said.

Spud shrugged. "Oh, it was easy," she said. "Once Wilson picked up that keylogger hidden in the catfish document I copied from the Met, I could get his password details." She turned to Karl. "Did you know he only uses two passwords for everything?"

Karl raised an eyebrow, but remained silent.

"Anyway, I put a new Host file in his system folder and added my favourite gateway blocker. Every time he accessed a file the Gateway IP address changed. Just using basic kernel commands, nothing out of the ordinary for the system to see, but he could never access his network files and these big systems are all server based. It was like his system got lost trying to find its way out." She began to chuckle. "I got his credit card details too. Do you want me to send him a truck load of pig swill? He can afford it."

Karl shook his head in bewilderment. "I didn't understand a word of that I'm afraid, but the important thing is it worked and for that I am extremely grateful, but I think we'll save the pig swill for another day, don't you?"

Spud's pale cheeks began to flush. "It was my pleasure," she said. "I hate cops."

Karl turned to Simon. "Has this young lady been rewarded?"

"Oh yes. I've got the money, thanks. Me and Jodie are using it for our honeymoon next month."

"Oh, you're getting married?"

"The twelfth of next month," she said, "that's Jodie's birthday, then we're off to Brighton for a week."

"Well, congratulations, and thank you again for what you did. By the way, I may need your services again in the future."

"No problem. Just let Lenny know and he can get in touch."

Karl frowned. "I hope you don't mind me asking, but why do people call you Spud? It's not a flattering name for a young lady, is it?"

Colour began to rise in Spud's cheeks once more. "It's a lot better than my proper name."

"Oh, what's that?"

"Marie."

"What's wrong with Marie? I think Marie is a pretty name."

Spud huffed. "Not when your surname is Piper," she said.

5

It was eleven o'clock that morning when Roger Laverick arrived at Karl's house. Karl was in his study. Paul knocked sharply on the door and stepped inside.

"Roger's here," he called, stepping aside to allow the visitor access.

Karl got up from his desk and walked towards Roger, arm outstretched. "Great to see you again," he said smiling. "And thanks again for arranging to get me and Paul home."

"Glad to see you got back safely," Roger said, shaking Karl's hand. "Sorry about the boat, it must have been bloody uncomfortable, but it was the best I could do at such short notice."

Karl shrugged. "It wasn't exactly a cruise liner," he said, "but it did the job."

"How was Venezuela?"

"Hot. Bloody hot."

Roger grinned. "Surely that's better than this awful weather here. It hasn't stopped raining for three days."

Roger ensconced himself in one of the two leather armchairs and taking out a cigarette from his pocket, commenced to light it. "Hope you don't mind," he said. "Mary will create merry hell if she ever catches me smoking."

"Carry on mate. I think I'll join you." Karl reached into his desk drawer and removed a cigar.

Roger frowned. "Never did take to cigars myself. The aroma's a bit too strong."

"Each to his own," Karl said as he proceeded to light the cigar.

Roger sank back in the chair, drawing heavily on the cigarette. "So, what's the plan now you're back in good old Blighty? I presume you have a plan?"

"Yes, I have a plan," Karl said. "I want you to sell the Emerald back to me."

Roger gave a short gasp as he sat forward. "The club is not for sale, and it's not The Emerald anymore. It's the Empire."

"Emerald, Empire, who gives a fuck? I want it back."

Roger sprang to his feet. "Like I said, it's not for sale." He pointed his finger at Karl. "You begged me to take the club off your hands when you were in trouble. Remember? If it hadn't been for me —"

"Yes, and I'm grateful," Karl said, "but all that trouble has been sorted. I'm back now and I want The Emerald."

"Well you can't have it. You do know the club's been closed for the last three months? There's an Abatement Order in place. Some bastard was using the club to peddle drugs."

"Shit happens," Karl said. "You have to be on guard against that sort of thing."

"The police are making me reapply for my licence. Can you believe that?"

"They could decide to close you down indefinitely if the Order isn't lifted. Do you want to take that chance?"

"Why shouldn't it be lifted? Have you heard something?"

Karl shrugged. "I've heard rumours," he said. "Now, if you sell the club back to me all that shit will just disappear. It will become my problem, not yours. So what do you say? Can we do business?"

Roger huffed and shook his head defiantly. "No. That place is a gold mine. I'll take my chances with the Court."

"The club's only a gold mine when it's open. Running a club like The Emerald takes certain skills. Skills which I'm afraid you don't have, Roger."

"What do you mean by that? I've been running a successful business for years."

"There's a difference between your line of business and running a club like The Emerald."

Roger drew heavily on his cigarette. "I'll have to think about it," he said.

"There isn't time to think about it. It has to be done now." Karl reached into his desk drawer and removed the prepared Sale Agreement, placing it on the desk. "All it needs is your signature and your troubles will be over."

Roger huffed. "How much were you thinking of offering?"

"I'll give you half of what you paid."

"Half? You're joking, right?"

"That's all it's worth. When I sold it to you it was making a healthy profit. Now, it isn't even allowed to open. It's been run into the ground."

Roger snorted, banging his fist on the desk. "I want the full price I paid you," he said defiantly, "otherwise I'll keep the damned club myself."

"Don't be stupid," Karl scoffed. "We both know you were using the club to launder money from your other businesses. That's not going to happen now, mate. Trust me."

Roger was silent for a moment. "If I sell it to you for what you're offering, I want a percentage of the profits for the next two years."

"How big a percentage?"

"Fifty."

Karl gave out a harsh laugh. "Are you serious? You want half the profits?"

Roger shrugged. "Take it or leave it."

"I'll give you ten percent."

"Twenty," Roger said, "and that's my final offer."

Karl scowled. "Alright, twenty percent," he said, "but you're a thieving bastard Laverick."

"And you're a choirboy I suppose," Laverick retorted as picking up the pen, he signed the document.

……

When Paul returned to the office, Karl was putting his mobile back into his pocket.

"That was the police,'" he said. "They want to speak to me at the station tomorrow."

"I'll come with you."

"No, that won't be necessary. You stay here. I need you to make some calls for me." He handed Paul a list of names.

"Tell these girls I want them in The Emerald as soon as it opens. Tell them it will be in the next couple of weeks."

"Okay," he said scanning the paper, "I'll see what I can do."

Karl poured himself a whisky and settled back into his chair. "After that's been sorted, we've still got the small matter of Patrick Flynn to deal with."

"You should have let me deal with him when we first saw him in Venezuela. He could be anywhere by now."

"I couldn't afford any trouble over there and risk getting deported. Flynn might have a new identity, but I have the advantage of knowing what he looks like."

"You think he's still out to cause you trouble?"

"I know he is. I closed down his dirty little racket that made him a fortune. He's not going to let that go unpunished, is he? Now I'm back in plain sight, you can bet he'll be around somewhere. I need to know where."

"I'll put out feelers," Paul said. "Somebody must know something."

6

Karl arrived at the offices of Beauchamp, Bonneville & Clements at precisely two o'clock. He was shown into a smart waiting area by an attractive dark haired young woman dressed in a smart navy-blue suit. She introduced herself as Deborah Wallace, Gina Beauchamp's secretary.

"Miss Beauchamp won't keep you a moment, Mr Maddox," she said. "May I get you anything? Tea? Coffee?"

Karl perched on the edge of the couch. "No thanks, I'm fine," he said.

Deborah gave a weak smile as she began pounding on her keyboard.

Karl looked around the room. He was impressed with the thick grey carpet, the lavender-coloured walls and the light oak furniture. On one wall was a portrait of the three founders of the firm. He recognised Jeramiah Beauchamp immediately. On the far wall was a door with a small glass panel bearing the name 'Georgina Beauchamp' in gold lettering. Karl strained to hear raised voices from beyond the door. It suddenly burst open and a well-dressed man in his mid-thirties bounded through.

"You're over-reacting, Gina," he said as he strode past Karl. "You're getting it all out of proportion."

A young woman with fair, shoulder-length hair followed him into reception. "I don't think so, Miles," she said. "What you did was unforgiveable."

The man turned sharply. “Let’s talk about it this evening when you’ve calmed down. I’ll pick you up at eight.”

“You’re not listening,” the woman shrieked, placing her hands defiantly on her hips. “I don’t want to see you again, ever. Do you understand?”

The secretary gave a discreet cough and it was then Gina Beauchamp noticed Karl sitting in Reception. “Oh,” she said, flustered, “I’m so sorry. I didn’t see you there.” She gave one last defiant glare at Miles as he hurried out of the building, banging the door noisily behind him.

“It’s Mr Maddox, isn’t it?”

Karl gave a slight nod as he got to his feet and followed Gina into her office.

“I’m sorry about that,” she said, holding out her hand. “I’m Gina Beauchamp.”

Karl shook her hand and sat on the chair across from her desk, indicated by Gina.

“Is everything alright? I couldn’t help overhearing your conversation with that young man.”

Gina took a deep breath, and Karl noticed her body was trembling slightly. “Everything’s fine,” she said unconvincingly. “Miles and I merely had a disagreement. It’s sorted now.”

Karl shrugged. “I was expecting to be dealing with Jeramiah today,” he said, “but I understand he’s retired.”

Glad to be changing the subject from her altercation, Gina smiled and Karl noticed two dimples in her flawless complexion. “Uncle Jed is living in the Isle of Wight. When Aunt Maud passed away he decided to retire and follow his passion of sailing again."

"Leaving you to hold the fort, eh?"

Gina grinned. "Something like that," she said. "By the way, Mr Maddox, I did some work for your son a few months ago."

"Please, call me Karl. I take it was you who dealt with his divorce?"

"Yes, that's right."

"Hopefully he'll move on now and find himself a suitable wife."

Gina shrugged. "I don't think Alex is ready to settle down any time soon. He seems to have a string of female admirers."

Karl raised an eyebrow. "Oh? And are you one of them?"

Gina laughed. "Alex and I have been out to dinner a couple of times, but like him, I'm not ready to settle down either."

Gina opened the buff-coloured file on her desk. "Now, I see you're wanting to purchase The Empire Club from Mr. Roger Laverick. Is that correct?"

"That's right. I owned the club previously and sold it to Laverick about a year ago."

"You do know that there is an Abatement Order in force regarding the club?"

"It's against Laverick and the Empire Club, not me. I ran that place for years without any trouble from the police. I want it back. I need you to get the Order lifted."

Gina frowned. "That's not going to be easy. Has Mr Laverick agreed to sell the club back to you? I don't have any record of a Sale Agreement between the two of you."

Karl removed the document from his briefcase and handed it to Gina. "Laverick signed it this morning," he said. "I think you'll find everything in order."

Gina studied the document for a few minutes. "Yes, everything seems fine. I'll get my secretary to make a photocopy for your records."

Gina got up from her desk and strode into the reception area. She handed her secretary the document and gave her instructions, returning to her office a couple of minutes later. "Deborah is dealing with it now," she said.

"Excellent. I want this matter concluded as soon as possible."

"I'll get onto the Court right away," Gina said. "Perhaps you could call into the office tomorrow afternoon for a progress report?"

Karl got to his feet. "I'm going to be busy tomorrow I'm afraid. The police want me at the station."

"Oh? Is it anything I can help with?"

Karl shook his head. "No, I can handle it thanks."

"If you do need legal advice, please let me know. I don't deal in criminal law myself, but my colleague, Arthur Bonneville, would be available to offer advice."

"I'll bear that in mind," Karl said. "Perhaps you'd care to join me tomorrow evening for dinner? We can discuss progress with the Order then."

Gina smiled. "I can see where Alex gets his charm," she said. "I'll text you the restaurant."

There was a discreet knock on the door and Deborah stepped into the room, handing copies of the Sale Agreement to Gina.

"Thanks," Gina said, passing a copy to Karl. "I think that concludes our business for today. Deborah, show Mr Maddox out, will you?"

Karl got to his feet. "Thank you, Gina. I'll see you tomorrow evening."

"I'm looking forward to it," she said, a slight flush to her cheeks.

"This way," Deborah said, as she led Karl to the main entrance.

7

At two o'clock the following afternoon, Karl dutifully arrived at Holbeck Police Station. Detective Inspector George Calvert, a forty-three-year-old ex-military man, was standing by the front desk holding a blue document folder.

"Ah, Mr Maddox," he said, striding towards Karl. "Right on time." He indicated a corridor off the main reception. "If you'd care to follow me." Karl followed the Inspector into a small, airless room with grey walls and a metal table with two plastic chairs.

"Take a seat," Calvert said, as he plonked down on one of the chairs.

Karl sat opposite, folding his arms across his chest. "Can we hurry up and get this over with. I'm a busy man."

Calvert placed the folder on the desk in front of him and slowly and deliberately took out a document. "That's quite a tan you've got, Mr Maddox," he said, not raising his head. "Been somewhere nice?"

"That's none of your business. Can we stop the bullshit? Why am I here? Am I under arrest?"

"No, at least not yet. I just wanted a little chat, that's all."

"Chat about what? I've nothing to say to you."

"I suppose you've heard Joe Stevens withdrew his statement?"

"Statement about what?"

"His statement accusing you of trying to kill him."

"Probably because it never happened."

"Oh, I think it did. Inspector Wilson was the officer dealing at the time. He was building quite a case against you."

"Wilson? Isn't he the cop who got sent down for kiddy fiddling?"

Calvert's posture stiffened and he banged his fist on the table. "John Wilson is a personal friend of mine. I've known him for nearly twenty years. He's no more a paedophile than I am." Beads of sweat appeared on Calvert's brow and his jaw tightened. "Do you know what I think, Maddox? I think he was set up by you or one of your cronies, and I have every intention of proving it."

"You're talking bollocks," Karl said. "From what I've heard, the man's computer was full of that shit. He wasn't fit to be a copper."

Calvert jumped to his feet. "When I find out what really happened, I swear to god you'll swing for this."

"If there's nothing else, I'd like to leave," Karl said, standing up and meeting Calvert's glare.

"Joe Stevens led us to the knife you used to kill that girl. It had your dabs all over it."

Karl huffed. "I'd like a second opinion on that."

"The knife was found next to Paula's body."

"Paula? Is that the tart Joe buried in the cemetery? I think he must have killed her. After all, he knew where to find the body, didn't he? I didn't. Why wasn't he charged with her murder?"

"Because we don't believe he killed her. That was you. Stevens was charged with unlawfully disposing of a body."

"So he's in jail?"

"Suspended sentence," Calvert said. "He co-operated with recovering the knife used to kill the girl."

"Where is this knife?"

"You know very well it was stolen from the police property store."

Karl raised an eyebrow. "Are you accusing me of taking it?"

"I'm saying you're as guilty as hell and I intend to prove it."

Karl gave a harsh laugh. "Well, Inspector, let's hope that you're more successful than your friend Wilson, eh?" He strode towards the door. "If there's nothing else, I have things to do."

"I'll be watching you, Maddox. One wrong move and—"

"Good luck with that," Karl said, a broad grin on his face.

8

Karl and Gina Beauchamp were sipping brandy after their three-course dinner at The Bon Appetit Restaurant in Alwoodley.

"That was delicious," Gina said, dabbing the corner of her mouth with her napkin. "The French cuisine is the best in the world in my opinion."

Karl nodded in agreement. "More brandy?" he asked, draining his glass.

"No thanks. I really must get home. I have an early start tomorrow."

Karl sighed his disappointment. "That's a pity. I was hoping we could make a night of it. Go to a club or something."

Gina smiled and placed her hand on top of Karl's. "I'd love to," she said, "but not tonight. I have an important client meeting first thing."

"More important than me?"

Gina pouted. "I'm afraid so. Oscar Wright is the firm's largest client. I have to keep him sweet."

"Oscar Wright? Where have I heard that name?"

"He owns one of the biggest security firms in the country. Actually you met his son at the office yesterday."

"That little pipsqueak that was hassling you?"

"Miles is alright. He just immature, that's all."

"What had he done to upset you?"

Gina hesitated. "Oh, it doesn't matter now. It's sorted and I'm sure it won't happen again."

Karl frowned. "What did he do?"

Gina attempted to stand up but Karl held her arm. "Tell me," he said, "I want to know."

Gina stared at the floor, avoiding eye contact. "I've told you, it's over. Please, just let it go."

"Did he hurt you?"

Gina shook her head. "No, no of course not. It was nothing like that."

"Then what? I won't let this drop until you tell me."

Gina gave a deep sigh. "Alright, if you must know. Miles and I had dated a few times. He was a perfect gentleman, but..."

"But what?"

"He was jealous. Really jealous. He wanted to know where I was and what I was doing all the time. It was driving me crazy so I called it off."

"From what I heard yesterday there was more to it than that."

"Miles... Miles bugged my apartment. I found concealed cameras and microphones in my lounge and in the bedroom."

"Why would he do that?"

"Someone had been in my apartment a few days earlier, rifling through my desk. Nothing was taken but... Miles thought I needed protection."

"It sounds a nutter to me," Karl said. "You did right to get rid of him."

"Perhaps, but I don't know what his father's reaction is going to be when he finds out his precious son has been dumped. I'm afraid it could affect the business."

"If his father's got any sense, he'll pack him off to the nearest shrink and get the lad's head sorted."

"I don't think he'll do that. Miles is the moon and stars as far as Oscar is concerned. He can do no wrong."

Gina got to her feet and Karl helped her into her coat.

"I'll call you as soon as I hear from the Court," she said. "We should hear something within the next couple of days."

"Good. The sooner I can get back into The Emerald the better."

"Oh, I forgot to ask how you got on at the police station this afternoon. What did they want?"

Karl shrugged. "Just fishing. Inspector Calvert tried flexing his authority, but it's nothing I haven't been through a thousand times before."

"Well don't forget my offer. Arthur Bonneville deals with criminal law and would be happy to represent you, should it become necessary."

"Thanks, but no thanks. I can take care of myself. After all, I'm a respectable businessman."

Gina chuckled. "Not according to Uncle Jed, you're not."

Karl turned sharply and grabbed Gina's arm. "What do you mean? What's Jeramiah been saying about me?"

Gina wriggled to free Karl's grasp. "You're hurting me," she whined.

"Tell me."

"Nothing specific. He just said was you had been involved in a couple of dodgy business deals, that's all."

Karl snorted and released his grip.

"You must understand, Karl, solicitors need to know everything about their client's business dealings in order to represent them properly. The more a solicitor knows, the better they can do their job."

"What is it you think you know about me?"

"Only what Uncle Jed told me about your financials being a bit suspect. Stuff like that. Whatever information I have is confidential. You do know that? I would never tell a living soul."

Karl frowned. "I don't like the idea of Jeramiah discussing my business with you, or anyone else for that matter."

"You're my client now. Uncle Jed had to fill me in on all of your activities to enable me to represent you properly. It's perfectly normal. You'd be amazed at the stuff I know about some of my clients."

"Who for instance?"

"I can't tell you that. It would be unethical."

"I'm not asking for details. I just want to know I'm not the only one who's affairs you're aware of, that's all."

Gina hesitated. "Well there's Oscar Wright for a start." She began to chuckle. "The things I could tell you about him would make your hair curl, but of course, as his solicitor I'm not at liberty to disclose anything about him."

They walked in silence towards Karl's Mercedes. Once inside, Karl drove off at speed.

He pulled up outside Murtagh Court, Gina's luxury apartment at The Calls. "Here we are," he said. "Home safe and sound and in bed before midnight."

Gina leant over and kissed Karl lightly on the cheek. "Goodnight, Karl," she said. "Thank you for a lovely dinner." Climbing out of the car, she quickly entered the block of apartments and got into the lift.

After Gina left, Karl sat in his car for a few minutes drumming his fingers on the steering wheel. He had an uneasy feeling he was being watched. A feeling that had persisted all evening. He turned on the ignition and the engine roared into life.

9

It was eight o'clock the following morning. Karl was surprised when he heard the doorbell ring and his son, Alex, strode into the kitchen, a broad smile on his handsome face.

"'Morning, Dad," he said, walking towards Karl with his arm outstretched. "Glad to see you back in one piece. You're looking well."

Karl shook his son's hand. "What brings you here this early?"

"And good morning to you too," Alex mocked, pouring himself a coffee from the cafetiere. "Where's Paul? I heard he was back too."

Karl shrugged. "He stayed out last night. He's probably shacked up with some bird."

"Well say hello from me when you see him." Alex perched on one of the kitchen bar stools and began to sip his coffee. "So, Dad, what are you going to do to keep busy now you're back in Leeds?"

Karl gave a mischievous grin. "I have plans," he said. "What about you? I hear you are back working at the hospital."

"I'm giving medicine another try."

"That's good to hear. Are you enjoying being back?"

Alex shrugged. "It's a job, I suppose," he said. "But if I'm honest, I'd rather be back working in the clubs. It was much more fun."

Karl scowled. "Well that's never going to happen," he said, banging his coffee mug down on the counter. "Are you keeping in touch with your mother and sister?"

"We skype at least twice a week. I'm sure they'd love to hear from you."

"Later," Karl said. "I'm busy at the moment. By the way, a little bird told me you've divorced Sarah."

"My, you're still on the ball. Nothing gets past you, does it, Dad?"

"I keep my ear to the ground. Actually it was my new solicitor, Gina Beauchamp who told me about the divorce."

Alex's posture stiffened. "You've met Gina?"

"Yes. She seems a nice girl. As a matter of fact I took her out to dinner last night."

"She's a bit young for you, isn't she?"

"It was a business meeting, that's all," Karl said. "Anyway, what is it to you?"

"Nothing I suppose. It's just that I quite like her. We've been out a couple of times and... and well, I'd rather you didn't go muddying the waters, that's all. She's a good kid. I'd hate to think she was mixed up in your shady business deals."

"Don't worry, son. Our relationship is purely professional."

Alex strode over to the door. "I'd best be going. My shift starts at ten." He opened the kitchen door, then turned to face Karl. "By the way, Dad, you didn't say what your plans were now you're back."

"No, I didn't, did I?"

10

Sarah was sitting in front of her illuminated dressing table mirror brushing her shoulder-length blonde hair. Joe Stevens was perched on the edge of the bed attempting to knot his tie.

"I was thinking of having my hair cut short," she said. "What do you think?"

Joe looked up and smiled. "Your hair looks perfect. Long or short, it really doesn't matter."

"Oh, Joe," she said in mock rebuke. "You're no help."

"Darling, in three days we'll be married. I don't care if you shaved your head. You'll still be the most beautiful woman in the world to me."

Sarah meandered over to Joe and slid onto his lap, kissing him lightly on the lips. "I can't wait to be Mrs Joe Stevens," she whispered. "Being married to Alex, was like a bad dream."

Joe gently patted her thigh. "That's behind us now," he said. "Alex and Karl Maddox are no longer part of our lives."

"I suppose not, but I don't understand why you withdrew your statement. After all that bastard did try to kill you."

Joe sighed. "There were no witnesses to the assault. It would have been his word against mine in the end, and I'm sure Karl would have produced half a dozen witnesses to swear he was with them all evening."

"Even so, he can't be allowed to get away with it."

"Trust me, it's for the best we keep a low profile. Let Karl get on with his life and we get on with ours."

Sarah got to her feet. "I suppose so," she said hesitantly, "but I still think you should have followed it through. Inspector Wilson said—"

"Inspector Wilson had problems of his own. He got sent down, don't forget."

Sarah got off Joe's lap and walked back to the dressing table. "I can't believe he's guilty of what they accused him of. He seemed such a decent, honourable man to me."

"From what it said in the papers, the evidence was overwhelming."

"But evidence can be planted, can't it? His conviction certainly got Karl Maddox off the hook."

"Like I said, Sarah, let's keep well and truly out of it."

"Alright, darling, if you say so, but I bet Karl's behind it somehow. I just know he is."

The front doorbell gave out it's familiar jingle.

"Oh, that must be Charlotte," Sarah said hurrying out of the room. "She's early."

Going down the stairs two at a time, Sarah flung open the front door. "Charlotte," she said, flinging her arms around her. "You look wonderful. Do come in."

Sarah led the way into the lounge followed closely by Charlotte, carrying a large blue suitcase.

"I'm a bit early," Charlotte said. "I couldn't believe how light traffic is here compared to the city."

"Joe and I moved here a couple of months ago. We loved living in Liverpool, but we both wanted to come back to Yorkshire."

"But isn't Roundhay a little too close to you know who?"

"Karl's left. Rumour has it he's somewhere in South America, but frankly I don't care a jot."

"But what if he comes back? Do you think there'll be trouble?"

"Joe says not. He's not frightened of Karl. Joe says..."

Joe entered the lounge, his necktie dutifully tied. "Joe says what?" He strode over to Charlotte. "Good to see you," he said, hugging her. "You're looking well."

Charlotte grinned. "So are you. Both of you."

"I love your new hairstyle," Sarah said. "It suits you short. I'm thinking of a change myself."

Charlotte began to giggle as she ran her hand through her short chestnut locks. "Lewis prefers my hair darker. He thinks it makes me look intelligent."

"Lewis?" Sarah and Joe echoed.

"Lewis Cameron. He's my fiancé."

Sarah plopped on the chair, mouth gaping. "Fiancé? When did this happen? The last time I heard from you, you were in the Caribbean with Marion and Bernard."

"I was, then I met Lewis. He was there on business and... well, we just clicked."

"Have you named a date?" Sarah quizzed.

"Not for a couple of months yet. Lewis has a couple of big deals on the go at the moment."

"What does he do?"

"He owns several hotels throughout Europe. He's got one here in Leeds, too. It's called The Galaxy. When we met, he had just bought a hotel in Barbados."

Joe placed his arm around Sarah's shoulders. "When are we going to meet him?"

"He'll be here in time for the wedding. I hope you don't mind my inviting him?"

Sarah laughed. "Of course not, darling," she said. "The more the merrier. It's only going to be a small affair. I have two cousins coming from Norfolk and half a dozen of our friends. Then there's Joe's sister, Angie and her family, but apart from you, that's the lot."

"What other family I have are in Barbados," Joe said. "Dad came to England before I was born so we've never met."

"Well I'm sure it'll be perfect," Charlotte said. "Now, if you'll show me my room I'll get freshened up. You say the restaurant is booked for eight?"

Sarah began to chuckle. "That's right," she said. "It's called The Bay of Naples. We'll be eating out every evening until the wedding I'm afraid. I'm far too busy to cook."

Joe picked up Charlotte's case. "This way," he said. He turned to Sarah. "Pour everyone a drink before we go will you, darling? Gin and tonic still your tipple, Charlotte?"

"It certainly is," Charlotte said as she followed Joe up the stairs.

Once in the bedroom, Charlotte closed the door. A serious look on her face as she grabbed Joe's arm.

"I heard about Karl trying to kill you," she said. "Why have you withdrawn your statement?"

"Just leave it, Charlotte," he said.

"No, I won't leave it. Not until you tell me what the hell's going on with you?"

Joe took a deep breath and plonked onto the edge of the bed. "I had no choice," he said quietly. "There were threats made. Lots of threats. Karl's gang knew where I lived, where I worked. They sent pictures on my phone of me and Sarah."

"I don't understand. You could have told the police. They could have put a stop to it."

"Could they? They couldn't provide protection for ever. Besides, it wasn't at me the threats were directed. They were towards Sarah."

Charlotte gasped. "Did she know about this?"

"No." Joe gave a slight shudder. "The things they threatened to do to her... it makes me sick just thinking about it." He took Charlotte's hand. "You must promise not to say anything to her. She mustn't know anything about this. Sarah thinks I withdrew my allegation for the sake of a quiet life."

"Alright, if that's what you want."

Charlotte began to unpack her suitcase. "By the way, Matthew sends his congratulations."

"Matthew? You've seen Matthew?"

"Yes. I went over to Australia last month to see my new nephew. Andrew is a gorgeous baby." She began to chuckle. "I must admit, I began to feel a bit broody."

"What about Christina? What did she have to say?"

"She was really upset and apologetic about what happened to you. She promised she had no idea what Karl was planning when she arranged to meet you that night."

"Do you believe her?"

Charlotte hesitated for a moment. "I know Christina is a proven liar. I caught her out a few times in the past, but about this... yes, I believe her. I don't think she had any idea what her father was planning."

"The drinks are ready," Sarah shouted from the hallway. "Hurry up you two."

Joe turned to go downstairs. "I'd leave the unpacking until we get back," he said. "We don't want to be late for the restaurant."

"Okay, I'll just freshen up," Charlotte said, "and Joe, I think you've done the right thing walking away from Maddox. That man's a monster."

Joe walked onto the landing, jaw set, hands curled tightly into fists. "I'm not walking away from Maddox," he murmured. "I'm just biding my time, that's all. That bastard's going to pay for what he did."

11

It was nine o'clock the following morning when Paul arrived at Karl's house. He went straight to the kitchen and poured himself a coffee. Karl came out of the lounge and joined him.

"She must be some bird, keeping you occupied for two days," he said, a broad grin on his face.

"Chance would be a fine thing. I've actually been recruiting for staff."

"How did you do?"

"I've got a couple of handy blokes lined up. They've both worked on the doors at The Sapphire."

"What about the girls on the list I gave you? Did you manage to track them down?"

"Ah, that's not so easy. Two of them were up the duff and one was loved up and her bloke didn't want her working in a club again."

"And the rest?"

Paul shrugged. "There are a couple of decent girls I suppose but we'll need to audition properly to get quality. How's it going getting the Order lifted?"

"I'm expecting to hear from Gina any time. She doesn't seem to think there'll be a problem."

"Let's hope not, otherwise you're going to end up with one hell of a white elephant."

Karl snorted. "Don't talk twat," he said. "I know what I'm doing." He poured himself a coffee. "By the way, Alex came round yesterday. He said to say hello."

"Oh, how's he doing?"

"He's working at the hospital but... I don't know... he didn't seem that settled to me."

"Give him time. He'll get there."

"Let's hope so. He's in regular contact with his mother and Christina."

"Haven't you spoken to Lisa yet?"

Karl shook his head. "If she wants to go to the other side of the world, that's her business. She needn't think I'll be joining her any time soon."

Paul drained his cup and took it to the sink. "Any chance of gaining access into The Emerald? I'd like to see what changes Laverick has made."

"According to Roger, the only thing he did was to take the Emerald sign down behind the bar and replace it with one of his own."

"I take it he didn't find the passageway from the office into the club?"

"No. I placed a heavy filing cabinet in front of the passage door before I left."

"Good. In that case we should be able to open more or less straight away."

"That's the idea. I'm just waiting for this damned Abatement Order to be lifted. I think I'll chase Gina. See if she's heard anything yet."

Paul smirked. "What's she like, this Gina?"

"What do you mean, what's she like? She's a solicitor, that's all."

"So there's nothing going on between you two?"

"For fuck's sake. You're as bad as Alex."

"Alex? What do you mean?"

"I think he's got the hots for her. He didn't say it in so many words but I got the impression he was warning me off."

Paul chuckled. "Boys will be boys," he said.

Karl huffed and strode back to the living room, followed closely by Paul.

"I was thinking of calling in at Danny's bar tonight. Fancy coming with me?" Paul asked.

"To a gay club? I don't think so. Besides, I might be taking Gina out tonight if the Order has been lifted."

Grinning, Paul made his way to the hall. "I'm going for a hot shower," he said, "then I'll go back recruiting. There's a new strip club opened at the end of Lower Briggate. I'll call in later and see if there's any suitable totty."

"I'm afraid that will have to wait. I might have a little job for you tonight."

"Oh?"

"I'll let you know, once I've heard from Gina."

12

It was four o'clock that afternoon when Karl received the call he had been waiting for. The Abatement Order had been lifted and the club could once again open its doors. At seven o'clock, Karl pulled up outside Gina's apartment. Before he could get out of the car, she came hurrying towards him.

"Congratulations," she greeted as she climbed into the front passenger seat. "You're now officially the owner of The Empire Club. I'll have the documents and the keys couriered to you tomorrow as soon as the Court release them."

Karl leant over and kissed Gina lightly on the cheek. "Thank you," he said. "You've done a great job. All I have to do now is change the club's name back to The Emerald."

"You're using its old name?"

"Of course I am. Why?"

"I just thought with it being a new venture you would give it a new name."

"Like what? I like the name Emerald."

Gina shrugged and fastened her seat belt as Karl turned on the ignition. "So, where are you taking me tonight to celebrate?"

"Simon recommended an Italian restaurant in Roundhay called The Bay of Naples. I thought we might give that a try."

"Sounds lovely. I adore Italian food."

"I thought you loved French?"

She smiled. "I do. I love all food really."

Karl smiled. "After dinner I thought we might do a few bars."

"Sorry, Karl, but it's a school night don't forget. I can't be too late."

Karl shrugged. "Okay. Perhaps we can do that at the weekend?"

"Perhaps," she said.

"By the way, how did your meeting with Oscar Wright go? Was he annoyed about you and Miles splitting up?"

"Actually he never mentioned it. I don't think Miles had told him. Anyway he had far more important matters to discuss."

"Such as?"

"I can't tell you that."

"Why not? I won't tell anyone."

"Karl, please…"

"What's the problem? I'm thinking of getting a quote from him for security at the club. I like to know the type of bloke I'm dealing with, that's all."

Gina was silent for a moment. Karl could sense the tension in her body.

"Is everything alright, Gina? You look a little… a little edgy."

"I'm fine," she said at last. "I'm tired, that's all."

Karl tutted. "You work too hard," he said turning on the ignition. "So, what do you think? Is Oscar Wright's security firm the right choice for the club?"

Gina turned to face Karl, placing her hand firmly on his arm. "If you take my advice," she said, a slight tremor in her voice, “you’ll keep well away from Oscar Wright and his damned company.”

13

The rest of the journey was in silence. Gina, with a glum expression, was staring out of the window as Karl pulled up in the car park of The Bay of Naples Restaurant.

"Gina, you look upset. Is there anything you want to talk to me about?"

Gina shook her head. "No, I'm feeling tired, that's all. I think you're right. I have been working too hard."

Karl turned off the ignition and was about to get out of the car when his posture stiffened and his jaw tightened as he saw, standing under the glittering lights of the restaurant, the unmistakable figure of Joe Stevens.

"Is everything alright, Karl?" Gina asked. "You look like you've seen a ghost."

Karl remained silent as he watched Joe open the door of his Lexus and his ex-daughter-in-law, Sarah, alight. The rear door opened and out stepped Charlotte, a little older than he remembered, but unmistakable, nevertheless. He didn't recognise the fourth person to get out of the vehicle, a powerfully built man in his late thirties.

Gina followed Karl's gaze. "Do you know those people?" she asked.

Karl inhaled deeply. "Yes, I know them," he said as he turned on the ignition and began to drive his car out of the car park. "I think we'll find somewhere else to eat tonight. I don't particularly like the clientele here."

Gina frowned. "Who are they?"

"It's best you don't know."

He drove back towards the city centre in silence. It was Gina who spoke first.

"Do you mind if we don't go out tonight after all?" she said. "I'm a little tired and you're obviously upset about something."

"You're probably right. I do have a few things to take care of before the club can open for business."

"I hope I'll be getting an invite on opening night. I've never been to a pole-dancing club before. It should be fun."

"Of course you'll get an invite."

Gina grinned. "I'm looking forward to it," she said as the car pulled up outside her apartment. "Good night, Karl."

"Good night, Gina," Karl said as he kissed her lightly on the cheek. "Speak to you tomorrow."

……

Karl arrived back at his house at nine o'clock. He went into his study and after taking out a cigar from his desk drawer, poured himself a large whisky. Five minutes later Paul arrived.

"You were right," Paul said. "You were being followed."

Karl punched his fist into his hand. "I knew it," Karl said. "Who was it?"

Paul handed his phone to Karl. "I managed to get a couple of shots. I think you'll recognise him."

Karl studied the first blurred image and frowned. The second picture was much clearer. "Alex," he gasped. "What the fuck is he playing at?"

"He followed you from Gina's apartment through to Roundhay and back again. He was still parked outside her apartment when I came here."

"The stupid bastard. What's his game?"

Paul shrugged. "By the way, what happened with the restaurant? I thought you were looking forward to having dinner with the pretty solicitor."

"Joe Stevens. That's what happened. He was there with Sarah and Charlotte. There was another bloke with them."

"I thought Joe was settled in Liverpool?"

"Not any more. You need to find him, and that bitch Charlotte. We have unfinished business."

"Okay, Karl, if that's what you want, but don't you think you've enough on with the club opening?"

Karl grunted. "I have to know what they're up to. I don't like them being around. They make me nervous."

"I'll put out feelers tomorrow," Paul said. "Joe shouldn't be too hard to find."

"What about Flynn? Have you heard anything about him yet?"

Paul shook his head. "Not yet, but I've got people out looking. I'll let you know as soon as I hear anything."

Karl drained his glass. "You do that. I've got an uneasy feeling things are about to happen."

14

It was ten-thirty the following morning when the courier arrived at Karl's house. Karl took the two packages and hurried into his study. Taking out a paper knife, he opened the first larger package which contained a bundle of documents. It was the top sheet that brought a smile to his face.

"Paul, they're here," he shouted. "The club is all mine."

Paul dashed into the study. "It's been released from the Abatement Order? That's great news." He took the documents from Karl's grasp and began to read.

Karl opened the second, smaller package. Inside were three sets of keys. "Ah, keys to my kingdom," he grinned as he picked up the telephone. "I'll give Gina a call and let her know they've arrived."

He dialled Gina's office. It was Deborah who answered.

"I'm sorry, Mr Maddox," she said. "Gina's not arrived yet."

"Oh? Well, tell her I've just received the documents."

"Good. I sent them over myself with Gina not being here. Should I ask her to give you a call when she gets in?"

"Yeah, you do that," Karl said. He turned to Paul. "Gina's not there. I wonder what's keeping her?"

Paul shrugged. "Probably working from home."

"I suppose so. That girl's a workaholic. Pity she doesn't want to dance in the club. She'd make a fortune." He laughed coarsely as picking up his jacket from the back of his chair, he headed towards the hall. "Fancy a quick peep? Let's see what Laverick did to the place."

"Sure. I'll ring Si and tell him to meet us there."

Karl hurried towards the front door with Paul in quick pursuit. Soon they were in Karl's Mercedes heading at speed towards The Emerald Club.

……

Karl opened the main door and was greeted with the musty smell of a building not having been occupied for some time. The windows were shuttered so there was little light.

"Gina was supposed to be getting onto the electricity people today to get the power on," Karl said, striding over to one of the windows. Opening it, he tugged at the shuttering and managed to pull it off the frame causing light to flood into the foyer. He squinted at the brightness as he slowly inspected his surroundings.

"Laverick doesn't seem to have changed much in here," he said at last, running his finger over the dusty reception desk.

He walked through into the main club.

"Let's get all the shuttering down before anything else, then we can see the damage."

Paul helped Karl take down the boardings and Simon joined them a few minutes later.

"It doesn't look too bad, boss," Simon said. "There's just the sign behind the bar to change."

Karl looked over towards the bar where a large glass sign 'Empire Club' was hanging.

"I'll see if I can find the old Emerald sign," Paul said. "We might still be able to use it."

"You do that. The Emerald is going to be bigger and better than it ever was."

Paul smiled. "If you say so, boss, but it's going to need a thorough clean first. The place stinks."

Simon took out his phone. "Leave that with me," he said. "I know the very people."

"Get them in as soon as you can," Karl said. "This place is filthy."

Accompanied by Paul, Karl strode back through the foyer and up the stairs to what had been the Emerald Club's VIP lounge. "The lazy bastard hasn't changed a thing," he said, wandering around the room. "Everything is exactly as I left it."

"That's good, isn't it boss? Apart from cleaning, there's not much for us to do. It means we can open sooner."

"I suppose so, but I still think Laverick's a lazy bastard. The only reason he wanted the clubs was to launder his dirty money."

Karl strode over to the room which had served as his office. Opening the door, he saw everything appeared as he had left it. Rushing to the stationery cupboard behind the desk he flung the door open. A broad grin spread across his face as he saw the heavy filing cabinet he had placed in front of the entrance to the secret staircase, was still in place.

"Give me a hand. I want to make sure Laverick didn't find this."

Both men pushed the cabinet to the side and Karl opened the door. He struck a match and it briefly illuminated the staircase which led behind the false wall in the main club. Boxes of cigarettes and bottles of spirits left on the shelving were still there as he had left them.

Karl gave a satisfied nod. "Everything seems to be here," he said.

He closed the stationery cupboard and both men returned to the main club where Simon had pulled down most of the shuttering.

"The dance poles are still here boss," he said. "The bar needs re-stocking, but apart from that we should be good to go in a couple of days. I've spoken to Sue and her mate about the cleaning. They're the ones who got your house ready. They can come round first thing tomorrow, providing the electric's on."

"I'll get onto Gina and see what's happening with that. Can you let the cleaners in tomorrow and supervise? I have stuff to do."

"Sure, boss. It's going to be great working here again. I've missed it."

"I'll need you to audition dancers in the next couple of days. Paul's managed to recruit a handful, but I'll need more. Lots more. Then there's the hostesses for upstairs. You know the sort of girls I want."

"Sure. Leave it with me. I still have contacts."

"Oh, and there's..." Karl's phone gave out its shrill ring. Looking at the screen, he saw it was Gina's office. "Hi, Gina. I was just about to ring you. I –"

"It's Deborah, Mr Maddox."

"Put Gina on, will you? I need to speak with her."

"I'm afraid that won't be possible."

"Why not? What's going on?"

"Gina Beauchamp was found dead earlier today. I'm afraid she's been murdered."

"Murdered? That can't be right. Are you sure?"

"Quite sure," Deborah said sternly.

"Do the police know who killed her?"

"I understand they've made an arrest."

"Who?"

There was a pause.

"What bastard murdered her?" Karl shrieked. "Tell me."

"The police have arrested your son, Alex," she said. "He's at the police station now."

15

Driving at speed, Karl arrived at Holbeck Police Station within twenty minutes. He raced into the crowded reception area where two harassed young constables were attempting to deal with the mayhem.

"You can't lock our kid up," a heavy-set man in his thirties yelled at one of the officers. "He's getting married tomorrow."

"Mr Jacobs will remain in police custody until his appearance at the Magistrates Court tomorrow morning," the officer said calmly. "I suggest you and your party leave the station immediately."

"Not without our kid," the man said, banging his fist on the counter. "He's done nowt I tell you."

"Mr Jacobs assaulted a police officer," the constable said. "That's an extremely serious offence."

"It was the copper's fault. He shouldn't have got involved in the fight."

The young policeman picked up the telephone on the desk. "I won't ask you again. Leave the station now and take your friends with you, otherwise I will have you all put under arrest."

"Come on, Uncle Steve," a skinny lad of about twenty said, grabbing the older man's elbow. "Let's get a solicitor for Dave. There's nothing we can do here."

Steve gave a defiant stare at the officer and turned to leave, muttering abuse as he did so. With his departure, the majority of the crowd followed.

Karl strode up to the front desk. "I demand to see my son," he said.

"Like I told your mate, he's not going to be released until he goes to court tomorrow. Now jog on before you get banged up as well."

Snarling, Karl pointed his finger at the officer. "I'm not here about that toerag. My name is Karl Maddox. My son, Alex, has been arrested for murder."

The officer raised an eyebrow. "Oh him?" He picked up the phone and dialled an extension. "Karl Maddox is in reception, sir." After a few seconds he turned to Karl. "If you take a seat over there, Detective Inspector Calvert will be down shortly."

Karl huffed and began pacing around reception. It was ten minutes before Calvert arrived.

"Sorry to keep you, Mr Maddox," he said. "If you'll come this way, please?"

Karl followed the inspector down the corridor to the same room he had been in earlier. Calvert stood aside to let Karl enter, before closing the door behind them.

"What the hell's my boy doing here?" Karl demanded. "Alex wouldn't hurt anybody. He hasn't got it in him."

"That's not what we've heard," he said. "Your son was heard arguing with Ms Beauchamp. It would seem he was the last person to see her alive."

"Apart from the killer," Karl spat. "I want to see Alex. I want to hear what he has to say."

"That won't be possible, I'm afraid. Your son is about to be interviewed."

"Who's his solicitor? I presume he does have a solicitor?"

"One will be appointed. Don't worry about that."

"I do worry. I want Alex to have the best. The very best. I'll get one for him myself."

"Mr Maddox, I assure you—"

Karl snorted. "Bollocks. You don't speak to my son until I have got him a proper solicitor. Do you understand?"

"You have one hour," Calvert said, "after that—"

Karl rushed out of the interview room, along the corridor and out into the car park. It was when he was inside his vehicle that he took out his mobile phone and dialled a number.

"Deborah? Deborah, I want you to put Arthur Bonneville on the phone."

"I'm sorry Mr Maddox, Mr Bonneville is with a client."

"Fuck the client. Get him on the phone now."

There was silence for a moment, then the receiver was picked up.

"Mr Maddox, this is Arthur Bonneville."

"I need you down at the police station right now," Karl said. "They're interviewing my son and I want you to represent him."

Bonneville gave a low, guttural cough. "I'm sorry, Mr Maddox," he said, "but that's impossible. Gina was my colleague. My friend. I can't possibly defend the person held responsible for her murder. I'm sure you can understand my position."

The veins on Karl's neck began to throb. "No, I don't bloody well understand. I need you at the police station now."

"But—"

"No buts, Bonneville. Get your arse down to Holbeck nick or else."

16

Arthur Bonneville was in his late fifties with receding grey hair and shrewd blue eyes. His trim moustache and beard helped disguise the fact that he had been born with a harelip. After a quick nod of acknowledgement to Karl in the police station's reception, he was bundled along the corridor by DI Calvert. An hour and twenty minutes later Bonneville emerged from the interview room and walked back through reception, a sombre expression on his face.

"Well?" Karl demanded. "What did Alex say?"

Bonneville sighed deeply. "Perhaps this would be best discussed elsewhere," he said, walking towards the exit.

Karl huffed his exasperation as he followed Bonneville into the car park. Bonneville took out a fob and pointed it at his dark-blue Jaguar, releasing the lock. "Let's talk in here," he said, "away from prying eyes." Bonneville climbed into the driver's seat and Karl went round the car, getting into the front passenger seat.

"What have the cops got?" Karl said, closing the car door. "Why have they arrested Alex?"

"According to the police, late last night your son was heard arguing with Gina in her apartment," Bonneville said. "The witness said the argument was extremely heated and Alex was seen to slap Gina across the face."

"He hit her? But why? What had she done?"

Unperturbed by the interruption, Bonneville continued. "Gina's body was found on the kitchen floor the following morning. She had been stabbed."

"When was she killed?"

"The pathologist thinks it was around the time Alex was there, but a postmortem will reveal exactly when."

"Anyone could have got into her apartment after Alex left."

"The apartment block employ a twenty-four-hour concierge service. The guard on duty is confident that no-one else entered the flat after Alex left the building,"

"Then he's a fucking liar. Someone must have got in. Alex is no killer."

Bonneville shrugged. "We'll have to wait for the postmortem for the exact time of death, but until that's completed, there's little else I can do."

"Who heard Alex arguing with Gina? Did you find out?"

"It was the concierge on duty. Gina and Alex were on the first-floor landing."

"What? They took the word of a bloody nightwatchman? Did Alex say what they were arguing about?"

"I'm afraid your son is not saying anything at the moment," Bonneville said. "An extremely foolish thing to do under the circumstances."

"When can I see him?"

"Alex is in no mood to speak with anyone at the moment."

"Has he been charged?"

"Not yet. They'll probably do that after they get the result of the postmortem."

Karl leant back into the plush leather upholstery and closed his eyes. "The bastards are out for revenge," he said, his voice solemn. "They can't get anything on me so they've gone after my son instead."

"Mr Maddox, I really don't think—"

"Don't think what? That the police aren't vindictive? That's bollocks. Calvert said as much the other day."

Bonneville reached for the ignition. "I really must be getting back to the office," he said. "I'll call you tomorrow and we can go to the station together."

17

When he left the police station, Karl went straight to The Emerald. He walked through the door to see the electricity had been restored. Paul and Simon were clearing away empty bottles from behind the bar. Both stopped when they saw Karl.

"How'd it go, boss?" Simon asked. "Is Alex okay?"

Karl strode up to the bar and perched on one of the stools. "The stupid little bastard isn't saying anything. He hasn't been charged yet but..."

Paul put his arm around Karl's shoulder. "What did the solicitor say?"

"Not much. Until Alex gives his version, what can he do?"

"But why would he want to kill Gina?"

Karl shrugged. "Who knows what goes on in that boy's head? We both know he was stalking her, so maybe he was jealous of some bloke."

Simon shook his head. "I don't think so. Alex is a good-looking bloke. Girls throw themselves at him. I can't see him getting hung up on a bird, can you?"

Paul took his jacket from the back of a chair and headed towards the door. "In the meantime," he said, "I'll dig around and see what I can find out about Gina Beauchamp. Alex can't be the only one interested in her."

Karl turned sharply. "I heard her arguing with Miles Wright at the office the other day. You might start there."

"Do you know what they argued about?"

"Someone had broken into her apartment a few days earlier. Nothing of value had been taken but Miles took it on himself to install hidden cameras without telling her."

Paul pursed his lips. "Naughty," he said as he headed for the foyer and out into the car park.

……

Simon returned to behind the bar and continued to gather the empty bottles. "Oh by the way, boss, I've spoken to the cleaners. They'll be here first thing."

Karl waved a dismissive hand. "Great. You deal with it Si. I've more important things on my mind at the moment."

"Are you going to ring Lisa and let her know Alex is under arrest for murder?"

"Why the fuck should I?"

"She is his mother. I thought—"

"If that silly bitch wants to live in Australia instead of with me, then let her. She's lost any right to know anything."

"But, Karl, she—"

"You heard what I said. Now, get me a bottle of whisky, will you? I can't think straight without a drink."

"Sure boss. It'll have to be from the supermarket though."

Karl tossed a couple of notes at Simon. "I don't give a fuck if you have to get it from the dry cleaners."

Simon took the money and hurriedly left the club.

Left alone, Karl took out his mobile phone and dialled a number. “Lisa? Lisa it’s me. I’m afraid I’ve got some really bad news about Alex...”

18

It was six o'clock when Deborah Wallace left her office. Pulling her woollen coat around her, she stepped out into the cold night air and hurried along the deserted street to the bus stop. Paul was in his car. He had been sitting in the car for the last half-hour waiting for his prey. He watched as Deborah got onto the bus. As the bus pulled away, Paul followed.

Deborah alighted at the third stop and hurried along Lowe Street, a smart, red-brick terrace. She stopped at number 35. Paul watched as she took out her key and entered the house. He waited twenty minutes before knocking on the door.

Paul rapped several times before the door was finally opened. He noted Deborah had changed from her smart office wear into denim jeans and a pretty pink top. Her long hair, which had previously been fastened up, hung loosely on her slender shoulders. "Yes?" she said, a puzzled look on her face.

"Ms Wallace?" he asked. "Ms Deborah Wallace?"

"Yes, that's right. Who are you?"

"My name is Paul Borowicz. I work for Karl Maddox."

Deborah gave a slight frown. "What can I do for you, Mr Borowicz?" she said.

"Forgive me calling at your home, but the matter is quite important. I did try your office but they said you had left for the day."

"How did you know where I lived? The office are not supposed to give out personal information."

"Oh, Gina told Karl where you lived. He asked me to speak to you."

"Did she indeed? Why couldn't Mr Maddox speak to me himself?"

Paul shrugged. "He's pretty busy at the moment, what with the club about to open and then this business with his son."

Deborah's frown deepened. "What exactly do you want to talk to me about, Mr Borowicz? I was on my way out to get something to eat. It's chaotic at the office at the moment. I haven't eaten all day."

Paul beamed his warm, sexy smile, the smile that left most women weak at the knees. "Perhaps I could join you?" he said softly. "I haven't eaten either, and by the way Deborah, the name's Paul."

Deborah hesitated. "I… I don't think…"

"It really is most important I speak with you," Paul insisted. "My car's just over there." He nodded in the direction of his Audi.

Deborah took a deep breath. "Alright," she said. "Give me a couple of minutes to get my coat." She closed her door and Paul strode over to his car to wait. Deborah came out of the house five minutes later and Paul noticed she had refreshed her lipstick and was wearing perfume.

"It's a damned nuisance not having my car," Deborah said as she climbed into the front passenger seat. "It failed its MOT. It's having new brake pads fitted. I should be getting it back tomorrow."

Paul grinned. "Never mind, you won't need your car tonight," he said, turning on the ignition. "Where would you like to eat? I know a good little Italian restaurant that's just opened."

"Sounds perfect," Deborah said. "I love Italian food."

......

"That was delicious," Paul said, finishing the last of the linguine. He refilled Deborah's glass with more pinot. "Do you fancy a dessert?"

Deborah dabbed at her mouth with her napkin. "Thank you, but I couldn't eat another thing."

The waiter came and cleared the table.

"Now, Paul," Deborah said, "you haven't told me what is so urgent that it couldn't wait until tomorrow."

"I want to talk about Gina," Paul said. "What sort of person she was and who you think might be responsible for killing her."

"Alex killed her," Deborah said. "The police have arrested him."

"Yes, but they haven't charged him. Not yet anyway."

"If he didn't do it, then who did?"

"Who indeed? How long have you been Gina's secretary?"

"Almost a year. I worked for her uncle before that, and when Jeramiah retired, I began working for Gina."

"Did you enjoy working for her?"

Deborah shrugged. "She was alright."

"You two were about the same age. Did you ever socialise?"

Deborah shook her head vehemently. "No, not at all. Gina made it perfectly clear she preferred the company of men."

"Any man in particular?"

"Take your pick. There was a different one every week as far as I could see. Alex was one of many."

"Who else did she see?"

"There was Miles, of course. They'd been seeing each other on and off for months."

"And it was Gina who finished the relationship?"

"That's right. They had a blazing row a few days ago. I don't think I've ever seen her so angry."

"How did she get on with Alex?"

"He seemed alright I suppose. He only came to the office a couple of times."

"Did you ever see them argue?"

"No, but that doesn't mean—"

"Do you know if there was anything bothering her? Anything in her personal or professional life?"

Deborah inhaled. "Like I said, Gina did like the men. From what I saw, I think she was giving your boss the come-on. I know he took her out to dinner a couple of times. Maybe she flirted once too often with the wrong person. Who knows?"

"What about her professional life?"

"Gina did work hard, there's no denying that, but I got the impression she was worried about something. Something to do with one of her clients."

"Which client?"

"Paul, I can't disclose that. It would be... unprofessional."

"Deborah, a man's liberty is at stake. I don't think for one moment that Alex was responsible for what happened to Gina. I'm trying to find out who was."

"Isn't that the job of the police?"

"The police are okay for directing traffic and finding lost dogs. Anything else..."

Deborah chuckled. "That's a cynical viewpoint."

"Cynical or not, it's the truth. Now, tell me who you think Gina was worried about."

Deborah was silent for a moment. "Well," she said at last, "I got the impression there was tension between her and Oscar Wright."

"Oscar Wright?"

"Miles's father."

"What was the problem. Do you know?"

Deborah shrugged. "All I know is there were meetings held between them after the office had closed for the day, and I was never asked to type up any notes for his file."

Paul stroked his chin. "Mmm... that is interesting. I wonder what that was about?"

"I did try to casually ask her once but she nearly bit my head off."

"So you've no idea?"

"None." Deborah stood up and took her coat from the stand. "Thank you for a lovely meal," she said, "but I really must be going. I have an early start tomorrow."

"Of course," Paul said. "I'll drive you home."

After settling the bill, Paul accompanied Deborah into the car park. "You must come to see The Emerald, once it's open," he said. "Karl's working on making it the best in the area."

Deborah grinned. "Yes, Mr Beauchamp said Karl was a formidable character. He'll be surprised when I tell him tomorrow about the club opening up again."

"Tomorrow?"

"Yes. Jeramiah is coming out of retirement to replace Gina at the firm. Didn't you know?"

19

"What time did you get back last night?" Karl said from behind his newspaper. "Out on the lash again?"

Ignoring the remark, Paul poured himself a coffee and began buttering his toast. "I went to dinner with Deborah Wallace if you must know."

"Who the fuck is Deborah Wallace?"

"She was Gina's secretary. We had an interesting chat."

"What about?"

"Amongst other things, she said Gina had the morals of an alley cat. She had a string of men."

"I'm not surprised. She was a pretty girl."

"She also told me Jeramiah Beauchamp is coming out of retirement. He's starting work at the office today."

Karl huffed. "I suppose I ought to pay him a visit and offer my condolences."

"Don't you think you should wait and see what happens with Alex? It could be a bit tricky if they charge him with murdering Gina."

Karl sighed. "Yes, I suppose you're right. I'll…"

The familiar shrill ring of Karl's mobile filled the air. Karl removed the phone from his pocket and recognising the caller, walked through into the lounge before he answered. A few minutes later he came back into the kitchen, a broad grin on his face.

"That was Bonneville," he said. "Alex has been released on bail."

"That's great news."

"Let's hope so. I'm going round to his to find out what the hell has been going on. I want you to go to the club and give Simon a hand."

"Sure. Give Alex my best."

......

Alex was in the shower when Karl arrived at his flat.

"Won't be long, Dad," he said from behind the bathroom door. "Put the kettle on and make me a coffee, will you?"

Karl huffed as he filled the kettle and switched it on. "I'm not your bloody daily," he muttered as he took two cups out of the wall cupboard. Five minutes later Alex entered the room wearing a blue and white corded bathrobe. "That's better," he said, rubbing his wet hair with a towel. "Police stations have a smell all of their own."

"I hear you haven't been charged."

Alex smirked. "They won't do that. I haven't done anything and they can't prove I did."

"I heard you'd been arguing with Gina shortly before she died."

"So what? When I left her apartment, she was in one piece."

"What were you arguing about?"

"It doesn't matter."

Karl grabbed Alex by the arm. "It does matter. The cops will twist and turn everything you say. Now, tell me. What was the fight about?"

Alex walked over to the kitchen counter and picked up one of the coffee mugs. "You've put too much milk in," he said frowning. "You know I don't like a lot of milk."

"Make you own fucking coffee in future," Karl said. "Now tell me what happened."

Alex sipped at the offending coffee before turning to face Karl. "If you really want to know, the argument was about you."

"Me? What do you mean?"

"I warned her to keep away from you, that you were bad news."

"You did what?"

"I've seen the way you were sniffing round her. Gina was a decent girl. I didn't want her getting involved in your shady business."

"She was my solicitor, you stupid bastard. Our relationship was purely professional."

"Professional? Do you usually take your solicitor out to dinner?"

"Yes, when it's cause for celebration, and the work Gina did for me was cause for celebration."

"I still think you were angling to get your leg over. I've seen how you operate."

Karl leapt forward; fists clenched. "Who the fuck do you think you're talking to? You ungrateful little maggot. I've a good mind to—"

Alex stepped back. "Still got your temper, I see. You'll never change, Dad. Once a thug, always a thug."

Karl gnashed his teeth. "You don't know what you're talking about. I came here to help you."

“Well you can’t. Now go back to your precious club and your dodgy mates. I don’t want anything to do with you.”

Karl strode to the door. “Suit yourself,” he said, “but be warned. Calvert is out for blood. If he can’t get mine, yours will have to do.”

20

Karl drove at speed to The Emerald. Simon was busy working in the foyer when he arrived.

"'Morning, boss," he said. "How's young Alex doing? Paul told me he's out on bail."

Karl huffed. "Forget about Alex. He's an arsehole." He strolled to the door leading to the stairs and his office. "How's the cleaning going?"

"Great. The girls have done upstairs. They're working in the main club now. Liz says they'll be finished by tonight."

"Where is Paul? He told me he was coming here."

"He called in earlier. He's gone to the wholesaler to get more glasses. The ones here have seen better days."

"Have you ordered stock for the bar?"

"Yeah. The delivery will be here the day after tomorrow."

"What about recruitment? Have you and Paul managed to find enough girls between you?"

Simon smirked. "Find them? They're coming out of the woodwork. The first set of auditions are down for eight tomorrow morning."

Karl nodded his approval. "That's great. I'll leave it to you to get it sorted."

Rushing upstairs to his office, he took out his mobile phone and rang a number.

"Bonneville? Its Karl Maddox. I've just been talking with Alex."

"How is he?"

"You tell me. You're supposed to be his solicitor."

"Alex had already been bailed in his own recognisance when I got to the station this morning. I did telephone him but got no reply. Your son really is being most uncooperative, Mr Maddox."

"Alex is an arrogant little twerp. He always has been. So, what happens now?"

"I will need to speak to him, of course. I need to know exactly what his relationship with Gina Beauchamp was and—"

"I'll get him to your office tomorrow afternoon. Is three o'clock convenient?"

There was a slight hesitation. "I... I suppose I can arrange that, but I really must insist that your son's attitude improves, otherwise..."

"Don't worry, it will." Karl put down the phone and walking over to the cabinet, poured himself a large whisky. Thirty minutes later, Simon entered the office.

"The funniest thing, boss," he said. "One of the cleaners has applied to be a dancer."

Karl frowned. "A cleaner? I don't think so."

"Don't be too hasty. She auditioned and I have to say she was good... in fact she was more than good. She was bloody fantastic."

"Well, if you say so. What's this cleaner's name?"

"Sue, but she's using Suki when she performs."

Karl shook his head and sighed. "Where these girls get their fancy names from beats me."

"Actually her sister Kelly worked here last year. You remember Kelly, don't you?"

Karl grinned, remembering how Kelly had been in his office performing oral sex the night Geoffrey Lawrence got shot.

"Oh yes," he smirked. "I remember Kelly. Proper little raver was Kelly."

Karl's phone rang. "Yes, Deborah?" After a short conversation, he put the phone down. "Jeremiah Beauchamp requests my company at his office," he said, reaching for his jacket. "When Paul gets back, send him round to Alex's will you? Tell him I want him at the solicitors tomorrow afternoon at three. No excuses."

"Sure, boss," Simon said as he turned and strode towards the door. "I've got some blokes to meet shortly to see if they're suitable for working the doors."

"Make sure they're handy," Karl said. "I can't get rid of this feeling that things are going to kick off very soon."

21

Jeremiah Beauchamp was dwarfed by the large oak desk in front of him. He made no attempt to rise or shake hands as Karl was shown into the office by Deborah.

"Mr Maddox to see you, Mr Beauchamp," she said officiously.

Beauchamp gave a slight nod. "Yes, thank you Deborah. Close the door, will you."

Leaving the room, Deborah dutifully did as she was asked.

"Well, Karl," Beauchamp said. "Here we are again."

Karl drew up a chair in front of the desk and sat down. "I'm sorry to hear about your niece," he said. "Bad business."

Beauchamp took of his spectacles and began polishing them vigorously with his handkerchief. "Yes, it is. Gina was a lovely girl."

"I want you to know my son had absolutely nothing at all to do with what happened to her. Nothing."

Beauchamp shrugged. "That's in the hands of the police," he said. "I'm sure they'll find out who was responsible."

Karl snorted. "I wouldn't bank on it," he said. "From what I've seen, they haven't got much of a clue."

Content with his polishing, Beauchamp returned his handkerchief to his pocket and replaced his spectacles onto his nose. "Actually, Mr Maddox," he said, "I didn't ask you here to discuss my niece. I believe it would be in both our interests if you found another firm of solicitors to represent you."

"Are you refusing to work for me?"

"I'm not refusing. I'm merely suggesting that perhaps it would be best if we severed our professional relationship."

"Because of Alex?"

Beauchamp inhaled, lacing his fingers in front of him. "Partly," he said. "It's understandable that I don't want the firm to represent the man accused of murdering my niece, but it's also in connection with the work I did for you in relation to Roger Laverick. Moving money around like that was really most unprofessional, bordering on illegal in fact."

Karl's jaw tightened. "Firstly, Alex did not harm Gina. He has not been charged with any offence, nor is he likely to be." Karl pointed his finger menacingly at Beauchamp. "Secondly, I don't understand your reticence regarding that business with Laverick. You got well paid for it, didn't you? I didn't hear you complain at the time."

"You must understand, I... I was under a great deal of stress at the time," Beauchamp said. "My wife was gravely ill and the firm were facing a damages claim from one of its clients. Fortunately the claim was rejected, but... well, I'm sure you can see why I did what I did."

"Have there been any repercussions from the authorities?"

"No, but... but well, there could have been. I really don't want to find myself in that position again."

"You won't. I give you my word," Karl said. "I'm back in Leeds and I mean to stay. I've bought The Emerald Club from Laverick so that business is finished with."

"What about the other clubs you sold him? Are you buying those back too?"

"I've no plans to."

Karl scraped his chair back and stood up. "Now that's settled, I take it we're still in business?"

"I... I suppose so," Beauchamp said hesitantly, "but there is the matter of your son's attitude. I understand from my colleague, Arther Bonneville, that Alex is being most un-cooperative in forming his defence."

"Don't worry about Alex. I'll speak to him." Karl leant across the desk, holding out his hand. "It's good to see you again, Jeramiah. Let's hope we can do lots of successful business together."

Beauchamp gave an unconvincing handshake. "Let's hope so," he said, pressing the connecting buzzer on his desk to the outer room. "Mr Maddox is leaving, Deborah. Show him out, will you?"

Deborah gave a weak smile. "Yes, of course Mr Beauchamp," she said. She turned to Karl. "This way Mr Maddox."

22

Detective Inspector Calvert arrived at West Top Manor, on the outskirts of Roundhay Park, at exactly three o'clock that afternoon. He was in the company of newly promoted Detective Sergeant Kate Burrows.

"This is quite a place, sir," she said, getting out of the car. "Security systems must be the way to go."

Calvert raised an eyebrow. "It looks like it," he said. "Hard to believe that Oscar Wright and his son had barely a pot to piss in five years ago." He knocked briskly on the door, and it was opened almost immediately by a young woman wearing a black and white maid's uniform.

"Good afternoon," she said politely.

"Inspector Calvert? Mr Miles is expecting you."

Calvert stepped into the hall. "Actually, it's Detective Inspector," he said, "and this is Detective Sergeant Burrows."

"Beg your pardon, sir," she said, giving a mock bow. "If you both follow me, I'll let Mr Miles know you're here."

The woman led the way into a spacious, ornately decorated room with a crystal chandelier hanging from the ceiling. An open fire was blazing in the marble fireplace. Two of the walls were lined from floor to ceiling with books. Several brocade-covered chairs were positioned around a large oval table containing three reading lamps. Several drinks decanters and glasses were on a small table by the window.

"Bloody hell," Burrows said, giving a low whistle. "It's like being on a set from Downton Abbey, complete with chambermaid."

Calvert frowned. "Yes, it is, isn't it?" he said quietly. "Not bad from a bloke brought up on a council estate in Chapeltown."

The heavy oak door flung open, and Miles Wright stepped briskly into the room.

"Ah, you must be the police officers here to ask me about Gina Beauchamp," he said, striding purposefully to the drinks table and pouring himself a whisky. "Well, ask away. I'll help in any way I can."

Calvert studied Wright. No more than thirty, he deduced. Well dressed, thick set and of medium height. His fair collar-length hair was brushed back off his rather high forehead and intense light-blue eyes.

"Mr Wright, I was hoping to speak to you and your father," Calvert began, "I..."

"Miles, please," he interrupted. "In this house I'm referred to as Mr Miles. It avoids confusion with my father." He walked over to one of the chairs and plopped down. "I'm afraid you can't speak to pops. He's away on business. He won't be back until late." He sipped at his drink. "Why do you want to speak to him anyway? He hasn't been speeding again, has he?"

"No, sir, nothing like that. Your father was one of Ms Beauchamp's clients. We'll be speaking to all her clients during our investigation."

Miles huffed. "Waste of time if you ask me. I thought you'd caught the bastard who killed her. It said so on the news."

"We did make an arrest, but the person has been released on bail."

"So, you're saying there's a murderer on the loose?"

Calvert ignored Miles's remark. "I understand you were a good friend of Gina Beauchamp?"

Miles shrugged. "I wouldn't say good friends, exactly. I took her out to dinner a couple of times, but there was nothing serious going on between us."

"I hear you and Ms Beauchamp had words the last time you were at her office. Could you tell me what that was about?"

"We had a disagreement, but what exactly has that got to do with what happened to her? Surely you can't think I'm responsible?"

"At this point in our investigation we must look at all the facts. What was the argument about?"

Miles took another sip at his whisky, then ran his tongue over his lips before he answered. "It was silly really," he said at last. "I'd installed a couple of cameras in her apartment, and she got upset about not being consulted."

"Why would you do that?"

"I did it to keep the girl safe. You do know her apartment had been broken into a few days earlier?"

Calvert frowned. "No, I didn't know that. Was anything stolen?"

Miles shook his head. "No, at least not according to Gina. She said they'd made a mess in her study rifling through papers, but nothing had been taken. If the silly girl had left the cameras in situ..."

"I take it the incident was not reported to the police?"

Miles gave a raucous laugh, throwing back his head. "Of course it wasn't. What could they have done, if they'd even bothered to turn up that is? No, Gina insisted the matter was left alone."

"Where were you the night Ms Beauchamp was murdered?"

"I was in London on business," he said, brushing an imaginary speck from his lapel. "I have all the details of my stay if you wish to see them. I only got back last night."

"Do you know if Ms Beauchamp had any enemies? Anyone who wished her harm?"

Miles drained the contents of his glass before answering. "Like I said, Gina and I were not close. I really don't know a great deal about her private life. I would have thought her secretary may be able to point you in that direction."

Calvert turned to DS Burrows. "Perhaps you could make a note of Miles's movements on the night in question," he said.

"Yes, sir," Burrows said, taking out her notebook.

……

Calvert and Burrows were halfway to the station before they spoke.

"Well, sergeant, what did you make of Mr Miles Wright?"

Burrows shrugged. "He seemed alright, I suppose, but there's something about him that... well, that doesn't seem real. It felt like he was playing a part. I can't explain it, but I don't think he was telling the whole story."

"Yes, I agree. I'm sure that young man knows a lot more about Gina Beauchamp's private life than he's letting on."

"I'll check his alibi of course, but he seems to have been in the company of other well-respected people for the entire time."

"Of that I have no doubt, but I still think he's hiding something, and I mean to find out what."

He turned the car into the police station car park and parked in his designated space. "What did you think to West Top Manor? Impressive, isn't it?"

Burrows grinned. "It was beautiful, like something from a bygone age."

"It is. The house was originally owned by the Westfield family. Back in the day, they owned coal mines and weaving mills all over Yorkshire. They had more money than you could count."

"So what happened?"

"Unfortunately, the Westfield's were not very fertile. The family dwindled down until there was just Felix and his brother, Robin. Both men never married. Robin went to live in America, California I believe. He had something to do with the film industry over there."

"What about Felix?"

"Felix chose to keep the house on. He was well into his nineties when he died five years ago. Robin decided to sell the house, together with most of its contents. That's when Oscar Wright bought the house."

"Ah, so the wonderful décor is nothing to do with him?"

Calvert shook his head. "Absolutely nothing."

Both officers got out of the vehicle and walked towards the station.

"What are you going to do about Alex Maddox? Do you still think he's involved?"

"I haven't written him off yet. I'm still not happy with his version of events."

Burrows frowned. "Sir, I hope you don't mind me saying, but is this anything to do with the fact that Karl Maddox is his father?"

Calvert turned sharply to face the sergeant. "Karl Maddox is as crooked as they come. He's got away with far too much for far too long. I intend to clip his wings for good."

"And you intend to do that through his son?"

Calvert snorted and strode towards the station door. "By any means at my disposal," he said, entering the station. "Type up your report and have it on my desk today."

23

After he left the offices of Bonneville, Beauchamp & Clements, Karl drove straight to Murtagh Court where Gina's apartment had been. Entering the lavish entrance foyer, he was confronted by the concierge, a stocky middle-aged man wearing steel-rimmed spectacles and a dark-grey suit. A metal badge with the name 'Henry' was pinned to the lapel of his jacket. Henry was seated behind a large, light-oak counter and on seeing Karl, pushed the copy of '*Racing Times*' beneath it.

"Good afternoon, sir," he said in a rather nasal voice. "May I help you?"

"Good afternoon," Karl said cordially. "My name is Karl Maddox. I want to speak with you about one of your tenants, Miss Gina Beauchamp."

"Miss Beauchamp is no longer with us, I'm afraid," he said. "The young lady died."

"I'm aware of that. I need to ask you a few questions about—"

Henry frowned. "Maddox, you say? Are you related to that man the police arrested for her murder?"

"He's my son, and he's not under arrest anymore."

The concierge sprang to his feet and rushed to the front of the desk. Karl was surprised at his agility. "I'm sorry, but I must ask you to leave. I have nothing to say on the matter." He grabbed Karl's arm to direct him to the door.

"Get you fucking hands off me right now," Karl snarled, pulling himself free from the concierge's grasp. "I intend to ask you some questions and I would advise you strongly to answer them. Do we understand each other, Henry?"

Henry nodded weakly, quickly returning to the relative safety behind the counter.

"What exactly is it you want to know?"

"The night Alex was here, was it you who saw him?"

"Yes. Me and Andy McCulloch. We work shift together."

"What exactly happened?"

"They were on the first landing," he said pointing to the staircase. "The young man was shaking her by the shoulders. The girl looked proper frightened."

"Did you hear what was said?"

"Not clearly. You're best asking Andy. His ears are keener than mine."

"Did I hear my name mentioned?"

Karl and Henry turned to see a tall, lean man in his early twenties approaching.

"Ah Andy, there you are," Henry said. The relief in his voice was evident. "I was just telling Mr Maddox about that argument between Miss Beauchamp and that chap."

"So I heard. What of it?"

Karl stepped towards him. "Did you hear what was said?"

Andy shrugged. "The bloke was insisting she kept away from someone. I don't know who. Then she started screaming at him to mind his own business and... well, you know how these things go. Before too long shouting and screaming turn to blows."

"Are you saying he hit her?"

"It was just a slap, but it did the trick. The stupid woman was becoming hysterical."

"Where exactly were you when this happened?"

"Here," Andy said. "Right here. Me and Henry are always here. Isn't that right, Henry?"

Henry nodded his agreement.

"You saw my son leave?"

"Yeah. He stormed out of here like a rocket."

"You never left the foyer unattended?"

"Not for a minute."

"Did anyone else come into the building after he left?"

Henry shook his head. "No, it was quiet as the grave. I think everyone was watching the England match on the telly that night."

"Ah, you mean the match when France beat England 3-1?"

Henry huffed. "Don't be daft. England were playing Italy and they won 2-0. It was a qualifier for the World Cup. It was a brilliant match."

Karl glanced around the foyer. "I don't see a television set in here."

"No, it's in the back."

"If you're in the back watching the football, how come you are so positive that no one came into the building?"

Andy stepped forward menacingly. "Look, mate, if you're trying to stir up trouble..."

"What I'm trying to do is get at the truth."

Henry exhaled. "Put the kettle on, Andy. I fancy a cuppa." He turned to Karl. "Alright," he said. "Maybe we did leave our post for a bit. This job doesn't pay a King's ransom you know."

"So it was possible someone could have got into the building without your knowledge?"

"I... I suppose so, but it's unlikely. We weren't gone that long, and the connecting door was left open."

"What about the night Ms Beauchamp's flat was burgled? Were you watching the telly that night too?"

Henry hung his head. "I defy anyone to sit behind this counter for twelve hours a night and not get bored out of their minds. A bit of telly now and again breaks the monotony, that's all."

Andy clasped his hands. "You won't tell the boss, will you? I need this job. I've got a kid on the way and—"

"I'm not a grass," Karl said, "but you'd better tell the police what you've told me. My son's not going down for something he didn't do."

24

It was almost six o'clock that evening when Karl arrived at The Emerald Club. The foyer was empty, so he made his way into the main club. Simon and Paul were arranging the newly delivered drinking glasses behind the bar.

Paul rushed over to him. "Everything alright, boss?" he said, "only I've been trying to get hold of you for the past hour."

Taking his mobile from his pocket, Karl frowned. "Oh, sorry. I turned it off when I went to visit Beauchamp. I forgot to turn it on again."

"Well, never mind that now. I rang to tell you Lisa's back. She's at the house now. She's brought Christina with her too."

Karl huffed. "I suppose I'd better get over to the house. Will you and Si be okay to finish off here?"

Paul grinned. "Of course we will. We've managed so far on our own, haven't we?"

"Fuck you," Karl grinned, as he hurried through to the foyer.

……

Lisa was reclining on one of the large couches in the sitting room when Karl arrived at the house. As he entered the room, she made no attempt to get up.

"At last," she said. "I thought I'd been abandoned."

Karl strolled over to the couch and kissed her lightly on the cheek. "Good to see you, Lisa. You're looking well."

Lisa pulled herself up onto her elbows and swung her legs down to the ground. "What's happening with Alex? Have you heard? I've tried ringing him but he's not answering his phone."

Karl shrugged. "Don't worry about him. He'll be alright."

"Who is he supposed to have killed?"

Holding Lisa's hand, Karl perched on the edge of the couch and began to relay the events of the last few days. "The police can't prove that no one was able to enter the building after Alex left, so they have no case against him."

Lisa frowned. "But he's still on bail?"

"A mere formality. Bonneville will sort it out. Now, when are you coming home? I've missed you."

"Home? You mean to Leeds?"

"Of course I mean to Leeds, where else? Christina and Matthew won't want you hanging round them forever, will they? Besides, you're my wife. Your place is by my side."

"Karl, I… I don't want to come back. I couldn't cope with the life we had before."

"What-the-fuck do you mean by that, the life we had before? We had a good life in case you've forgotten, and we'll have a good life again."

Tears began to trickle down Lisa's face and she brushed them away with the back of her hand. "I… I can't live like that anymore, wondering who is out there wanting to hurt you. Paul said you've got The

Emerald back. If that's what makes you happy then I'm glad, but it's not for me. Not anymore."

Before Karl could respond, the door flung open and Christina rushed towards him, flinging her arms around his neck. "Dad," she cried, "how lovely to see you again. How's Alex? Is he going to be alright?"

"Don't worry, Alex hasn't been charged."

Karl got to his feet and strolled over to the drinks cabinet. "Anyone fancy a drink?" Both women declined as he poured himself a large whisky.

Lisa scowled. "I thought you were cutting back on the booze. You know what the doctor said."

"And you know what I think about doctors." He turned to Christina. "I want to know all about Australia," he said, "but first tell me all about my grandson."

25

Oscar Wright banged the front door shut after him as he entered West Top Manor at eleven-thirty that night. Trish, the young housemaid, came running into the hallway.

"Good evening, Mr Oscar," she said, taking his coat which he flung at her.

"Where's Miles? Where's that bloody useless son of mine?"

Oscar thundered past Trish and went into the lounge.

"Mr Miles has gone to bed," Trish said. "Do you want me to wake him?"

"Of course I want you to bloody wake him. Tell him to get his idle arse down here now." The veins in Oscar's neck pulsated and his face flushed with anger.

"Did I hear my name spoken?" Miles said from the lounge doorway, rubbing his eyes with his knuckles. "What... what time is it?"

Oscar snarled, pointing his finger menacingly at his son. "Never mind what time it is. What the fuck were you doing talking to the cops without me being present? How many times do I have to tell you? Are you stupid?"

Miles yawned as he sprawled over an armchair. "Chill out," he said. "They just wanted to ask about me and Gina."

"What about you and Gina? I thought you said that was all over."

"It is. They'd heard about us rowing at her office and wanted to know what it was about, that's all."

Oscar plopped into an armchair. "Those bloody cameras," he said. "This is all your fault."

Miles sprang to his feet. "Wait a minute. It was your idea, not mine."

"It was a good idea if you hadn't ballsed it up. Just goes to show, don't send a boy to do a man's job."

Miles walked over to the door. "I'm going back to bed," he said. "Oh, by the way, the cops want to talk to you. Apparently, they're talking to all of Gina's clients."

Oscar huffed, slapping his fist into his cupped hand. "Damn it! I could do without this. There's another job coming up soon. I don't want the cops nosing around."

"Don't worry. They've already got a suspect. They're not interested in us."

"You'd better be right. We're answerable to some pretty violent bastards."

26

Joe and Sarah arrived home late that evening after their brief honeymoon in Paris.

"I'll put the kettle on," Sarah said, making her way to the kitchen. "Charlotte said she put fresh milk in the fridge this morning."

Joe followed and gently put his arms around her slim waist. "Don't bother with tea," he whispered, nuzzling her neck. "There's champagne in the fridge. Let's have that instead."

Sarah began to giggle. "Darling, we have work in the morning. I think we'd better stick to tea, don't you?"

Joe sighed. "I suppose you're right. Does this mean the honeymoon is really over?"

Sarah kissed Joe on the lips. "No. It's not over, darling. Just postponed until the weekend, that's all."

Joe raised his hands in mock surrender. "Okay, you win. I'll check the post and leave you to get on with the tea."

He returned to the lounge where Charlotte had placed a dozen envelopes on the coffee table earlier that day. Joe meticulously read each piece of correspondence before stacking them in a neat pile. Most of the post referred to his business, a small fleet of private hire cars. His manager, Mike Pearce. had been dealing with the day-to-day running of the business in Joe's absence. He put the final letter on the pile just as Sarah came into the room with two mugs of steaming-hot tea.

"Anything interesting in the post?" she asked, placing the mugs on the table.

Joe shook his head. "Nothing that can't wait until tomorrow," he said, handing an envelope to her. "This one is for you."

Sarah opened the envelope. It contained a hand-written letter from her friend Molly who worked at the same boutique.

"Oh, I don't believe it," she gasped, handing the letter to Joe. "Alex has been arrested for murder."

Joe took the letter and read it, a wry smile on his lips. "Well, well, what is it they say? An apple doesn't fall far from the tree?"

Sarah shook her head in disbelief. "No, Joe. I can't believe Alex would murder anyone. He wasn't a good husband but he's not a killer."

Before Joe could respond his mobile rang. Scowling at the disturbance from his manager, Joe picked up the phone. "Yes, Mike. What's so urgent it can't wait until tomorrow?" Joe listened intently to what Mike had to say. "Thanks for letting me know," he said. "I'll deal with it tomorrow."

He put his phone on the table, a serious expression on his face. Sarah took his hand in hers.

"Whatever's the matter, Joe? You look like you've seen a ghost."

Joe remained silent as he got to his feet and began pacing the room.

"Joe, what is it? You're frightening me."

Joe blinked rapidly, then perched on the couch next to Sarah. "Darling," he said softly, "I want you to stay with Charlotte and Lewis for a few days."

"Why? What's happened?"

Joe held Sarah's hand reassuringly. "There's absolutely nothing for you to worry about, but—"

"I'm you wife. Don't lie to me. What's going on?"

Joe lowered his head. "That... that was Mike on the phone."

"Yes, I gathered that. What did he say to upset you like this?"

"A couple of blokes have been hanging around the garage. They were asking where I was and when I'd be back."

"Who were they? What did they want?"

"Mike recognised one of them. He said his name was Paul Borowicz, Karl's right-hand man."

Sarah gave a slight shudder. "Joe, I don't want Karl back in our lives again. Please, you must do something."

Joe put his arm protectively around Sarah. "Don't worry, love. I'll take care of it, but first I want you out of the way. I'll ring Charlotte and arrange for you to stay."

"But Joe—"

"No buts, Sarah. Until I know what the hell's going on, I need to keep you safe."

27

It was midnight as, whisky in hand, Karl leant back into the plush office chair, a satisfied grin across his face.

"So, Joe's actually gone and married Sarah, has he?"

"According to the bloke at the garage they'll be back from their honeymoon tonight."

"Well, I'll say one thing for Joe, he's got some balls. How close is the garage from here? Three miles?"

"Four," Paul corrected, "and his house is a further two miles away on the edge of Roundhay Park."

"And you're sure this bloke at the garage knew who you were?"

"Yeah. His name's Mike something or other. We worked on the doors together in Manchester a few years back. He recognised me, although he didn't let on."

Karl began to chuckle. "You can bet he's let Joe know you were sniffing round. What I wouldn't give to be a fly on their wall tonight."

"What exactly are you planning to do? I wouldn't have thought he was a threat to you anymore. All the evidence has been taken care of."

"It's nothing to do with evidence. Just let's say me and Joe Stevens have got unfinished business."

There was a tap on the door and Simon came into the office. "I'm off now, boss," he said. "I've got the auditions with the girls first thing tomorrow."

"Okay, I'll lock up."

"By the way, how's Lisa and Christina? Are they well?"

"They're both fine."

"Will they be coming to the club for the opening? It'll be like old times."

Karl shrugged. "I've no idea what their plans are. Lisa's worried sick about Alex and Chris... well Chris will do exactly as she wants, just like she always does."

Karl drained his glass and reached for his jacket. "I'd better be getting back," he said. "We've a lot on tomorrow."

Paul followed Karl out of the office and down the stairs into the foyer.

"I don't suppose you've heard anything about Patrick Flynn?"

"Not yet, but if he's in England I'll find him."

After locking the door and setting the alarm, both men walked out onto the street.

"Oh, before I forget, can you arrange for Oscar Wright Securities to call in to give me a quote. I think we need to update our security."

"Sure, I'll give them a ring tomorrow."

"Good, and make sure it's the organ-grinder who comes, not his monkey."

Chuckling to himself, Paul walked across the car park to his vehicle, got in and drove away. Karl was about to get into his Mercedes when he realised there was someone standing in the shadows.

"Who's there?" he said, walking in the direction of the figure. "Fuck off, you're trespassing."

The figure stepped forward. "That's no way to speak to an old friend."

Karl blinked in astonishment. "Joe. What the fuck are you doing here?"

"I was told you were looking for me. Well, here I am."

Karl's posture stiffened. "I'd heard you were back in Leeds. I was wondering what you were up to, that's all. By the way, I hear congratulations are in order. You and Sarah, eh? Who'd have thought it?"

Joe took a step closer to Karl. "I don't know what your game is but stay away from me and from Sarah. You're bad news, Karl. You always have been."

Both men stood toe-to-toe glaring at one another for a few seconds, Karl's fingers automatically curling into fists. It was Karl who broke the silence.

"Well, pleasant as this is to rekindle old friendships, I really must be going." He turned and walked towards his car. "Nice seeing you again, Joe," he said. "I'll be in touch."

Joe watched as Karl drove his Mercedes out of the car park. The fingers of his right hand tightly wrapped around the handle of a steel knife.

28

The following day, Karl drove Lisa to visit Alex at his apartment. Although it was almost noon, Alex was still in his dressing gown when they arrived. Lisa rushed over to her son, throwing her arms around his neck.

"Darling, are you alright? My poor baby. What have the police had to say? Are they going to charge you?"

Alex pushed his mother away. "For goodness sake, leave me alone. I'm not a child."

Karl stepped forward. "Then stop behaving like one, and don't let me hear you speak to your mother like that again. We have an appointment with the solicitors this afternoon so hurry up and get ready. We'll just have time for a bite to eat before we go."

Alex pouted. "Not hungry," he said, plonking down on the couch.

Lisa sat next to him and gently took his hand in hers. "Alex, tell me what happened. You didn't hurt that girl, did you?"

"Of course I didn't hurt Gina. I... I loved her."

"Where did you go that night after your argument with her?"

Alex made no reply.

"I asked you a question," Karl said. "Where were you?"

Alex remained stubbornly silent.

Karl leant down and placing his hands on Alex's shoulders, pulled him to his feet.

"Stop being a twat," he said, shaking him violently. "You have to provide an alibi, otherwise the cops will hang you by the balls. Now, for the last time, where the fuck were you?"

Alex wriggled unsuccessfully to get free from Karl's grasp.

"Well? I'm waiting."

Lisa jumped up and attempted to pull Karl off her son. "Leave him alone, you're hurting him," she said.

In frustration, Karl pushed Alex back onto the couch.

"You're not doing yourself any favours keeping quiet," he said. "Just tell the police where you were and this will all be over."

"Will it? If I tell them where I was, things will only get worse. Much worse."

Karl scowled. "How? Tell me how things could get any worse."

"Because... because I was sat in my car outside her apartment watching her. That's how."

Lisa gasped. "Darling, why would you do that?"

"I thought she was meeting someone. I needed to know who."

"And was she?"

Alex shook his head. "Not whilst I was there, so you see, if I tell the cops I was stalking her... well, there's your evidence."

Karl was silent for a moment. "Did anyone see you parked up outside the building?"

"No, I don't think so."

"What time did you leave?"

Alex shrugged. "About midnight. I came back here and went straight to bed."

"No one saw you?"

"No, not at that time."

"In that case we need to get you an alibi."

Lisa frowned. "What are you talking about, get him an alibi?"

"Leave it with me," Karl said, taking out his phone. He dialled a number. "Danny? Danny mate, I need you and Lenny to do me a favour."

29

Karl got back to The Emerald about four o'clock that afternoon. Simon was standing by the bar with a couple of young women. On seeing him, Simon rushed over.

"How did Alex get on with the solicitor?" he said. "Is everything sorted?"

Karl shrugged. "I think so. Danny and Lenny are giving him an alibi for that night."

Smiling, Simon raised an eyebrow. "Really? I wouldn't have thought Bar Dalziel was his cup of tea."

"He was there to see two of his mates. There's nothing wrong with that, is there?"

"No, of course not."

"How did the auditions go?"

"Great. I've signed up seven hostesses for the VIP lounge and a dozen dancers for down here. All we need now is a start date."

Karl gave a quizzical look at the two women at the bar. "Who are they?" he said, "and what are they doing here?"

"The red-head is Suki, the cleaner I was telling you about. The blonde is Kelly, her sister. You might remember her. She worked here last year."

"So, why are they still here? The auditions finished hours ago."

"Kelly wanted to speak with you. She said it was important so I said she could wait."

Kelly strode over to Karl and smiled. "It's good to see you again, Karl," she said. "Might I have a word?"

"What about?"

"In private?"

Karl studied the woman. Her blonde hair cascaded over her slender shoulders and her blue eyes were still as stunning as he remembered. Her flawless complexion bore little makeup and her perfume was subtle yet tantalizing.

"This way," he said, turning towards the foyer and the staircase to his office. "I can spare you five minutes, that's all. I'm a busy man."

Karl led the way up to his office and Kelly followed.

"Well?" he said, taking his seat behind his desk. "What do you want to talk to me about that's so urgent?"

Kelly inhaled, clenching her hands tightly by her side. "It's about my sister," she said. "She's the girl downstairs."

"What about her?"

"I... I don't want her working here. She's too young, too innocent to be working in a place like this. Please, Karl, tell her no."

"Have you spoken to her?"

"Of course I have. I've pleaded with her, but she's got it into her head that working here as a dancer is more glamorous than being a cleaner."

Karl smirked. "She does have a point."

"But—"

Karl raised his hand. "This isn't a knocking shop, it's adult entertainment. I'm sure Sue, or Suki as she prefers, will be perfectly safe working here."

"I wasn't," Kelly said. "I was made to do things I didn't want to do."

"I don't remember you objecting at the time," Karl said, "in fact I think you were enthusiastic, especially with all that money you were paid."

"I don't want that kind of life for Sue. She's better than that."

"I would have thought she's better than cleaning toilets too."

"Can you promise me that nothing like that will happen to her? Please, Karl. I'm begging you."

Karl opened his desk drawer and took out a cigar. "Suki is paid to entertain the customers, just like you," he said. "Now, your five minutes are up. I'm sure you can find your own way out."

……

Kelly rushed down the stairs, through the foyer and into the main club. Sue was standing at the bar talking with Simon. She grabbed her by the elbow, swinging her round.

"Come on," she said, "we're going."

Sue hurriedly picked up her bag from a bar stool as she was unceremoniously steered to the exit by Kelly.

"What's your problem?" Sue wailed as she entered the street. "I was talking to Simon."

"This isn't the place for you," Kelly said. "Please say you won't work here. I'm begging you."

"You work here."

"I have no choice. We're on our own, Sue. We need the money."

"I hate my cleaning jobs. Why shouldn't I work at The Emerald and earn good money too?"

"Because... because it can be dangerous. You know that a bloke got shot in there last year?"

"That's not likely to happen again, is it? Anyway, a bloke got shot in Kirkgate Market last week. Does that mean I shouldn't go there to shop?"

"That's not the same, and you know it. Now promise me you'll stay away from The Emerald. Please, Sue."

Sue threw back her head in a gesture of defiance. "I'll do no such thing. I think you're jealous that I'll be more popular with the punters than you."

"Don't be ridiculous, you silly girl. I—"

Sue pulled away from her sister and began to run along the road, leaving a distraught Kelly behind.

30

Inspector Calvert watched as Alex Maddox and his solicitor, Arthur Bonneville, left the police station. DS Burrows was by the inspector's side.

"What do you think, sir?" Burrows said. "Do you believe his story?"

"Do I fuck. His alibi's been concocted by Maddox."

"But there are half a dozen customers from the Bar Dalziel who will swear that Alex was there from the time he left Gina's apartment until long after she had been stabbed."

"Tomorrow we'll visit each and every one and take statements from them. You can bet your pension they'll all give exactly the same story."

"Unfortunately, unless we can prove they're lying, there's not much we can do about it, is there?"

Calvert huffed. "In the good old days before this PACE shit came into force, we'd give them a going over in the cells. We'd soon find out the truth."

"Yes, sir, but those days are long gone."

"More's the pity," Calvert said. "I'm going for a cuppa. Are you coming?"

Both officers made their way to the canteen.

"Well, sir," Burrows said as she sipped her tea in the police canteen, "what's our next move? We've eliminated Miles Wright and it looks like we're going to have to eliminate Alex Maddox too."

Calvert shook his head slowly. "My money's still on Maddox. That dozy pair of nightwatchmen are unreliable witnesses. It would have been easy for him to slip back into the building whilst they were watching the footie."

"It would have been easy for anyone to do the same for that matter," Burrows said. "It's a pity there is no CCTV in the building. It would have made our job a lot easier."

"Talking of surveillance cameras, has Oscar Miles made contact yet? We need to speak to him about his dealings with Gina."

"No, not yet. I'll call him later for an appointment."

"Good. In the meantime, I'm going to do a background check on him and Miles. There's something very wrong there. I'm sure of it."

31

Oscar Wright was in his early fifties. Just under six feet tall, stocky with receding grey hair and, like his son, piercing blue eyes. Well-dressed in a dark-blue suit and white shirt with a black woollen overcoat, he emitted an aura of importance. It was one o'clock in the afternoon when he entered The Emerald Club to be greeted in the foyer by Simon.

"Ah, so this is the famous Emerald Club that everyone is talking about," he said, gazing around the room. "Impressive, I must say."

Simon stepped forward and held out his hand. "Mr Wright?" he said as they shook hands, "Mr Maddox is expecting you, if you'll follow me?"

Both men made their way up the stairwell, through the VIP Lounge to Karl's office. Simon knocked briskly on the door and entered. "Boss, Mr Wright to see you."

"Show him in," Karl said, rising from his chair.

Oscar Wright walked confidently into the office. "Good afternoon, Karl. You don't mind if I call you Karl, do you? I've never been one for formalities."

"Thank you for coming so promptly, Oscar," Karl said, indicating the two armchairs in the office. "Please take a seat. Can I get you anything to drink? Tea, coffee or perhaps something a little stronger?" indicating the drinks cabinet in the corner of the room.

"Not for me, thanks," Oscar said. "I never touch the stuff when I'm doing business. I like to keep a clear head."

Karl shrugged as he walked over to the cabinet and poured himself a large whisky. "I'm just the opposite. I find I think clearer with a drink."

Oscar lifted his briefcase onto the desk. "I was sorry to hear about your son being nicked for murdering that girl. You must be worried sick."

"Worried? Why should I be? Alex is innocent and the cops can't prove otherwise."

"Let's hope you're right." He busied himself for a few seconds taking out various brochures from his briefcase and displaying them on the desk. "I've taken the liberty of bringing some of our systems to show you," he said. "Perhaps you could tell me what level of security you're looking for? I noticed as I came in that the system you have installed is quite high-spec."

"That's true, but it's been in a while," Karl said. "I want it updating. You can't be too careful these days, can you?"

"Well, you've come to the right place. Wright's Securities are the right security for you." Oscar began to chuckle. "That's our motto. Catchy don't you think?"

Karl gave a weak smile. "Tell me about your company. How long have you been operating and what type of clients do you have?"

"Our clients are corporates mainly," Oscar said. "We used to do domestic, but as our reputation grew, we decided to go after the big fish. That was about five years ago. We've never looked back since."

"Who's we? I take it you have partners in the business?"

"Just my son, Miles. He's the one that usually gives the quotes, but I understand you specifically asked for me. Do you mind if I ask why?"

Karl shrugged. "What I'm planning for the club is going to be expensive. I like to get to know who I'm doing business with before I start handing out money. I'm sure you understand, Oscar?"

"Absolutely, Karl. I couldn't agree more. Now, times pressing. Perhaps you could show me around and I'll make notes."

Karl picked up the internal phone on his desk. "Si? Can you come up, please?" He turned to Oscar. "My manager will show you what needs to be done. I have briefed him."

"Oh, very well. I'll send you my recommendations within a couple of days."

Simon tapped on the door and entered the room.

"Si, I want you to show Mr Wright around the club like we discussed."

"Sure thing, boss." He turned to Oscar. "If you'd follow me Mr Wright, we'll start with the VIP lounge."

Left alone, Karl picked up his phone and dialled a number. "Lenny? I want you to get in touch with Spud. I have a job for her."

32

Christina was reclining on the couch watching television when Karl returned home that night.

"Where's your mother?" he asked.

"She's gone to see Alex. She said she might be late back so not to worry."

Karl casually walked towards the drinks cabinet and began pouring himself a generous Macallen. "Want one?"

"Sure, why not?" Christina said. "I'd best make the most of not having Matthew constantly breathing down my neck."

Frowning, Karl poured the drinks and handed a glass to his daughter. "Matthew has a problem with you having a drink?"

"Dad, these days Matthew has a problem with everything I do. He seems to think that once you become a mother you cease to become who you are, what you enjoy. I... Oh, I'm sorry Dad. I shouldn't be burdening you with my problems. You've enough on your plate with Alex."

"No, I'm interested. What exactly is the problem?"

Christina sipped at the whisky, then carefully placed the glass on the table before she answered. "Ever since Lydia died, he's changed. He's become more... I don't know, it's hard to explain, but he's dictating what I do and where I go all the time. He's constantly checking up on me."

"That doesn't sound like Matthew," Karl said. "Have you tried speaking with him about it?"

"He barely talks to me these days. When he's not working, he's spending all of his time with the baby."

"That's good, isn't it? A father taking an interest in their child?"

Christina shrugged. "He's employed a nanny you know. There's me and Mother in the house, but he goes and pays for a nanny to look after the kid."

"I suppose he's thinking it's giving you more time to enjoy yourself."

"You think so? He wants to know where I am, what I'm doing, who I'm doing it with. He's driving me crazy."

"What does your mother have to say about it? It's not like Lisa not to get involved."

"Mother... well, mother has her own interests. She's rarely at home."

Frowning, Karl leant forward. "What do you mean, rarely at home? Where exactly does she go?"

Christina picked up her glass and sipped at the whisky. "You'd better ask her."

"I'm asking you. What the fuck is she up to?"

Christina shuffled uncomfortably, staring down at the floor. "She has... she has a friend who she sees a lot of."

"What's this friend's name?"

"Dad, it's not important. I don't want you to think—"

"Answer me, damn it! I take it this friend is a man?"

Christina nodded. "His name is Alan Dawson. He owns a haulage firm. But Dad, I'm sure there's nothing going on between them."

Karl took out his mobile and rang a number. It was answered almost immediately. "Lisa? Lisa, I want you back here right now."

33

Lisa arrived at the house at ten-thirty. Christina had gone to bed and Karl was standing by the window in the lounge.

"What's so urgent?" she said, taking off her coat and throwing it onto the back of the couch. "Alex and I were enjoying a late supper together."

"I hear you've made a new friend in Australia," Karl said.

"I've made lots of new friends in Australia."

"But this is a special friend. Alan Dawson. Tell me about him."

Lisa perched on the edge of the couch; her hands clasped in front of her. "Alan's a friend. A good friend."

"Are you fucking him?"

"What? How dare you?" Lisa attempted to get to her feet but Karl sprung forward and pushed her back onto the couch.

"I asked you a question," he snarled. "Are you fucking him?"

"That's none of your damned business," she said. "I've told you, Karl, you and I are finished. Once Alex is cleared of all charges, I'm going back to Australia, and you can't stop me."

Karl grabbed her by the hair and raised his fist as if to hit her, then suddenly stopped. "You're going nowhere," he said. "You're my wife and you'll do what I say."

Lisa managed to wriggle free. "You don't scare me," she said. "I'm not Erica. You can't bully me like you did her." She got to her feet and shakily stumbled to the hall door. "I assume it was your daughter told you about Alan?"

"She says you spend days away from home with him."

"Then she's lying. Alan and I go out to dinner sometimes. He's good company and it gives him a break from attending to his invalid wife. She's in a hospice."

"But you spend the night with him."

"I have never spent the night with Alan, nor have I had sex with him either. When I'm away from the house overnight, I'm usually staying with one of my friends from the book club or the wine tasting society. The atmosphere in the house is toxic. I have to get away."

"But Christina says—"

"Christina is a liar; she always has been." Lisa walked cautiously over to Karl. "Ask her why her husband keeps her on such a short leash, and why she has such little contact with her son."

"What the fuck are you talking about?"

"You might also ask her about Matthew's mother."

"What about her? Christina said Lydia had a heart attack."

"Really? Did she tell you there was a lethal amount of drugs in her system when she died?"

"Lydia's always been unhinged. She probably committed suicide."

"Matthew didn't seem to think so."

"What are you saying?"

"He thinks Christina was somehow responsible for his mother's death. After all, getting Lydia out of the way was what Christina always wanted."

"You're crazy if you think she would do something like that."

"Am I?"

"What are you saying, Lisa?"

"I'm saying that I believe Christina is capable of anything, including murder."

34

Inspector Calvert was sitting at his desk the next morning. Across from him was Oscar Wright.

"Tell me, Mr Wright, how long had Gina Beauchamp been your solicitor?"

"Please, inspector, do call me Oscar. Everyone does."

"Please answer my question."

"Gina began representing my company a few months ago. Her uncle, Jeramiah Beauchamp had been my solicitor for many years prior to his retirement. Gina replaced him in the firm."

"When was the last time you spoke with Gina?"

Furrowing his brow, Oscar began to stroke his chin. "Let me see, it must have been the day before she died. I'd called into the office to sign some documents."

"Did Gina seem worried or upset in any way?"

"No, not that I recall."

"How did the breakdown of her relationship with your son affect her? I understand they were close at one time."

Oscar smirked. "If Gina had expectations towards Miles she was wasting her time. When my son does decide to settle down and take a wife, it will be to a much bigger and more influential fish than a junior solicitor. I can promise you that."

"What exactly was Gina Beauchamp's involvement in your business?"

"Involvement? I don't know what you mean."

"We've checked her phone records. She seems to have spent a great deal of time talking with you this last couple of weeks. Why was that?"

Oscar shrugged. "Gina dealt with several of my company's legal affairs. They are confidential and I do not intend to discuss them with you."

"Who'll be handling your business from now on? I hear Jeramiah's back in the office."

"Yes, I'm seeing him this afternoon. There are one or two matters which need putting to bed." Oscar glanced at his watch. "If there's nothing else, Inspector, I really do need to be going. I've a couple of things to do before my meeting with Beauchamp."

Calvert closed his notebook and placed his pen into its holder. "I think that's everything for now," he said. "I may need to speak to you later though."

Scraping back his chair, Oscar got to his feet. "As you wish," he said, walking towards the door, "but I really don't think I can throw any light on what happened to poor Gina." Opening the door, he bounded down the corridor and out into the car park.

"Arrogant twat," Calvert muttered, firmly closing the door behind him.

35

It was two o'clock that afternoon when Spud arrived at the club. She was clad in the same black leather clothes she had worn at their first meeting, but this time her short, spiky hair was bright pink. She followed Simon into Karl's office and timidly nodded by way of greeting.

Karl was behind his desk, smoking a cigar. He gave his broadest smile. "So glad you could find the time," he said. "I have another little job for you. Take a seat." He indicated the chair in front of his desk.

Curiosity piqued; Spud perched nervously on the edge of the chair.

"Have you heard of a company called Wright Securities?" he said. "They're based in Leeds."

"Yes, of course. I'd actually been thinking about having a crack at them and test just how good their systems really are."

"Do you think you could break into their company files for me?"

"Access their data?" she corrected. "And yes, I'm sure I could."

"Okay, Spud," he said, handing her a sheet of paper. "This is a list of things I want you to find for me. Do you think you can do that?"

Spud studied the document for a few seconds. "No problem. I could do an even deeper search if you want. It's no trouble."

"Well, I'll leave that to your discretion young lady, as long as you find out the information I have written down on the paper."

Smiling, Spud jumped to her feet. "Sure thing, Mr Maddox. It shouldn't take more than a couple of days."

"That's fine. Just make sure you don't get caught. I don't want this coming back at me."

"Don't worry, it won't. I'm the best in the business at this sort of thing."

"I'm sure you are, Spud," Karl sat back in his chair and put his cigar to his lips. "If you see Simon downstairs, he'll give you half of your fee in advance."

"Thanks," Spud said, opening the door. "I'll see you in a couple of days then."

......

Jeramiah Beauchamp paced nervously around his office. Oscar Wright was lounging on one of the leather armchairs.

"For goodness sake sit down and relax, Beauchamp. You're making me nervous."

"I... I'm sorry Oscar," Beauchamp said, "but this has to stop. I can't help you anymore."

"Yes, you can," Oscar said. "You're in this too deep to back out now."

Beauchamp plonked onto the second chair; his fingers tightly intertwined. "It's too dangerous," he said. "We've been lucky so far but—"

"Luck has nothing to do with it," Oscar sneered. "We've been meticulous and careful, and we will continue to be meticulous and careful in the future."

"But Oscar, what about Gina?"

Oscar scowled, banging his fist down onto the chair arm. "I've told you; Gina's death has no connection with our arrangement. It was a lover's tiff, that's all. That lad of Karl Maddox is responsible. Everybody knows that."

"No, that's where you're wrong. Alex had nothing to do with it."

"How do you know? He's been arrested. It's in all the papers."

"The police have let him go."

"Who told you that?"

"Arthur Bonneville. He's been representing him."

Oscar jumped to his feet. "What? Your partner has been defending that little scrote? I don't believe this."

"There wasn't enough evidence against him to secure a conviction. The police had no choice."

"You shouldn't have let Bonneville anywhere near this, you fucking idiot. What if he finds out about—"

Beauchamp raised his hand. "He won't. Arthur's a lazy bastard. He won't go digging."

"You'd better be right. There's too much at stake for slipups now."

There was a tap on the door and Deborah Wallace discreetly entered the room. "Your three-thirty appointment is waiting in Reception, Mr Beauchamp," she said.

"Oh, thanks Deborah. Tell Mr Reynolds I won't keep him a minute."

Deborah smiled weakly, closing the door.

Oscar snorted. "I don't like it. I don't like it one little bit."

36

"Well, boss, it won't be long now. Twenty-four hours and The Emerald will be back in business."

"You've done a great job, Si. All the lads have," Karl said as he walked around the main club. "The place looks bigger than I remember."

"Oh, that'll be because we took some of the tables out. Most of the blokes like to stand whilst they're watching the girls."

Karl strode over at the far wall with the fleur-de-lis panelling and scowled. "Where's the tables that were here?"

"I got rid of them to create more space."

"Well you'd no business doing that. I want them putting back immediately."

"But Karl, there's much more room without them and—"

"Stop arguing with me and just do as I fucking tell you," Karl yelled. "I want the three tables back there as they were. Understand?"

Simon looked shaken at Karl's outburst. "Sure, no problem. I'll get it done right now." Shoulders slouched, he turned and began to walk away.

"Sorry I was a bit short, mate," Karl said, following him. "My head's up my arse at the moment." He placed his hand on Simon's shoulder. "How many VIP responses have we had? We'll need to get a bit of catering in for upstairs."

"That's all sorted," Simon said. "We've had thirty-six so far. Two of the councillors have sent apologies. They're both going to be abroad on holiday, but apart from that, everyone's coming that you invited."

"Even Oscar Wright?"

Simon nodded. "Yeah, I received his RSVP this morning. He's bringing his son with him too."

"Make sure you put some handy lads in the car park. I don't want a repeat of last time."

"Don't worry, that's taken care of. All of the security staff are coming in later for their final briefing. If you want to come along and have a word...?"

Karl shook his head. "No, too busy. I'll leave that to you."

"I've got the bar and reception staff coming in first thing tomorrow morning for their briefing."

"What about the dancers?"

Simon inhaled deeply placing a hand on each hip. "Karl, I have done this before, remember? I do know what I'm doing."

Grinning, Karl shrugged. "I'll piss off up to my office and leave you to it then, eh?"

"I think that's a good idea," Simon said, a broad grin on his face. "I'll go and replace the tables."

......

Oscar Wright was in his dining room finishing lunch when Miles burst through the door, his breathing was erratic with colour rising in his cheeks and his eyes blazing. He strode over to the table and plonked down on a chair across from his father.

"Are you going to tell me what's the matter, or do you want me to guess?" Oscar said.

"It's Millers Motors," he said. "The bastards have decided not to renew their contract with us."

Oscar laid down his knife and fork. "Did they say why?"

"They said they can get the same deal a lot cheaper elsewhere."

"Did they indeed? And who is going to provide this cheaper deal?"

"Fontaines. That's twice those bastards have pinched our business."

"Did you offer Millers a fair price?"

"Of course I did. We must get their business, Dad. The guys are already beginning to set things in motion."

Oscar picked up his glass and took a sip of the wine. "Leave it with me," he said. "I'll let our friends deal with Fontaines."

"They will be... they will be discreet? The last thing we need is bad publicity."

"Have they ever let us down?"

"No, I suppose not."

"Then stop whittling. I said I'll get it sorted and I will." He dabbed his mouth with a napkin. "By the way, I may have a new client coming on board."

"Oh, who's that?"

"Karl Maddox. He wants a quote for his club, The Emerald."

"What, Karl Maddox the gangster? Dad, you've got to be joking. That bloke's dangerous."

"He didn't seem dangerous to me when I met him."

"When was this?"

"Yesterday. I'm working on the quote today. It should be ready to give him tomorrow night when we meet."

"You're meeting Maddox tomorrow?"

"He's invited me to his opening night."

Miles began to chuckle. "I wouldn't have thought watching a load of skinny-arsed birds twirling round a pole was quite your thing."

"It isn't, but I want the business. Having a finger in The Emerald could be really useful."

Miles got to his feet. "Well good luck with that. I hope you have a lovely evening. You must tell me all about it when you get back."

Oscar pushed his plate to one side, a large grin on his face. "No need, son. You're coming with me."

37

It was nine o'clock. Karl was on his second cup of coffee when Christina came into the room.

"Morning, Dad," she greeted, kissing him lightly on the cheek. "Where's Paul this morning?"

"At the club," Karl said. "He left at seven."

"He's keen. Last night he said everything was ready."

"It is, but there's always something else to be done. I want tonight to be perfect."

Christina smiled as she placed a slice of bread into the toaster. "I would have thought that opening up a club was like shelling peas to you. What will this be, the fourth time?"

"The fifth," Karl corrected. "You've forgotten The Amethyst."

"Oh, of course, The Amethyst. The cause of my little brother's downfall."

"That's a strange thing to say."

"Well it's perfectly true. That's the club he put in hoc to Joe and Matthew. By the way, have you seen Joe lately?" The toast popped up out of the machine and Christina began busying herself with the butter.

Karl drained his cup. "He's around. He's just got back from honeymoon."

Christina huffed. "Alex is well shut of her." She plonked down onto a chair at the table and began pouring herself a coffee.

"Chris, whilst we're on our own, I need to talk to you about something your mother said."

Christina scowled. "Oh? What's she been saying?"

"She thinks things aren't working out too well between you and Matthew. Is she right?"

"That's none of her business, or yours either for that matter."

"You're my daughter and I love you very much so I'm going to ask you right out. Did you have anything to do with Lydia's death?"

Christina gasped. "Is that what she said? How dare she?" She flung the toast across the table and turned to leave the kitchen. Karl sprang to his feet and steered her back to the table.

"I want an answer, and I want the truth."

Christina glared at her father with an air of defiance.

"I'm waiting," he said. "Did you play any part in her death?"

Christina pursed her lips and lowered her head. "I hated that witch so much," she whispered. "She was always interfering and trying to turn Matthew against me."

"So what did you do?"

Christina shrugged. "It was just a few of her sleeping pills. I crushed them up and put them in her drink." She turned to Karl. "I didn't mean to kill her, Dad, honest. I just wanted to make the silly cow sick, that's all. It serves her right for the way she treated me."

"Matthew knew what you did?"

"No, of course not. He thought Lydia had committed suicide. Everybody did."

"And Matthew suspects you were involved?"

"Maybe... I'm not sure. He knows Lydia and I didn't get on."

"Is that why Matthew doesn't allow you much contact with the baby?"

"Probably, but that suits me fine. If he wants to look after the kid, he's welcome. I don't think I'm cut out to be a mother anyway."

"Are you planning to go back to Australia?"

Christina ran her tongue across her lips. "I... I was thinking perhaps I could stay here with you?"

"You want to stay here and abandon your son?"

"Why not? You abandoned me and Alex."

Karl scowled. "That was different, and you know it."

"I... I'm sorry, Dad. I didn't mean it. I want to come back to England to live. I can be really useful to you; you know I can." She flung her arms around Karl's neck. "Please let me stay. I don't want to go back. Please let me stay."

38

"So, what do you think to my hotel?" Lewis asked, addressing Sarah. "The Galaxy isn't quite the Ritz, but it does have style."

"It's beautiful, Lewis," she said, gazing around the elegant suite she was sharing with Charlotte. "You wouldn't think you were so near to Leeds, would you? There's so much countryside around."

"You and Joe will have to visit my hotel in Barbados when it's completed. That should be in about a month's time."

"Oh, we'd love to. I've never been to the Caribbean before. Is it as lovely as they say?"

"Better," Lewis said, "in fact—"

Suddenly the door burst open and an ashen-faced Charlotte rushed into the room. Lewis was quickly by her side, his arm protectively around her shoulders.

"Darling, what on earth's the matter?" he said, leading her to the couch. "Sit down here before you fall down. I'll get you a brandy."

Charlotte was trembling uncontrollably as she took the glass. "Thanks," she managed to mumble, tears trickling down her cheeks. "I... I..."

"Take your time," Lewis coaxed, sitting next to her on the couch. "Tell me what's wrong in your own time."

Charlotte gulped at the brandy, almost choking.

"Steady, love," Lewis said, as he took the empty glass from her.

Charlotte took several deep breaths before she managed to regain her composure. "He… he's here," she said shakily. "I saw him in Reception just now."

"Who? Who did you see?"

"It was… it was Patrick."

Sarah frowned. "Are you sure? I thought he was in hiding abroad somewhere?"

"He's here, I tell you. He's changed his appearance, but I heard his voice. I'd know his voice anywhere."

Lewis jumped to his feet and marched to the door. "I'll get the bastard thrown out," he said. "Don't you worry, love. Nobody's going to hurt you whilst I'm around."

Sarah rushed over to Lewis. "Wait," she said. "Let's find out what he's up to first."

"I don't care what he's up to. Whatever it is he's not getting up to it in my hotel."

Sarah turned to her friend. "Did Patrick see you?"

Charlotte shook her head. "No, I was behind the petition in Reception. I could see him, but he couldn't see me."

"You say he's changed his appearance?"

"That's right. His face looks more angular somehow and his hair's different, but it was definitely

Patrick. He might be able to change his face, but not his voice."

"What name has he booked in under?"

"Phelan Donnolly."

"Was he alone?"

"No, he had another man with him."

Lewis turned to Sarah. "Ring Joe and tell him what's happened, then I suggest you both stay in the suite until this is sorted."

39

Joe was deep in thought, as he perched on the edge of an armchair in Charlotte's suite. Sarah, Charlotte and Lewis were sat together on the couch.

He turned to Charlotte. "You're absolutely sure it was Patrick Flynn you saw? You couldn't be mistaken?"

"No, Joe. I was not mistaken. Patrick is here in this hotel I'm telling you."

Lewis lit a cigarette. "What should we do? Call the police? Patrick threatened to kill Charlotte, don't forget. I think we should—"

Joe got to his feet. "Lewis, let's think this through. If this bloke is Patrick Flynn, and I'm sure Charlotte is right in recognising him, we have to be careful. Flynn is dangerous. We need to know what he's up to, why he's back in Leeds."

"I don't care what the bastard is up to. He's wanted by the police so I think we should—"

"Should what? If he's arrested, the chances are he'll be out on bail within the hour. If that happens, Flynn will never be seen or heard from again and Charlotte will always be looking over her shoulder. Is that what you want?"

Lewis drew heavily on his cigarette. "Then what do you suggest? Turn a blind eye? Leave Charlotte locked up here hiding from that mad bastard of an ex-husband until he decides to fuck off?"

"What I'm suggesting is that we use our brain," Joe said. "Flynn being here might have nothing at all to do with Charlotte."

"Then what is he doing in Leeds?"

"Who knows? Maybe he has unfinished business with Maddox. Karl was responsible for him going on the run in the first place, don't forget."

Sarah wrung her hands nervously on her lap. "You don't think he's… you don't think he's still into sex trafficking, do you? Maybe that's why he's back."

Joe shrugged. "I doubt it. His network was totally destroyed, thanks to Maddox."

Lewis sighed. "Yes, Charlotte told me about that. I hear Karl's daughter was kidnapped by Flynn's people."

"That's right. There's certainly no love lost between those two."

Charlotte leant forward, a wry smile on her lips. "Call the idea crazy," she said, "but what do you think would happen if Karl got to know the whereabouts of Patrick Flynn?"

Joe smirked. "I was thinking along those lines myself," he said.

40

It was seven o'clock. Karl and Simon were standing at the bar of The Emerald surrounded by over sixty people, mostly men. Strobe lights danced around the room which was engulfed in a cacophony of loud music. Scantily clad young women gyrated around the poles. Men's whooping and whistling added to the mayhem.

"It's great to have things back as they should be," Simon said, taking a gulp of his lager. "It's like you've never been away."

"I see most of the regulars and back," Karl said, studying the crowd. "That's a good sign."

"What do you think to the dancers? Pretty good, eh?"

Karl pouted. "Not bad," he said hesitantly, "but most of them are new. I'd prefer the regular girls."

"A year's a long time in this business, Karl. You know that. They move on and... oh look, there's Kelly and Suki."

Karl turned as the two women approached. "How's it going?" he asked Suki. "Are you looking forward to starting work here?"

Before she could answer, Kelly grabbed Suki's upper arm and briskly steered her in the direction of the staff quarters. "We have to get ready," she said. "Come on Sue."

Simon smirked. "Not your greatest fan, I think."

Karl shrugged. “Kelly was in the office when that bastard took a pot shot at me. She’s still got the hump.”

“I’m sure she’ll get over it. By the way, are Lisa and Chris coming tonight?”

“Christina said she’d pop in, but Lisa won’t be coming.”

“Boss, I know it’s none of my business, but is everything alright between you two?”

“You’re right, Simon. It is none of your business.”

“Sorry, boss, I only thought… oh look, there’s Danny and Lenny.”

Glad to make his escape, Simon hurried across the room towards his two friends.

Karl began to drum his fingers repetitively on the bar top. It was then he saw Paul approaching. He was surprised to see Gina’s secretary, Deborah, by his side.

“’Evening, Karl,” Paul said. “I think you’ve met Deborah?”

“Debbie, please,” she said, lightly tapping his arm. “Deborah is purely for the office.”

“Glad you could make it,” Karl said, a weak smile on his face. “I didn’t know you and Paul were such… such good friends.”

“Paul insisted I come. I think he wanted to show the club off.”

“So, what do you think of it?”

"It's great." She turned to Paul. "It'll be even better if I had a drink."

"Your wish is my command. G and T?"

"Perfect," Debbie purred seductively. "Don't forget the ice."

"Of course not. I think I'll have the same." Paul signalled the bartender and ordered the drinks.

"So tell me, Debbie," Karl said, "what's it like having your old boss back?"

"Jeramiah? Oh, he's okay. He's still grieving for poor Gina, of course."

"You must miss her."

Debbie shook her head. "No, not really. Gina and I were never what you would call good friends. I did my job and got paid. That's all there is to it."

Paul handed Debbie a glass. "Here you are," he said, clinking his glass with hers. "Cheers."

Debbie sipped at her drink. "Let's sit over there," she said, indicating the table and chairs by the far wall. "It's a bit quieter."

Paul turned to Karl. "Give me a shout if you need anything. I'll just be over there." He placed his arm around Debbie's shoulders and steered her through the ever-increasing throng of men standing around.

It was then Karl saw Oscar and Miles Wright arrive. Oscar looked cagily around the room, then smiled as he spotted Karl by the bar. He walked briskly over to him, hand outstretched.

"My, my, Karl," he said, "this place is amazing. Well done."

Karl gave a slight nod. "Thanks," he said. "I have a good team."

The two men were joined by Miles. "Can I get you a drink, Dad?" he asked, captivated by the mayhem around them.

"Let's go upstairs and get a drink," Karl suggested. "It's quieter in the lounge."

All three men made their way up to the VIP area, where there was soft background music. Apart from the four hostesses, the lounge was empty as it did not officially open until nine o'clock. One of the girls came over with a tray of drinks and Karl handed Oscar and Miles a glass of champagne. Oscar slowly scanned the room before deciding to sit in one of the armchairs nearest to the bar.

"Now, this I could get used to," he said, leaning back into the soft upholstery, a contented grin on his face. "You and I have a lot in common, Karl. Did you know that?"

Karl looked puzzled. "Do we?"

"Absolutely. We both like the nicer things in life. We won't settle for anything less. I'm right, aren't I?"

Karl shrugged. "Well..." he began.

"That reminds me," Oscar said, reaching into his inside pocket and retrieving a brown envelope, "I've prepared that quote for the surveillance equipment you wanted. It's not cheap, but it is the best." Karl took the envelope.

Miles snorted. "For goodness sake, Dad, don't talk business tonight. Can't it wait until tomorrow? This is supposed to be a social evening."

Oscar leant forward, pointing a finger. "Haven't you learnt anything?" he said. "Business always comes first. Always, you hear me?"

Miles exhaled, took a sip of champagne, then turned to leave. "I'm going downstairs to watch the girls," he said. "I'll see you later."

Karl plonked on a chair next to Oscar, placing the envelope into his inside jacket pocket. "I'll look at this tomorrow," he said. "I'm a bit busy tonight. I… Oh, here's Christina."

Dressed in pale blue chiffon, Christina glided across to her father, kissing him lightly on the cheek.

"I'd like you to meet my daughter, Christina. Chris, this is Oscar Wright. We may be doing a little business together soon."

Christina smiled and nodded. "Very nice to meet you, Oscar."

Oscar ran his tongue over his lips. "You never mentioned you had such a pretty daughter.," he said, taking her hand and kissing it softly. "Will you be helping your dad with the club, Christina?"

Karl snorted. "No she won't. Chris will be going back to her husband and son in Australia very soon."

"Pity," Oscar said, draining his glass. "Well, I'll speak later Karl. I'm going downstairs to see what that son of mine is up to." He gave a curt nod, then hurried to the landing, leading down to the club.

Christina frowned. "Who's that?" she said. "He seems a bit creepy to me, and what sort of business are you doing together?"

"Never mind, it's not important. Have you seen your brother? He said he'd be calling in."

"Alex is downstairs chatting to some girl." She turned to Karl. "He is going to be alright, isn't he, Dad? The police are going to leave him alone, aren't they?"

Karl shrugged. "Who knows? I've done all I can. The solicitor doesn't think they have enough to charge him, but... well, we'll have to wait and see, won't we?"

The door swung open and half a dozen couples, laughing and joking, bounded into the lounge. The hostesses rushed forward to greet them with trays of drinks as they settled into the booths.

Smiling, Karl turned to Christina. "Well, it looks like I'm back in business," he said. "I'm going through to the office. Will you be alright downstairs?"

Christina sashayed to the landing. "Sure. I'll find Alex. See you later, Dad."

41

After leaving Karl, Oscar hurried down the stairs into the main club. It was crammed with people on the dancefloor, all eager to see the beautiful, scantily clad young girls writhing around the dance poles. He made his way to the bar where Miles was standing, his arm wrapped around the waist of a young woman with long blonde hair.

"Buying your old man a drink?" Oscar said, nudging Miles gently with his elbow.

"Hi, Dad," Miles said, turning around. "What would you like?"

"Whisky. A large one."

Miles ordered the drink and handed it to his father. "Oh by the way, this is a friend of mine, Kerry. She works here."

"It's Kelly, not Kerry," the girl scowled.

Miles shrugged. "Kelly? Kerry? What does it matter? It's probably not your real name anyway."

"Fuck you," Kelly snarled, forcing his arm from her waist. She turned and pushed her way into the crowded dance floor.

Grinning, Oscar turned to his son. "Not lost your charm with the ladies, I see."

"Plenty more fish," Miles retorted, "in fact there's a pretty little tiddler over there dressed in blue I wouldn't mind getting to know."

Oscar turned in the direction of Miles's gaze. "Oh, I'd forget about that one, son. I've met her. Her name's Christina."

"Then you'll have to introduce me," Miles said, draining his glass.

"I don't think so. She's married with a kid."

"It won't be the first married woman I've had in my bed."

"Maybe not, but it will certainly be the last."

"What do you mean?"

"I mean stay away. That young woman is Karl Maddox's daughter."

......

Paul was deep in conversation with Debbie when Oscar approached. Oscar sat on a chair opposite.

"Ah, I know who you are," he said, taking a sip of his whisky. "You were Gina's secretary, weren't you?"

"Yes, that's right. I work for Jeramiah now."

"Good chap, Jeramiah Beauchamp. I've known him for years."

Debbie turned to Paul. "Paul, would you mind changing my drink? I've gone off gin."

Paul took the glass from Debbie. "No problem," he said. "What would you like?"

"Pinot, I think. A large glass of Pinot."

Paul strode over to the bar leaving Debbie alone with Oscar. As soon as he was out of earshot, Oscar's demeanour changed.

He grabbed her roughly by the arm. "I got your email this morning. Just who the fuck do you think you are?"

A malicious grin crept across Debbie's face. "I'll tell you who I am," she said, wriggling from his grip. "I'm the person who can bring your fucking crooked scam crashing down. That's who I am."

"You know shit," Oscar spat. "You know less than shit."

"That's where you're wrong. I know everything. That dumb-arsed son of yours not only bugged Gina's home, he bugged her office too. Did you know that? Gina certainly didn't."

"I… I don't understand what you're saying."

"What I'm saying is that I found the recordings. I know exactly what your late-night meetings at the office were about. I could send you and that hapless son of yours down for years."

Oscar tightly clenched his hands into fists. Beads of sweat began to form on his brow. When he spoke, his tone was calm and even. "What exactly do you want from me?"

"Money, darling," she said. "What else?"

"How much?"

Debbie ran her tongue over her red-painted lips and smiled. "That's flexible," she said. "Let's start with, say, a thousand a month."

"Don't be ridiculous."

"I don't think so, in fact I think it's an extremely generous offer in view of what I know."

"Don't blackmail me, you stupid bitch. I work with some dangerous people. If I tell them about this conversation..."

"Before you start making threats, you should know I have placed copies of the recording in a safe place. Just in case."

Oscar inhaled. "We can't talk here. We'll discuss this later."

"I'll be waiting and... ah, here's Paul with my drink."

"Sorry it took so long," Paul said, "the bar is manic at the moment. Not that I'm complaining."

Oscar got to his feet. "Well, I think it's time I was leaving. Pole dancers are not really my thing I'm afraid."

"Well thanks for coming," Paul said. "I'm sure Karl appreciates it."

......

Karl was deep in thought as he climbed the hidden stairs behind the fleur-de-lis panelling leading to the cupboard in his office. Closing the cupboard door, he strode purposefully to his desk.

42

It was eight o'clock the following morning. Karl poured himself a coffee when his mobile rang. He recognised the number immediately.

"Yes, Spud," he said, "I take it you have something for me?"

"I certainly do. Can I come over this morning?"

"Sure, as long as it's before ten. Do you think you can do that?"

"I can be at your house in fifteen minutes. She began to giggle. "I have some information that's pure dynamite."

"Good girl. See you then."

Karl put his mobile back into his pocket as a bleary-eyed Paul meandered into the kitchen.

"Good night?" Karl asked as Paul collapsed into a chair.

"Great," Paul said, "what I can remember, that is. That Debbie is some girl."

"You like her?"

"Sure. She's a great girl. I'm taking her out for dinner tonight."

"I think you might have to change your plans," Karl said. "I may have a job for you tonight."

"Oh? What kind of job?"

"Get the lads over here for ten this morning. I'll tell you about it when we're all together."

Paul shrugged. "Sounds intriguing."

The doorbell rang.

"Ah, that'll be Spud. Let her in, will you, and bring her through to my study."

……

Spud bounded into Karl's office, still wearing black leather, but this time her spiked hair was lime green.

"Good morning, Karl," she greeted with a new found confidence, as she flung herself into a chair opposite Karl's desk. "Have I got some goodies for you."

"Great. I could do with some good news. But before you start, can I ask you to speak in plain English. I don't understand a word of your computer gobbledygook. No offence."

Spike shrugged. "None taken, I'm sure." She placed the leather shoulder bag onto the desk and took out a bundle of papers. "I've made notes. They cover all the stuff you asked me to find out and more. Much more."

Karl leant back into his chair. "Go ahead," he said. "I'm listening."

Spike took a deep breath of self-importance. "To start with, Oscar Wright keeps two sets of business records. One for the tax man that shows a healthy, if not moderate profit. He pays his taxes on time, and no doubt HMRC are more than happy to take the cash he hands over."

"What about the second set?"

"Ah, that's where it gets interesting. These are encrypted, that means they're well hidden behind lots of crap. It took me a couple of hours to get in, I can tell you. Anyway, once I did gain access, what a tale they told."

Karl leant forward, his fingers steepled. "Go on," he encouraged. "I'm listening."

"You were right to think Oscar's company is dodgy. He keeps detailed records of all the alarm code installations going back about five years. Not only that, but he can also see when codes are changed. That software he's been using is very naughty and very illegal." Spud rifled through her papers before picking out one which she handed to Karl. "This is a list of companies who had been clients of Wright Securities. I've highlighted those which have been robbed during the last five years."

Karl studied the paper. "Christ, are you sure about this?"

"That's only the tip of the iceberg," Spud said. "Whilst security alarms were being fitted, Oscar also planted hidden recording devices so he knew when stock was arriving."

"But surely the authorities would become suspicious of Oscar?"

"That's where it gets clever. Shortly before each robbery, the security system starts playing up and developing faults. It's orchestrated by Oscar, of course, but it's assumed that some hacker has caused the problem."

"There's some big names on this list," he said. "The haul must be enormous."

"It sure is. I estimate it at almost a million pounds. I also found out that Oscar has a partner."

"Who?"

"All I can tell you is that Oscar makes a lot of calls to him in Venezuela on a withheld number. No names are used, but this bloke, whoever he is, is the one who does the heavy lifting. Last month, half a million cigarettes were taken from a warehouse in Surrey. The month before that it was whisky from a distillery in Scotland."

"And nothing's ever been recovered?"

Spud shook her head. "Disappeared without a trace," she said. "There's obviously some big organization dealing with the stolen goods, but unfortunately Oscar's computer didn't give details of that part of the operation."

"Were you able to find out where Oscar stashes his cash? I presume he has accounts abroad?"

Spud began to chuckle. "He certainly does. I have details of everyone involved. They all use the same bank. That was a stupid thing to do in my opinion. Give me a few days and I can clean them all out if you want."

Karl raised an eyebrow. "Maybe later," he said.

"By the way, there's someone else involved, apart from this bloke in Venezuela."

"It wouldn't be Jeramiah and Gina Beauchamp by any chance, would it?"

"How did you know?"

"Never mind. Explain to me what their role is in all of this."

"Jeramiah Beauchamp is Oscar's solicitor. He puts the stolen cash into the client account away from prying eyes. Then he opens up the accounts abroad on behalf of his client, Wright Securities, and transfers the money direct. I followed the pattern going back about five years. Then, about six months ago, Gina Beauchamp took over from Jeramiah."

"So Gina and Jeramiah's role was setting up accounts and moving cash from the client account to the overseas accounts?"

"That's right. Nobody asks too many questions when cash is coming directly from a solicitor's office, do they?"

"Do you have any more names hidden away?"

"The bloke in Venezuela refers to 'his men,' but I can't trace them I'm afraid. There's one thing I do know from the text messages on Oscar's phone. This bloke is coming to England. To Leeds in fact."

"When? Did you manage to find that out?"

Spud gave a wry smile. "If his flight is on time, he should have arrived today."

43

When Spud left the house, Karl went to the lounge where Paul and Simon were sitting on the couch, each absorbed in reading the local newspapers.

Karl scowled. "Where's Danny and Lenny?"

"They'll be here," Paul said, not looking up from his newspaper. "It's only half-past nine."

The lounge door opened and Lisa walked into the room. "Christina and I are going shopping," she said. "We'll probably have lunch out."

Karl thrust his hands into his trouser pockets. "I thought we were all having lunch together."

"Another time, Karl. Chris and I have things to talk about."

She turned and made to leave the room, Karl in pursuit.

"What the fuck are you playing at?" he said, grabbing her arm and spinning her round.

"You haven't changed, have you, Karl? Getting the men together like this. You're chasing trouble, and I don't want any part of it."

Karl raised his hand and slapped Lisa hard across the cheek. "You're my wife. You don't tell me what I can and can't do," he spat. "I tell you."

"Dad, leave her alone," Christina yelled as she ran down the stairs. "Are you alright, Mum?"

Lisa nodded. "Come on, love. Let's get out of here."

Christina turned to Karl. "You shouldn't have done that, Dad," she said. "You really shouldn't have done that."

……

It was ten minutes past ten before Danny and Lenny arrived at Karl's house.

"The club did well last night, Karl," Danny said as he entered the lounge, flinging himself into one of the armchairs. "It was still buzzing at two o'clock this morning."

Karl nodded. "Yeah, I hope you all had a good time."

"Great," Lenny said. "It's just like old times, Karl."

"Not quite. Unfortunately, we have a problem. A serious problem, and I need your help to resolve it."

Paul leant forward. "What sort of problem? I thought the evening went perfect." He gave a mischievous wink. "I know mine did."

"Dirty dog," Danny scoffed. "What did you get up to?" Simon and Lenny began to chuckle.

Karl banged his hand down on the table. "For fuck's sake, stop pissing about like silly schoolgirls. This is serious."

Simon frowned. "What's up, Karl? I didn't detect any problems last night."

"That's because you're too busy eyeing up the talent, just like Paul over there."

Paul jumped to his feet. “Be fair, Karl. It’s been a tense few months for all of us. We need to cut loose occasionally. So what’s the problem?”

“The problem, Paul, is that woman you were with last night.”

“Debbie? I don’t understand.”

“Well let me spell it out for you…”

44

Karl told them what he had learnt from Spud.

Simon shook his head in disbelief. "The clever bastard. No wonder Oscar can afford the lifestyle he has."

Paul sighed. "I can't believe Debbie's involvement. She seemed such a nice kid."

Karl huffed. "You're losing your touch, Paul. Too much time in the sun chasing totty has made you soft."

Paul glared at Karl but said nothing.

Lenny walked over to the window and stared down into the street. "What do you want us to do? Me and Danny can—"

"Do what? You don't know where he's staying or even what he looks like these days. Me and Paul saw him a couple of times in Venezuela after his surgery and his face had changed completely. We're the only ones that can identify him."

Danny turned to Karl. "What's he doing here in Leeds, that's what I want to know? Do you think he's come to settle old scores?"

"No. I think he's too much going on with Oscar at the moment to dig up more trouble."

"But if he's in league with Oscar, and Oscar's touting for your business... just a thought."

Karl's phone gave out its familiar ring.

"Yeah?" He listened intently for a few seconds. "What? Tell him I'll be right over."

Paul looked pensive. "Who was that? It sounded serious."

Karl got to his feet and hurried towards the door. "Security at the club," he said. "You'd better come with me."

"Why, what's up?"

"I have a visitor."

Paul scowled. "Who?"

"Joe Stevens."

……

Joe and Lewis were sitting in one of the booths at the side of the dancefloor when Karl and Paul arrived. Karl strode over to them with purpose.

"I never expected to see you in my club again," he said. "Want a drink?"

"No thanks," Joe answered. "I'm not here to socialise."

Karl plonked on the chair opposite. "Then why are you here?"

"Did you know Patrick Flynn's back in Leeds?"

"I'd heard rumours. I don't suppose you know where he's hanging out?"

Lewis leant forward. "As a matter of fact we do. At this moment, Patrick Flynn is staying in a suite at my hotel."

"Which hotel are we talking about?"

"Before we discuss that," Joe said, "what exactly are you planning to do about him?"

"Flynn and I have unfinished business."

Paul, who had been standing beside Karl, stepped forward. "You do know that bastard kidnapped my cousin as well as Christina? The man's an animal."

"I don't know what Flynn's planning, but I don't think he's into trafficking again, not after all the trouble last time."

"I know exactly what he's planning," Karl said. "All I have to do is find him."

Lewis steepled his fingers. "There's a bloke with him at the hotel. I think they call him Luke."

Karl tightened his jaw. "Yeah, they've worked together before, but I have it on good authority there are others on his payroll."

"So, what's his game? Drugs? Contraband?"

Karl turned to Lewis. "Why are you so interested in Flynn anyway?"

Lewis jerked his head back. "I intend to marry Charlotte, Flynn's ex-wife," he said. "The last time they met, Flynn vowed to kill her. That's not going to happen, and I won't have Charlotte in constant fear of this man."

"And what about you? Why are you taking such a keen interest, Joe?"

"Charlotte means a great deal to me."

Karl huffed. "Like I said before, you're too soft for your own good."

Joe got to his feet. "We can sit here swapping insults all day, or we can work out a plan. What's it going to be?"

Karl rubbed his chin. "There's no doubt that this bloke at the hotel is Patrick Flynn?"

"None," Joe said. "He's had facial surgery, but there's no doubt it's him."

"I take it he's using a different name?"

"Yes. He's calling himself Phelan Donnolly. According to Charlotte, Patrick has a cousin called Phelan Donnolly."

"How long is Flynn's stay at the hotel?"

"A week, but he said it may be longer depending on business."

"I wonder what kind of business."

"He's booked a table at the restaurant this evening for four people," Lewis said.

Karl smirked. "In that case, we'd better get things moving. I need a table for two tonight. Book the table in the name of Danny Davis and make sure it's in earshot of Flynn and his cronies."

Lewis looked alarmed. "What exactly are you planning to do? I can't have any violence in my hotel."

"Don't worry. I've no intention of harming a hair on his head, not for the moment at least. He's much too valuable."

Joe frowned. "Valuable? I don't understand."

"Let's just say Flynn has information I want. Information I intend to get."

"What sort of information? You're talking in riddles."

"I'll deal with Flynn, that's all you need to know. It's what all of you need to know."

Lewis reached out and grabbed Karl's arm. "What about Charlotte? As long as that bastard's around she's in danger."

"He won't be around for long, believe me. Now, I think that concludes our business." Karl got to his feet and began to walk towards the exit. Joe followed.

"Not quite," Joe said. "A word of warning, Karl. If I see you or your goons hanging around my home or business again, I'll come looking for you."

Karl smirked. "Well, you know where I am, don't you Joe?"

45

Inspector Calvert stared glumly at the report in front of him. "Is this all there is?" he said, addressing DS Burrows. "According to this, Oscar Wright is a saint waiting to be crowned."

"What makes you think he isn't, sir? You've no reason to suspect him of anything other than making lots of money."

"I have a well-trained nose for a crook, Burrows. Believe me, he's hiding something. Both him and his son."

"According to his bank records, all transactions are legitimate."

"Then the records are wrong. They must be. Nobody can get out of the gutter and raise to his dizzy heights without being bent. I'm going to ask for a deep forensics sweep into his affairs."

"Good luck with that, sir. Money's tight in the Force, don't forget."

Calvert huffed as he slammed the file down. "How did the interviews go with Alex Maddox's alibi? I take it they all sang from the same song sheet?"

"Yes, sir. It would appear Maddox is in the clear."

"I think I'll pay another visit to Murtah Court and speak with those two goons. You never know, they might have remembered something."

"I have a couple more interviews lined up for this afternoon with Gina Beauchamp's former clients," Burrows said, "but after that..."

"What about her colleagues? Have you taken a statement from them?"

"Only verbally, sir."

"Well, let's make it official. You'd better ring up and make an appointment. You know how busy these people get."

"Very well, sir." Burrows headed towards the door. "By the way, there was an invitation in the post this morning from The Emerald."

Calvert scowled. "I don't think so. The missus would skin me alive."

"I thought I might pop in," she said. "You never know what titbits I might pick up."

"I can't stop you, of course," Calvert said, "but I would strongly advise against it."

Burrows shrugged as smiling to herself, she left the room.

......

Detective Sergeant Burrows arrived promptly at two o'clock for her interview with members of staff at Gina Beauchamp's office. She had been shown into the boardroom to conduct the interviews and by three-thirty, had spoken to all members of staff except for Gina's secretary, Deborah Wallace. There was a faint tap on the boardroom door and Wallace entered, carrying two cups of tea.

"I thought you could do with this," she smiled, as she handed Burrows a cup and took her seat next to her.

"Thanks, Miss Wallace," Burrows said.

"Oh please, call me Deborah."

Burrows nodded. "Well thank you, Deborah," she said, taking out her notebook. "This won't take long. I need a few details of your relationship with Gina Beauchamp."

Deborah frowned. "There was no relationship. She was the boss, and I was the secretary. At five o'clock I went to my home, and she went to hers."

"Being roughly the same age I thought you might have socialised?"

"We went out for a drink after work a couple of times when she first joined the firm but that's all."

"Have you ever visited Gina's apartment?"

"Once. I went to collect some paperwork she'd forgotten."

"You never visited her apartment socially?"

"Of course not. I've told you; our relationship was purely professional."

Burrows leant back into her chair. "Did you like your employer?" she asked.

"What a strange question."

"Did you?"

"I wasn't paid to like Gina. I was paid to type, do the filing, answer the phone and a million other things."

"Yes, I appreciate that, but did you actually like her?"

Debbie inhaled deeply before she answered. "I don't see the relevance, but no. I did not like Gina Beauchamp."

"Why was that?"

Deborah took a sip of her tea. "I thought she was too full of herself for one thing. Always buying expensive clothes and jewellery. To be honest, I don't know where she got the money. After all she was only on a junior solicitor's salary."

"I understand she replaced her uncle in the firm?"

"When Jeramiah retired Gina took on some of his clients. Is that nepotism or what? She was barely out of law school."

"But she was efficient at her work?"

Deborah shrugged. "I suppose so, when she wasn't partying or chasing men."

"Gina was young and attractive. Why shouldn't she enjoy life?"

"I didn't like the way she treated men, like they were disposable objects. She really could be quite ruthless."

"Any man in particular?"

"Miles Wright for one. He adored her but she dropped him like a hot stone for no reason. I think she broke his heart. She also tried it on with Oscar, Miles's dad. I don't think she got very far there though." Deborah took another sip of her tea. "Then there was that handsome young doctor, Alex Maddox. She had him running after her like a puppy dog."

"So, you think her rejection of Alex could have led to him killing her?"

"That's not what I said. I'm not accusing Alex of murdering Gina. I'm only telling you what I witnessed. By the way, do you know Karl Maddox had taken her out a few times?" She began to chuckle. "Maybe she had a thing for father and son?"

"Did Gina have any enemies that you know? Anyone who bore her a grudge?"

Deborah huffed. "I think any of the men she toyed with would be justified in stabbing the bitch, don't you?"

"Can you tell me where you were, the night Gina died?"

"Me?" she said indignantly. "Surely you don't suspect me of killing her?"

"I'm not accusing you of anything. Please answer the question. Where were you the night Gina was murdered?"

"If you must know, I was at home."

"Were you alone?"

"No. I was with Thomas."

"Thomas?"

"My cat." Deborah scraped back her chair and got to her feet abruptly, picking up her empty cup. "If you don't mind, sergeant, I must get back to work. I have correspondence to type that must go in the post tonight."

DS Burrows closed her notebook and placed it in her pocket. "Thank you for your time," she said, walking towards the door. "You've been very helpful."

46

Whilst DS Burrows was taking statements at the offices of Beauchamp, Bonneville and Clements, Detective Inspector Calvert drove to Murtagh Court. Both security men he had seen previously were in the foyer.

"Good afternoon, Inspector," Andy said, quickly pushing his copy of The Racing Post beneath the counter. "More questions?"

Henry held up his tea mug. "I was just about to put the kettle on. Do you fancy a cup?"

"No thanks," he said. "I won't keep you long. I need to go over the events of the night Ms Beauchamp was killed." He placed his briefcase on the counter and took out the statements made by the two men. "You both seem adamant that Alex Maddox was on the landing directly outside her flat when the argument began, but that he did not go inside the flat. Is that correct?"

"Absolutely," Andy said. "They had a bit of a set-to and she got hysterical. That's when he slapped her."

"It wasn't a thump," Henry said. "Just a slap. She was shouting and screaming at the poor lad. He didn't have any choice, did he? And the lad did apologise straight away."

"That's right. He tried to put his arms around her, but she pushed him away and told him to get out."

"And did he?"

"Oh, yes. He came down the stairs like a rocket."

Calvert replaced the statements into his briefcase. "Are you absolutely-positive no one else came into the building that night after Maddox left? Think carefully. This is extremely important."

Both men looked furtive and were silent for a few seconds. It was Henry who broke the silence.

"Well… Andy and I did go into the back room to watch the footy for a bit," he said, "but we made sure the front door was locked. Nobody could get in without either of us unlocking the door from the inside."

"What about leaving the building? Could anyone get out without you knowing whilst you were both in the back room?"

"I suppose so," Andy said, "but why would any tenant want to go out in the pouring rain at ten o'clock at night?"

"Did Ms Beauchamp have many visitors?"

Andy grinned. "Men you mean?"

"I mean anyone."

"She did have a few gentleman callers, you might say. Miles Wright spent a lot of time here and that bloke you arrested, but to be honest, Gina Beauchamp was the type of girl who liked the bright lights. She was out on the town most nights."

"Apart from the two men you mentioned, could anyone have called earlier in the day?"

Both men looked at each other, as if for inspiration, before shaking their heads.

"I don't recall seeing anyone," Henry said. "I don't think she had many friends."

"That secretary of hers has called a few of times," Andy said, "but it was to do with business. She seemed to be either delivering documents or taking them back to the office. She never stayed long."

"Did she visit the day Ms Beauchamp died?"

Andy shrugged. "I don't remember seeing her, but this place does get busy."

There was the sound of laughter on the stairs as a young couple came down. Breaking away from the interview for a moment.

The man addressed Henry. "Won't be late in tonight, we've decided to have an early night for a change."

"Very well, Mr Baldwin," Henry said. "Did you have a good night at the casino yesterday?"

Baldwin scowled. "No, I bloody didn't, I lost a packet."

The young woman patted him on the back. "Never mind Ross," she said, "we'll try again tomorrow night. Take the buggers to the cleaners, eh?"

They both laughed as they made their way through the foyer and out onto the street.

"Who's that?" Calvert asked.

"That's Ross Baldwin and his girlfriend, Jenny Roe," Henry said. "They rent one of the apartments on the top floor. They're going on a cruise to the Caribbean next week, the lucky bastards."

"He's something big in the city," Andy said. "He's got more money than he can count."

"He won't have it for long if he keeps losing at the casino. Bloody mugs game if you ask me."

Andy chuckled. "I just wish I had his stamina. Doesn't go out until late almost every night and leaves for work at seven every morning, fresh as a daisy."

Calvert frowned. "He leaves the building late every night?"

Andy shook his head. "Not every night, but most nights. I think he's really got the gambling bug."

"I'll want to speak to that young couple," Calvert said, handing his card to Henry. "Can you see Mr Baldwin gets this, please? Tell him to ring me as soon as possible."

Henry squinted at the card and placed it on the countertop. "No problem, inspector. I'll pass on the message as soon as they get back."

47

Patrick Flynn adjusted his tie in the dressing table mirror and stared at his reflection. He smiled his satisfaction as he gently traced his jawline with his forefinger before running his finger up and down his newly constructed nose.

"They know what they're doing, those doctors in Brazil," he said, addressing his companion who was slouching on a chair by the window. "A completely new face, but still as handsome as before. I don't think my own sweet Mother would recognise me."

Luke huffed. "Let's hope you're right. I still think coming back to Leeds is risky after everything that happened. It's asking for trouble. You do know Maddox is back in town?"

"You worry too much," Patrick scoffed. "This deal we've got with Oscar Wright is too good to let old adversaries get in the way."

"But if Maddox finds out you're here, right in his backyard, you'll really be in the shit."

"I can handle Maddox if I have to, so stop worrying."

"Are you sure you don't want me to come to dinner with you? I can be ready in five minutes."

Patrick laughed. "No, Luke my friend, I do not. You have many qualities, but table manners and polite conversation are not amongst them, I'm afraid."

Luke scowled. "I suppose it'll be McDonalds for me then?" he said. "But you will be careful, won't you? We're onto a good thing with these guys."

......

It was seven-fifty-five when Patrick entered the dining room of the Galaxy Hotel. He was surprised to see Oscar Wright and Jeramiah Beauchamp already seated at the table.

"Glad you could make it," Patrick said, shaking them both by the hand.

"Oh, I'm honoured to finally meet you in person," Oscar said. "Online business relationships can be a little... a little taxing sometimes, don't you think? In the five years we've been working together, this is the first time we've actually all met together in person."

Patrick shrugged. "As long as it gets the job done, I don't really mind whether we meet in person or not."

Oscar tilted his head and smiled. "Patrick, did you—"

Patrick raised his hand. "If you don't mind Oscar, I would prefer it if you called me Phelan tonight. Just a precaution you understand."

Oscar grinned. "Absolutely, Phelan," he said. "I was about to ask if you had managed to sort out that little problem I was having with Fontaine Securities."

"Don't worry about them," Patrick said. "They won't be nicking any more of your clients. I've made sure of that."

Beauchamp looked alarmed. "I hope you didn't resort to violence. I can't be associated with violence."

The veins on Patricks neck began to protrude and the colour rose in his cheeks. "I did what had to be done if you want to keep receiving your fees," he said, pointing his finger menacingly at Beauchamp. "It's too late now to start questioning my methods. All you have to do is sit behind your big desk in your nice warm office and sign a few papers, so don't you dare criticise my methods. Understand?"

Beauchamp sank back into his chair, a forlorn look on his face. "I'm sorry, Patrick... I mean Phelan. I only meant..."

"Just stick to your role and I'll carry on with mine. Understood?"

Beauchamp nodded weakly.

Oscar cleared this throat as he reached for the glass of water. "So, you say Fontaines won't be competing with me in future. That's great news, Phelan."

Patrick began to chuckle. "It would be pretty difficult for them to compete with anyone now their office has been burnt to the ground. Millers Motors will be back in touch tomorrow begging to renew their contract with you. I give you my word."

"Let's hope so. Millers trade in high-end motors so there's lots of dosh to be made from them. By the way, I may have another client lined up soon."

Patrick raised an eyebrow. "Who's that?"

"I'll tell you about them later."

Patrick checked his watch. "Talking of making dosh, where's the distributor? You did tell him to be here at eight?"

"Don't worry, he'll be here," Beauchamp said. "I spoke to him only this afternoon. He's looking forward to meeting you in person at last."

The waiter came to the table and the drinks order was placed.

"Ah, here he is," Beauchamp said as a middle-aged man hurried towards the table. "I've ordered you a drink. Whisky, isn't it?"

The man took his place at the table. "Thanks, Jeramiah. So sorry I'm late everyone. Some last-minute business to deal with. You know how it is."

"Glad you could make it at such short notice," Patrick said. "I must say, you've been doing a great job for the syndicate."

The man smiled and held out his hand to Phelan. "Thanks. I appreciate that, and can I say how good it is to meet you in person at last. I'm Roger Laverick."

......

Danny and Lenny were at the nearest table to Patrick. Lenny had managed to record the conversation at the table using a tiny device provided by his cousin, Spud. Danny discreetly photographed all those present round the table on his phone.

"Karl's going to love this," Danny said as he heartily tucked into the roast lamb on his plate.

"I think we've got enough info," Lenny said. "We should be going."

Lenny shook his head. "Not until I've had my pud. Karl's picking up the bill, don't forget."

Both men began to chuckle.

48

Wearing a black velvet mini dress with matching gold bag and shoes, Detective Sergeant Kate Burrows arrived at The Emerald at exactly ten o'clock. She was accompanied by her long-time friend, James Moore, a karate instructor at the local dojo. At six-foot-four, handsome James made a formidable companion.

As they entered the club, James screwed up his nose in distaste. "Why did you want to come here, Kate? I thought you had more class than this?"

Kate gently squeezed his arm. "I'm not here to enjoy myself, James. I'm here to snoop. I told you that. Get me a glass of wine from the bar, will you, and try not to look so miserable."

James made his way to the bar and ordered the drinks. When he returned, Kate was chatting to one of the girls.

"It must be fun working here," Kate said. "Like going to a party every night."

The girl began to giggle. "Oh, it is. This is only my second night working here but I love it."

"All the gymnastics on the pole must be really tiring," Kate said sympathetically.

"No, not really. I only perform for twenty minutes, then I get a ten-minute break. I'm on my break now."

James handed Kate her wine. "Kate let's sit over there," he said, indicating the area near the panelled wall. "You can't swing a cat around here."

Kate smiled. "Alright. Save me a seat. I'll be along in a minute. I want to have a look around. first"

"Okay, but..." He nodded to the girl talking with Kate and smiled. "Will your friend be joining us?"

"No, she has to work."

Frowning, James made his way to a vacant table.

"He looks nice," the girl said, her eyes following James. "Is he your boyfriend?"

Kate grinned. "Not exactly. James and I were at school together. We've been best friends since then."

The girl tilted her head to one side. "Does he... does he have a girlfriend?"

"I don't think he does at the moment. Would you like me to introduce you?"

The girl blushed and looked uneasy. "No... no of course not. I was just saying..."

"If you change your mind let me know," Kate said. "James is a nice guy. By the way, I saw there was a staircase in the foyer. Is there another part of the club?"

The girl nodded. "There's the VIP lounge upstairs."

"VIP lounge? That sounds interesting."

"It's reserved for members and special guests. They have their own hostesses, but you have to hold a full membership to gain access."

"Have there been any VIP guests yet? Anyone famous I mean? A footballer or actor for instance?"

The girl shook her head. "No, no-one like that. The men that come here all look a bit stuffy to me, but—"

"Suki, it's time you were back at work."

Both women turned sharply.

"Oh, Kelly, this is… this is a friend of mine. She wants to look around the club."

Hands defiantly on her hips, Kelly threw back her head. "Temporary members are not allowed anywhere in the club but this room," she said. "Now Suki, get on with your job whilst you still have one."

Suki smiled weakly at Kate. "It's been nice speaking with you," she said as giving one more glance over at James, she turned and disappeared through the crowd in the direction of the podium.

Kate turned to Kelly. "She seems a nice girl."

"Yes, she is. Suki is my sister."

"I heard Karl Maddox has bought this place back again. Is that right?"

Kelly frowned. "Yes. Karl is the owner."

"Is he working tonight?"

Kelly's frown deepened. "Why do you want to know that? You're not thinking of applying for a job here, are you?"

Kate shook her head vigorously. "No, of course not. I just—"

Suddenly, two men rushed past Kate, pushing her into Kelly and causing her to drop her bag.

"Oh, I'm so sorry," Kate said as they collided.

"Are you alright, dear?" Kelly asked with concern as she picked up Kate's bag from the floor. "Those two clumsy oafs want locking up."

"Who are they?"

"They work for Karl sometimes. Their names are Danny and Lenny. They own a gay bar in Leeds, The Bar Dalziel."

"Oh, I think I've seen that. It's over in Elland, isn't it?"

Before Kelly could reply, Lenny hurried over to her. "Where's Karl?" he said. "I'm supposed to be meeting him here. It's urgent."

Kelly scowled. "He's in the office, but you'd better ring through first. The phone's on the bar."

Lenny huffed and hurried towards the bar.

"Karl doesn't like anyone barging in on him when he's in the office," she said.

Kate smiled and glanced over at James. "Well, it's been nice talking to you, Kelly, but I'd better join my friend. He'll be thinking I've deserted him."

Kelly followed her gaze. "Poor guy. He looks like a fish out of water, doesn't he? I don't think a poll dancing club is quite his thing."

"You're probably right. I..." Danny and Lenny barged past her once again as they headed through to the foyer and began clambering the stairs to Karl's office.

Kelly shook her head slowly. "I can only apologise for those two clowns," she said. "I don't know what their business is with Karl, but it looks important."

Kate nodded in agreement. "Yes, it does. Doesn't it?"

49

Patrick returned to his room and after telling Luke what had been discussed at the meeting, began nervously pacing the floor.

"I don't see the problem," Luke said. "So what if Oscar has lined Maddox up to be fleeced? That's not a bad thing is it, getting one over on him?"

Patrick huffed. "I don't want to get one over on him. I want to punish him. Really punish him. That bastard lost me an empire."

"I think you should forget about Maddox. Let's do what we came to do and then get the hell away from here. I haven't slept a wink since we arrived in England."

Patrick snorted. "I'm not leaving until I've made Maddox suffer. I'm going to give him hell."

"How do you propose to do that?"

"Don't worry, I'll think of something."

Patrick continued pacing the room. After a few minutes he stopped abruptly. "I've got it," he said. "I know what I'm going to do."

"What?"

"What's the things he most treasures?"

Luke shrugged. "I've no idea."

"His wife and daughter, of course."

"Oh fuck, Patrick. You're not going down the trafficking route again, are you?"

"No, not trafficking, although the thought of them in some brothel in Saudi Arabia does have a certain appeal."

"I can arrange a shooter," Luke said. "I know a couple of guys who could do the job. No questions asked."

"No, that would be too quick. I want Maddox to really suffer."

"Then what are you going to do?"

A sinister grin spread across Patrick's face. "How do you fancy making a movie?"

Luke looked perplexed. "A movie? What sort of movie?"

"A snuff movie."

"Fuck it, Patrick. You've got to be joking."

"Do I look like I'm joking? Tomorrow we'll go looking for premises that we can use as a red room."

"This is crazy. If you want them dead just shoot the bitches."

"I've told you; I want Maddox to really suffer. I'll send him videos of them being tortured and abused, instalment by instalment." He began to chuckle. "It will drive him insane."

"You're actually going to kill them on camera?"

"Of course, but slowly. Very slowly."

"I still think it's madness. We should get on with what we came here to do and move on, just like we always have. Messing with Maddox will end badly. I know it will."

"You know your trouble, Luke? You've no imagination."

"You do realise, if you're recognised, you'll be locked up for ever?"

"Stop worrying. My own mother wouldn't recognise this face."

Patrick went to the drinks cabinet and began pouring himself a whisky. "Want one?" he asked.

"No thanks," Luke said. "I'm ready for some shuteye." He meandered over to his bedroom door. "Don't do anything hasty, Patrick. We've a good thing going with the syndicate. You don't want anything to get in the way of that."

Patrick sipped his drink. "Goodnight, Luke," he said.

"Goodnight, boss."

50

Karl and Paul listened intently to Lenny as he relayed the conversation he had overheard in the restaurant.

"It's all recorded," he said, handing the small device to Karl. "Spud leant me this. It's very powerful."

"And I have pictures of all four of them," Danny said, handing his phone to Karl. Karl studied the images before handing the phone back.

"Thanks fellas. You've both done a great job. Go downstairs and grab yourselves a drink."

Danny sniffed. "No thanks. Women's tits and arses don't do it for me." He got to his feet. "We'd better be getting back to our bar."

Lenny joined him as they moved towards the door. "You must come to the Bar Dalziel for a drink one night, Karl. We'd love to see you."

Grinning, Karl shook his head slowly. "I'll pass on that if you don't mind. That's definitely not my kind of thing either."

Danny shrugged. "Suit yourself, but you don't know what you're missing."

"So, Roger Laverick's got his nose in the trough too," Karl said, after playing the recording for a second time. "That is a surprise."

Paul huffed. "We always knew he was dodgy, but to export stuff in the quantities he does is mammoth."

"It was interesting hearing Oscar Wright's plans for this place. The man's deluded if he thinks he can get into my overseas accounts."

"Is he? Spud says she can, so why not Oscar?"

Karl frowned, rubbing his chin. "If we don't do business with him it's going to look suspicious. The deal he's offered is too good to turn down. We're going to have to find a way to delay him somehow."

"How?"

"Don't worry. I'll think of something."

"What about Patrick? When he heard, Oscar was planning to deal with you and The Emerald he went ballistic."

Karl grinned. "No, he wasn't very happy, was he?"

"What are your plans?"

"Observe," Karl said. "We know now who the key players are, so with Spud's help we can keep track of their movements."

"What do you want me to do about Debbie?"

"Nothing for the time being. Oscar didn't tell the others about the secretary blackmailing him. He's scared what Patrick might do if he finds out that Miles planted the cameras at Gina's office in the first place." Karl poured himself another whisky from the bottle on his desk. "You need to keep close to the bitch. See what else you can find out." He smirked. "You've always been good at that type of thing."

51

Paul had just finished breakfast when Lisa entered the kitchen.

"Good morning," he said.

"Good morning, Paul," Lisa replied. "Where's Karl this morning? He'd gone when I woke up."

"He had business to see to at the club. He said he'd be back in time for lunch."

Lisa huffed. "He thinks more of that damned place than anything else, including me and Christina."

"I'm sure that's not true. Karl has a lot on his plate at the moment, that's all."

Lisa shrugged. "If you say so," she said. "What are your plans? Are you staying on here with Karl permanently when me and Chris leave?"

"No, I've been looking for a place for a few days now. I think I've found one out in Alwoodley. I'm going there this morning as a matter of fact."

"Oh, that's a pity. Me and Christina are going back to Australia in a few days so Karl will be all alone. He'll hate that."

Paul looked surprised. "You're definitely going back to Australia?"

"Yes. I only came back to England because of Alex. That seems to be resolved now, thank goodness, so there's no reason for me to stay."

"But what about Karl?"

"What about him? He has his club and his friends. He doesn't need a family in tow as well."

There was a sharp rap on the front door.

"I'll get it," Christina shouted as she came down the stairs and into the hallway. She opened the door to find the postman standing on the step.

"Mrs Christina Glendenning?" he said. "I need a signature." Christina swiftly signed the form before he handed her a brown A4 envelope with Australian stamps in the corner. Christina took the envelope into the kitchen and plonked down on a stool at the breakfast bar.

"Who's that from, dear?" Lisa asked as Christina tore open the envelope.

Christina was silent for a moment, the colour visibly draining from her face.

"Christina, are you alright? Is it bad news?"

Christina replaced the documents into the envelope. "It's from Matthew," she said.

"Oh, how is he? Is he coping on his own with the baby?"

Christina pushed the envelope towards her mother. "He's served me with divorce papers, Mum. Matthew wants a divorce and full custody of our son."

Lisa sat bolt upright, reached for the envelope, and began reading the documents. "What is that silly boy thinking? He can't divorce you, and he certainly can't have full custody of Andrew. I won't allow it. Your father won't allow it."

Christina began pouring herself a coffee. "I've no intention of going back to Australia, and I've no intention of staying married to Matthew either. If he wants to take care of Andrew, then let him."

"Don't be ridiculous. Matthew loves you and you love him. This is just a blip. You need to get back home as soon as you can and sort this out."

Christina banged her coffee mug down on the counter. "For fuck sake, Mother, just for once, why don't you mind your own business? This is between me and Matthew." She turned abruptly and hurried into the hall and up the stairs to her room.

Lisa remained visibly shaken. "I don't know what's got into that girl," she said. "She's always been difficult but this... this is too much even for her."

Paul walked over to the dishwasher and placed his mug and plate inside. "I'd best be going," he said, somewhat embarrassed at witnessing the family outburst. "Hopefully I'll have a place to call home by the end of the day."

Lisa smiled weakly. "Good luck with that, Paul," she said, "I hope it works out for you."

52

Inspector Calvert did not get to the station until after nine that morning. DS Burrows was busily working at her computer when he arrived.

"'Morning," he muttered as he made his way to his desk.

"Good morning, sir," Burrows said, picking up a buff-coloured file from her desk and briskly walking through to his office. Once inside, she closed the door. "This file has just arrived from headquarters. It seems Oscar Wright has been under surveillance by the Fraud Squad for some time." She handed the document over to Calvert and sat expectantly on the chair opposite his desk with her hands clasped tightly.

Calvert opened the file and slowly perused its contents for several minutes.

Frowning, he closed the file and sighed. "This is all conjecture," he said. "Suspected of passing on information of his client's security to a third party. There's no proof. Absolutely no proof."

"But surely, it's too much of a coincidence that so many of Wright Security's clients have either had their goods hijacked or their premises broken into? He must be involved somehow."

Calvert shrugged. "Apparently the Fraud Squad have had Oscar under surveillance for some time. They have not been able to connect him to any known criminals."

"Maybe they connect online somehow. After all that is his area of expertise, isn't it?"

"His finances have been gone through with a fine toothcomb, you know that, Burrows."

"Only those we have been able to trace. I thought you had requested a deep forensic sweep?"

"I did. The chief constable is considering it, which means it will probably never happen."

"But sir, if we show him this file from the Fraud Squad..."

"That's exactly what I intend to do," Calvert said. "I'll ring for an appointment now. By the way, did you go to The Emerald last night?"

"Yes, sir. I went with my friend, James Moor."

"The karate bloke I met at the Christmas party last year?"

"Yes, sir. James and I have been mates forever."

Calvert grinned. "Good looking bloke, but a brain the size of a pea, as I remember."

Burrows frowned. "That's a little harsh, sir if you don't mind me saying. He might not be academic, but he is astute. Anyway, I didn't take James with me for his intelligence, but for protection. By the way, you really shouldn't underestimate him. James owns four karate clubs in Yorkshire, as well as three gyms and a couple of spa centres. He is extremely wealthy."

Calvert shrugged his indifference. "Good for him," he said. "Now, how did you get on at the club? Did you see Maddox?"

"No. He was in his office all night, but I did see two blokes in a hurry to speak with him."

"Who were they, do you know?"

"They were the two blokes who own the Bar Dalziel. The same two who gave Alex Maddox his alibi."

Calvert stroked his chin thoughtfully. "Mm, that is interesting."

The telephone on his desk rang.

"Inspector Calvert... oh good. Show them to the interview room, will you? DS Burrows will be conducting the interview."

Calvert replaced the receiver and turned to Burrows. "Ross Baldwin and Jenny Roe are here at my request. They live in an apartment at Murtagh Court where Gina Beauchamp lived."

"I thought all the residents at Murtagh Court had been interviewed?"

"Not these two. They're elusive, always out and about. According to the concierge, they pay late night visits to the casino a few times a week. You never know, they might have seen someone hanging around."

Burrows huffed. "Very well, sir," she said. "Let's hope they did. The Beauchamp murder case is going nowhere."

53

Ross Baldwin was of slight build in his early twenties His fair hair was tied back in a ponytail. He was clean-shaven and smartly dressed in a dark-grey suite and pink shirt. Burrows was aware of the overpowering fragrance of his aftershave as soon as she entered the interview room.

Jenny Roe was sat next to Ross at the small table. She was dressed in a pale-blue dress and matching jacket. Her short dark hair was thick and unruly; she wore little makeup.

"Good morning," Burrows said, introducing herself and taking her seat behind the table. "Thank you both for coming in today."

Ross leant forward. "Henry, the security bloke, told me this morning that someone had been murdered in the building a few days ago. This was the first we'd heard of it."

"It was Gina Beauchamp, wasn't it?" Jenny said. "The young solicitor."

"Yes, that's right," Burrows said. "Did either of you know Ms Beauchamp?"

Ross shook his head. "No, not really. We'd say hello if we met on the stairs, stuff like that, but we didn't know her. Not properly."

"I went to her apartment one night to borrow a corkscrew," Jenny said. "We had a few friends round and our corkscrew broke. I did invite Gina to join us, but she said she was going out herself."

Ross nodded. "That's right. I'd forgotten about that. In fact, I don't think we returned it, did we?"

"Well, she won't be needing it now, will she? We might as well keep it." She turned to Burrows. "That's not stealing is it, being as though she's dead?"

Burrows pursed her lips. "I'm sure her family won't mind," she said. "Now, getting back to Ms Beauchamp, have either of you seen anyone hanging around the building during the last couple of weeks. Anyone acting suspicious?"

Ross shook his head. "Sorry," he said, "I can't say I've noticed anything out of the ordinary."

Jenny reached over and gently shook Ross's sleeve. "There was that bloke she'd been seeing on and off. He often sits in his car outside the building. He's a doctor at the hospital."

"Who, Alex Maddox?"

"Yes, that's him."

"Oh, Alex is alright. He wouldn't murder anyone. He just had the hots for Gina, that's all."

Burrows frowned. "You know Alex Maddox?"

"Not well. I've seen him sometimes at the apartment when he visited Gina."

"On the night Gina died, that would be last Thursday, did either of you see Alex in the building, or outside in his car?"

Ross furrowed his brow in concentration. "I heard them arguing on the landing early on. I think all the tenants heard them as a matter of fact, the way Gina was screaming. Then Alex left, but I don't know where he went after that."

"What time did you leave your apartment that night?"

Ross furrowed his brow in concentration. "It was late, very late in fact. We usually leave about half-ten, but that night we... well let's just say we got distracted, so it was almost midnight."

Jenny blushed and began to giggle.

"When you left the building did you see anyone hanging around the entrance?"

"Some madman wielding an axe you mean?"

"Not exactly," Burrows said. "You didn't see anyone entering the foyer or on the stairs?"

Ross shook his head. "No, sorry," he said. "I don't remember seeing... oh wait a minute, there was someone."

Jenny nodded. "That's right, I remember now. You'd opened the front door and they pushed their way in. I thought they were bloody rude."

"Did you recognise this person?"

They both shook their heads.

"They were wearing a hoodie, I remember that," Ross said.

"Was it a man or a woman?"

"I've no idea, I'm afraid. I didn't see their face. The lighting in the foyer is pretty shit."

"So, you can't give a description? Age? Height? Build? Anything you can remember could be vitally important."

Ross inhaled deeply. "Sorry, sergeant. I didn't pay much attention. I was too eager to get to the casino that night."

"You went straight to the casino?"

"That's right," Jenny said. "We got there just before half-past-twelve." She began to giggle. "Albert, the big bloke at the desk, said he'd given up on us that night because it was so late."

Ross got to his feet. "Well, if that's all, sergeant, me and Jenny have got to pack."

"Going somewhere nice?"

"We're flying to Barbados," Jenny said as she followed Ross to the door. "Then we're going on a three-week cruise around the islands."

"Very nice," Burrows said. "I quite fancy a cruise myself."

Ross made to leave the room. "Oh, by the way, you might want to cross Alex Maddox off your list of suspects."

"Why is that?"

"I've just remembered. When we got onto the gaming floor at the casino, Alex was already at the roulette table."

54

"And this is the second bedroom," Mr Wynter, the estate agent said as he opened the white painted door to reveal the small, windowless room.

Paul frowned. "Good job I haven't got a cat," he said. "I'd have a problem swinging it in here."

Oblivious to the sarcasm, the estate agent readjusted his spectacles on his large nose. "Like I said, if you decide to take it, it's three month's rent in advance, plus the deposit, and by the way, sir, there are no pets allowed."

Paul returned to the kitchen, a square room with ample fitted units, just as the doorbell rang.

Wynter frowned. "Oh, I wasn't expecting any other viewer this morning," he said as he strode to the front door and opened it.

"Is Mr Borowicz here?" said a female voice.

"This way, madam," Wynter said as he retraced his steps back to the kitchen, followed by Deborah Wallace.

Paul raised an eyebrow. "Debbie, I wasn't expecting to see you here," he said.

"You invited me to come to look around the apartment the other night, Paul. Don't you remember?"

Paul shrugged but remained silent.

Deborah glanced around the room. "It's in a good location," she said, "but a bit on the small side, don't you think?"

"There'll just be me living here. I don't need a lot of space."

Debbie sidled up to Paul. "But what's to say you'll be on your own in the future?"

Wynter coughed discreetly and glanced at his watch. "I'm going to have to rush you, I'm afraid," he said. "I have another property to show in fifteen minutes so—"

"I'll take it," Paul said. "Have the paperwork drawn up and I'll come to your office and sign it."

"Very well, Mr Borowicz," Wynter said, a hint of a smile on his forlorn face. "Shall we say, three o'clock?"

"Three o'clock will be perfect."

Debbie linked her arm into Paul's as they made their way onto the street. "How about an early lunch? I know this lovely little place—"

"Sorry, Deb. No can do I'm afraid. I have to get to the club. Karl's expecting me. I'll give you a ring later." Paul quickly got into his car and gave a wave as he pulled into the line of traffic, leaving an open-mouthed Debbie staring after him.

55

After Paul left her house, Lisa drove to The Emerald. She was greeted in the foyer by Simon.

"Hey, great to see you, Lisa," he said, kissing her lightly on the cheek. "It's been a while."

Lisa smiled weakly. "Good to see you too. You're looking well," she said. "Is Karl around?"

"Sure. He's in his office. Do you want me to—"

"That's alright. I know the way." She hurriedly made her way up the stairs.

Karl was behind his desk studying the accounts from the previous night when she entered. He raised an eyebrow but made no attempt to stand. "Christ, Lisa, what brings you here? I thought you vowed never to set foot in the club."

Lisa ignored his remark as she plonked herself on the chair opposite his desk. "It's Christina," she said. "You have to do something, Karl."

Karl exhaled. "What has she done now?"

"It's not really her, it's Matthew."

"Matthew? I don't understand."

"He wants a divorce. He sent the papers through to her this morning."

Karl leant back in his chair, steepling his fingers in front of him. "What do you want me to do? Surely, it's between the two of them?"

"He says he's going to apply for full custody of our grandson. You've got to stop him."

"Lisa, I think we both know Chris and Matthew are not suited as a couple. Maybe getting divorced and moving on with their lives is best for both of them?"

"What about our grandson? Are you suggesting we abandon him?"

Karl shrugged. "I've never met the kid, so I have no attachment, and to be honest, I don't think our daughter is cut out for motherhood. Do you?"

Lisa became agitated as tears began to trickle down her cheeks. "So, you're going to do nothing? You're going to let that man tear our family apart?"

"What does Christina say? Does she want me to get involved?"

"She's in shock. She doesn't know what she wants."

"I've got an important meeting in a few minutes. I'll speak to her when I get back to the house."

"But Karl—"

Karl slammed his hand down on the desk. "I said I'll deal with it later. Now, if there's nothing else, I have a busy morning."

Lisa huffed as she strode over to the door. "You really are a heartless bastard," she said. "You put this damned club before your own family. You always have." She left the office, slamming the door on her way out.

......

Hurrying down the stairs Lisa passed Paul who was on his way up.

"Hi Lisa," he said, "I—"

"Not now, Paul. I don't have time to chat." She rushed through the foyer and out into the busy street.

Paul knocked briskly on Karl's office door and strode in. "Lisa seems in a hurry this morning," he said. "Is everything alright?"

Karl shrugged. "She's getting her knickers in a twist about Christina and Matthew getting divorced. I don't know what she expects me to do about it."

Paul smirked. "That's why I'm happy being single. I've found a furnished place to rent over in Alwoodley, so I'll be out of your hair pretty soon."

"With all the female hormones flying around at my house, I might come and stay with you." Both men laughed.

"By the way, Debbie Wallace turned up at the apartment whilst I was there."

"Oh? What did she want?"

"She said I'd invited her to look around when we were out together the other night."

"And did you?"

Paul frowned. "If I did, I don't remember."

"Maybe she's stalking you."

Paul's frown deepened. "That's so not funny."

"Make sure you keep her onside. That girl knows a lot more about Oscar's business than she's letting on."

"I suppose I could give her a ring later and invite her to the club tonight," Paul said hesitantly, "but I think she's too astute to let anything slip."

"Keep trying. We have to know everything that's been going on. Oscar's coming round in about an hour to discuss his quote."

"What about Joe and that other bloke, Lewis? What are they doing?"

"Joe's keeping an eye on Patrick, seeing where he goes and who he meets."

There was a light tap on the door and Simon entered the room. "Karl, there's a bloke called Laverick here to see you. Do you want me to get rid of him?"

"No, show him in. Our business won't take long."

A few minutes later, Roger Laverick entered the office, a broad smile on his face.

"Well, well, well," he said, taking a seat across from Karl's desk. "You have been busy. The club is looking great."

"When I'm in charge, it always does," Karl said.

"I hear business has been booming. I'll need to see the books to work out my share of the profits."

"Can I remind you, Laverick, that you own a mere twenty percent. I'm the majority shareholder so I'll decide when you see the books. Okay?"

Laverick scowled. "That wasn't the agreement. We decided—"

"We agreed to you having a percentage of the profits for the first two years," Karl said. "Because of your neglect when you were in charge, the money I have outlaid to bring the club back to this level far outweighs what profits have been made in the short time The Emerald has been operating. If you want to take it to the wire, you actually owe me a substantial amount of money."

"What the fuck do you mean, I owe you? I almost gave this club to you."

"And for that I am grateful," Karl said, "but I think you will find that no profits have been recorded, nor will they be for quite some time due to the refurbishments taking place."

"What refurbishments? This place looks fine to me."

"New surveillance equipment for one thing. We have to have the premises secure. As a matter of fact, I have someone coming round later to discuss security issues. From the quote I've been given, it's not going to be cheap."

Laverick got to his feet. "Karl, stop fucking about. I want the money I'm owed. I get it today or else..."

"Or else what? I don't recall any documents being signed. Do you?"

Laverick clenched his hands into fists. "Damn you. We had a gentleman's agreement."

Karl smirked. "That's just the point, Laverick. Hasn't anyone told you? I'm no gentleman."

56

Patrick Flynn left the Galaxy Hotel just after lunch. He hailed a taxi from the street and was driven to Balby Quay, a rundown area by the side of the river. He walked a few yards along the path to Amber House, a derelict three-storey building where a man was standing outside the front door. The man wore a long black leather coat and had a dishevelled appearance.

"Richard?" Patrick said.

The man scowled at him suspiciously. "Who wants to know?"

"I was given your name by a mutual friend."

"Which mutual friend?"

"Arnie. He said you might be able to help me find what I'm looking for."

Richard scratched his stubbled chin. "And what might that be?"

"Somewhere private where I'm not likely to be disturbed," Patrick said.

The man grinned. "Ah, you're making a porn film, eh? I thought so." Richard took out a key from his coat pocket and opened the door. "Follow me."

Patrick followed Richard up the flight of stairs and along a dimly lit corridor covered in graffiti. He stopped outside an iron door and took out a bunch of keys from his pocket. "This is the room. How long do you want it for?"

"A few days," Patrick said.

The man scowled. "A few days? It's usually rented by the hour. What sort of film are you making that's going to take a few days?"

"That's my business. Now, can we get on? I'm in a hurry."

Richard shrugged as he opened the heavy door and turned on the light, bathing the room in a red glow.

It was a large windowless room with bare floorboards. The walls were painted white with a large mirror suspended from the ceiling. In the centre of the room was a four-poster bed with red velvet drapes and matching bed cover. There was also a black leather recliner chair against the wall. Several tripods were positioned around the bed and an assortment of handcuffs, leather whips and sex toys filled a metal box at the bottom of the bed.

Richard pointed towards the box. "If you want to rent any of that lot it'll be extra."

"No, I don't think so," Patrick said, "but thanks for the offer."

Richard smirked. "Ah, got your own, have you? You've done this sort of thing before, eh?"

"What about the other rooms in the building? Are they rented out?"

"No mate, just this one, so don't worry, you won't be disturbed."

"Okay, I'll take it for a week, starting today," Patrick said. "And Richard..."

"Yeah?"

"I need absolute discretion. Understand?"

"Don't worry, discretion is guaranteed." He began to chuckle. "Half the porn films made in Leeds are shot in that room. Now, when we agree a price, the key is yours."

......

Patrick walked to the end of the quay and summoned a taxi. Two minutes later, Joe, who had been parked down the street, got out of his car and hurried towards Amber House. Whistling to himself, Richard was locking the outer door and making to leave.

"Oh, shit. I've missed him," Joe said as he hurried towards him. "The bloody traffic has been murder in town today."

Richard looked sympathetically at Joe. "Your mate's only just gone," he said. "He took a taxi."

"Never mind, I'll catch him at the hotel. I take it he... he did the business?"

"Oh, the room you mean? Yeah, he's renting it for a whole week. It must be some film he's making. I wouldn't mind a copy myself when it's done, if there's a spare going."

"I'll see what I can do," Joe said as he turned to leave.

57

"A porn film? I don't believe it," Charlotte said when Joe told her about Amber House. "Trafficking girls across the world is one thing, but making films of orgies, however wild... well... it's simply not Patrick's thing."

"The bloke I spoke to said Patrick had rented a room for a whole week."

"But you can watch that sort of rubbish on television these days. You don't have to buy under the counter porn anymore."

Lewis took a sip of whisky. "Charlotte, you know Patrick better than any of us. What do you think he's up to?"

Charlotte shook her head. "I've no idea, but knowing how devious he can be, I don't think it will be pleasant."

Sarah was nervously pacing the room. "Do you think we should mention to Karl what he's up to?"

Joe scowled. "Why? Karl says he knows the reason Patrick is here in Leeds but he's not telling us. If he wants to keep secrets, so will we."

Charlotte sighed. "But surely—"

Joe raised his hand. "Let's just keep an eye on him until we find out what he's up to. He hadn't a clue I was following him this morning so we have the advantage. Agreed?"

"I... I suppose so," Charlotte said, "but—"

"What about you two?"

"Okay, Joe," Lewis said. "We'll do it your way for now but be careful. Whatever you do, be careful."

......

After his meeting with Oscar Wright, Karl left the club and returned home. Christina was lounging on the couch watching television.

"Where's your mother?" he asked, pouring himself a whisky.

"Shopping," Christina answered. "She's not been gone long."

Karl tutted. "That bloody woman is always shopping."

"I think she was calling at the travel agents. She's determined to go back to Australia."

Karl snorted. "Over my dead body." He strode over to an armchair across from his daughter and plonked down. "Anyway, what's this I hear about you and Matthew getting divorced? I thought we'd agreed you were going back to Australia to patch things up?"

Christina swung her legs down from the couch and sat upright, her arms folded defiantly across her chest. "We agreed no such thing," she said. "I'm not going back to him, and you can't make me."

"So, you're going to just walk away from your marriage and your kid?"

Christina pouted but remained silent.

"At least speak to Matthew on the phone."

"Why? What do you want me to say? Matthew hates me and I… I hate him." Christina got up from the couch and hurried to the door. "Please don't ask me to go back, Dad."

Karl sighed. "I can't make you, of course I can't, but I can advise you. I think it would be best if you at least tried to put things right."

"No, it's too late for that. I never want to see him again. Ever."

"And what about your son? What's he done to make you hate him so much?"

"Don't be ridiculous. I don't hate Andrew, I love him. He's a beautiful baby."

"But you're prepared to abandon him? How does that work?"

Christina was hesitant for a moment as tears began to well. "Matthew… Matthew is a much better father than I am a mother. Andrew will be well looked after; I know he will." She opened the door into the hall and rushed up the stairs, slamming her bedroom door behind her.

"Bloody women," Karl murmured as he drained his glass.

58

Oscar Wright hammered on Roger Laverick's door with his fist. After a couple of minutes he could hear bolts being drawn back and keys turned. Once open, Oscar pushed his way into the apartment, poking Laverick in the chest with his finger.

"What the fuck are you playing at, you stupid bastard?" he growled.

Roger stepped back in alarm. "What's the matter? What have I done?"

"Maddox wouldn't sign the papers this morning. He said he is having a dispute with you over money, and until it's settled, he is not in a position to spend any more cash on the club."

"Yeah, that's right. Maddox owes me. He agreed to give me twenty percent of takings and the bastard is welching on the deal."

The veins in Oscar's neck began to pulsate. "Fuck your twenty percent. When I get this surveillance contract signed, we can gain access to his accounts. Can't that birdbrain of yours understand that?"

Roger scowled. "But Maddox owes me."

Oscar gave a deep sigh of exasperation. "When my deal goes through, your take will be a hundred times more that your twenty percent, you stupid bastard. Can't you see that?"

Frowning, Roger walked over to an armchair and perched on the arm. "Okay. I suppose you're right. What do you want me to do?"

"Give Maddox a call. Tell him to go ahead with having the new surveillance installed and to deduct half the cost out of your share of the profits."

Roger took out his mobile phone from his pocket. "I have a bad feeling about this job," he said. "I think we should walk away."

Oscar huffed. "Don't be bloody stupid. It'll be like taking candy from a baby. Now hurry up and make that call."

......

Luke was in the hotel bar when Patrick arrived back from his meeting with Richard at Amber House.

"How did it go?" he asked as Patrick took a bar seat next to him and ordered a drink.

"Fine. Your mate Arnie was right. That place is exactly what I want."

"So you're really going ahead with it?"

Patrick raised an eyebrow. "Of course I am. I'm going to give Karl Maddox hell." He began to chuckle. "To witness his wife being tortured and killed is bad enough, but when we start on his daughter as well..."

"Whoa," Luke said, raising his hand. "Less of this we business. I'm not getting involved in murdering two women on film. I've told you I think it's a crazy idea."

Patrick turned to Luke, a steely look in his eyes. His voice was low but firm. "If you want to keep working for me and earning the cash, you'll do exactly as I say."

The bartender brought Patrick's drink and placed it in front of him.

"Thanks," Patrick muttered, his gaze still firmly fixed on Luke.

Luke drained his glass before he spoke. "Alright," he said hesitantly, "but I don't want my face on film."

"Don't worry, it won't be. We'll both be wearing masks."

"When… when are we going to do this?"

A malicious grin slowly crept across Patrick's face. "Soon," he said. "Very soon."

59

It was almost nine o'clock that evening when Debbie Wallace entered The Emerald Club. She hurried over to Paul who was standing by the bar. Leaning forward, she kissed him lightly on the cheek.

"Hi," she said smiling, "it's good to see you."

Paul casually put his arm around Debbie's shoulders. "I'm glad you could come," he said, drawing her close. "You're looking great, by the way."

Paul ordered a bottle of wine.

"When do you move into your apartment? I thought we might arrange a small housewarming."

Paul frowned and shook his head. "I don't think so. More than half a dozen in there at the same time and you'll be standing on each other's shoulders."

"Actually, I wasn't thinking of inviting anyone else," she said. "Just you and me."

Paul grinned. "Maybe, in a couple of weeks," he said, picking up the bottle and two glasses. "Let's go and sit over there. The bar's getting crowded." He made his way to the far wall and put the drinks down on a table before drawing up two chairs. "There, that's better. You can't hear yourself think over there."

Debbie flopped into the chair. "On the phone you said you needed to speak to me about something?"

"Did I? Maybe I just wanted to see you."

She began to chuckle. "I thought you sounded… mysterious, that's all."

"Actually, Deb, there is something I wanted to ask you. What do you know about Wright Securities?"

Her demeanour suddenly became defensive. "Why do you want to know about them?"

"They've quoted to do some work at the club. Karl asked me to find out about them, and as they were clients of Gina, I thought you might have some insight, that's all."

"Paul, they're clients of my employer. It would be unethical for me to make any comment about their professionalism, surely you know that?"

"I suppose so, but do you know them personally? I understand Miles was involved with Gina for a while."

Debbie fidgeted uncomfortably as she laced her fingers on her lap. "I'm sorry but I don't think I should be discussing them with you."

"Alright, suit yourself. But tell me, do you think they'd do a good job of security for this place?"

"I'm sure they would. They have an excellent reputation. By the way, has Oscar invited Karl to visit his house yet?"

"No, I don't think so."

Debbie grinned. "Oh, he will. He loves to impress people with his house. He likes to compare it with Downton Abbey."

"Sounds intriguing. Have you been?"

"Just the once. I went with Gina a couple of weeks before she died."

"And were you impressed?"

"A bit too ostentatious for my taste, I'm afraid, but Oscar and Miles seem to think it's wonderful."

"How well do you know Miles?"

Debbie shrugged. "Not very well. When he came to the office, he only had eyes for Gina. I don't think he even noticed me; the little secretary stuck behind her desk."

"Are you saying he never flirted with you?" Paul kissed her lightly on the back of her hand. "You're an attractive woman, and he's a good-looking bloke."

The colour in Debbie's cheeks began to rise. "And you're an outrageous flirt," she said, sipping her wine. "Miles and I never really got into any sort of conversation. I did get the impression he was an extremely jealous person though, the way he tried to keep tabs on Gina."

Paul frowned. "What do you mean?"

"When he rang the office and she wasn't able to take the call, he quizzed me about where she was, who she was with, that sort of thing. It could be quite unnerving."

"What caused them to split up, do you know?"

Debbie lowered her head. "His jealousy got too much, I think. He wanted to know where she was all the time."

"No wonder she packed him in," Paul sympathised.

"She did have a word with Oscar about his son's unreasonable behaviour."

"What did Oscar do?"

"He was furious and couldn't apologise enough to Gina. He sent her an enormous bouquet."

"What do you think of Oscar? Do you like him?"

Debbie shrugged. "He can be quite charming when he wants to be, but there's something about him I don't like."

"Oh?"

"It's hard to explain. I just go out of my way to avoid him when he comes into the office."

"Well, from what you've said, I think they both sound a bit odd. Maybe Karl should look elsewhere to do business."

"No, I'm sure they'll do a great job for the club. They're just not nice individuals, that's all."

"Another wine?" Paul asked, picking up the bottle.

Debbie nodded. "I'd love one," she said, "then maybe we can spend the evening somewhere else."

"Where do you suggest?"

Debbie shrugged. "Oh, I know a place," she said mischievously. "It's not a big place but—"

Paul laughed. "I think I know where you mean. Drink up and let's go."

60

James Moore looked nervous and uncomfortable standing at the bar of The Emerald Club with a lager in front of him.

"Good evening," said a voice to his left. He turned sharply to see Kelly standing at the bar. "I didn't think we'd be seeing you here again."

"I... I came to talk to Suki," he said, "but I can't find her."

"Suki's working in the VIP lounge this evening, but I'm afraid you're not allowed in there unless you're a member."

"But I only want a quick word," James said. "Do you think you could get her to come down here?"

"The staff are not allowed to fraternise with members, you do know that?"

James inhaled. "I don't want to fraternise," he said. "I want to... I want to take her away from all this."

Kelly raised an eyebrow. "Take her away? Where exactly do you propose to take my sister?"

"I don't belong here," James said, "and I don't think Suki does either, not really. Please, just get her down here for a minute."

"Don't be ridiculous. She doesn't know you and you don't know her."

"But I want to get to know her. I think she's the most beautiful girl I've ever seen." He leant forward and grabbed Kelly's arm. "Please, I'm begging you. Just let me talk to her for one minute."

Kelly threw back her head. "You really are a naive romantic, aren't you?" she scoffed. "People don't fall in love across a crowded room. That only happens in books."

"I need to speak with her, and if I have to stand here all night I will."

Kelly huffed. "For goodness sake, you're being ridiculous."

"Then get Suki down here," James pleaded.

Kelly was quiet for a moment. "I'll tell you what I'll do," she said at last. "Suki finishes work at two in the morning. If you're that keen, wait in the all-night coffee shop up the street. She'll meet you there, but I warn you, James, I will be coming along too."

"That's fine. I'll be there, and Kelly..."

"Yes?"

"Thank you." He leant forward and kissed her lightly on the cheek before hurrying to the club's exit.

Kelly shook her head and sighed. "Bloody idiot," she murmured.

......

Wearing her new pink-sequined mini dress and matching stiletto heels, Suki felt excited at being promoted to the VIP lounge in such a short time of joining the club. Although the clients, overall, were much older than the men in the main club, they were far more generous with their tips.

Deloris, the supervisor on the VIP lounge, came over to her.

"Suki, Karl wants you to take him a bottle of whisky to his office. He only drinks Maclaren so you'd best get Simon to get it from store."

Suki strode over to Simon who was in conversation with three well-known local figures.

"Sorry to interrupt," Suki said timidly, "but Karl wants a bottle of Maclaren. Deloris said you would have to get it."

Simon huffed as he turned to the three men. "I'll just be a minute, if you'll excuse me." He hurried across the room, stopping outside a small door, and took out a bunch of keys. "This is where we keep the special stuff," he said, reaching into the cupboard. He took out a bottle of Maclaren whisky and handed it to Suki. "For fuck sake don't drop it. Karl will go ape."

Suki took hold of the bottle. "Thanks, Simon," she said as she hurried towards Karl's office. She knocked lightly on the door and opening it, stepped into the office.

Karl was lounging on the large couch, cigar in hand. "Ah, my whisky at last," he said. "Pour me a glass, that's a good girl." He indicated the crystal glass on his desk. "Pour one for yourself."

Smiling, Suki shook her head. "No, thank you. I don't like whisky." She began to pour the golden liquid into the glass before handing it to Karl.

"If you don't like whisky, there's gin over there, or vodka."

"Thank you, but I don't drink alcohol."

Karl smirked and patted the seat next to him. "Sit down for a minute," he said. "You and I haven't had a chance to talk properly yet, have we?"

Suki perched nervously on the edge of the couch.

"So, Suki, are you enjoying working in the VIP lounge? Better than working downstairs, eh?"

Suki nodded. "Yes," she said meekly.

"This job is all about making as much money as you can. In this business you have a short career, you do know that? No bloke is going to pay good money to watch a girl who's past her prime. How old are you?"

"I was eighteen last month," she said.

"Good, so you've got a few years ahead of you, as long as you take care of yourself, of course."

Suki blushed but remained silent.

"Tell me, how would you feel about earning more cash? A lot more cash."

She frowned. "I... I don't understand."

"Well, let me spell it out for you. Punters are remarking on what a pretty girl you are. Did you know that?"

She shook her head.

"They are looking for a little more... how can I say... more interaction with you. That's why I've decided you would do well working for me at my agency, Cupid's Angels."

"What is Cupid's Angels?"

Karl smirked. "It introduces beautiful young women, just like you, to extremely rich clients. You're going to become an escort, Suki. Instead of teasing clients in the club, you're going to be satisfying the sad bastards. For a price of course."

Suki jumped to her feet. "You want me to become a prostitute? How dare you? I'm a dancer, not a whore."

"You work for me now, and you'll do exactly what I tell you to do."

"I won't do it, Karl. I won't."

"Think of all that money you'll be making. Far more than you earn twirling around the poles half naked, unless of course you get a kick out of being a prick tease. Do you?"

Suki ran towards the door, but Karl reached out and grabbed her arm.

"Think about it. As an escort you have empowerment over men. You have control, and best of all, you have a load of cash just for lying on your back. Now, what's not to like?"

Suki struggled to free herself from Karl's grasp. "No, I won't do it," she said, "and you can't make me."

Lunging forward, Karl knocked her to the floor, resting his full bodyweight on top of her. "You don't have a choice, Suki," he hissed. "You'll do as you're told. From tomorrow night you'll be working for Cupid's Angels, and that an end to it." He began to stroke her hair and pressed his lips on hers. "I'll send a driver round for you at seven, so make sure you're ready." He leant back onto his knees and grinned. "Now, what do you say your boss is your first client?"

61

Deloris was about to leave the VIP lounge for the evening when Suki came out of Karl's office.

"Oh, there you are at last. How long does it take to deliver a bottle of whisky?"

Suki remained silent as she made her way to the staff cloakroom.

"Is everything alright?" Deloris said, following her in. "You look upset."

Suki fought back the tears as she reached for her coat. "I'm fine. I just want to go home."

The two women went through the lounge and began descending the stairs. Deloris reached out and gently held Suki's hand. "Is it Karl? Has he... has he hurt you?"

Suki began to tremble as tears trickled down her cheeks. Deloris put her arms around Suki's shoulders and held her close. "I'm so sorry this has happened to you," she said. "I'm afraid seducing new staff is one of Karl's little weaknesses."

Suki pulled away and flung back her head. "You mean he does this to all the girls?"

"Not all, but some. Didn't your sister warn you about him before you came to work here?"

"She tried to persuade me not to come. She said Karl could be dangerous, but I ignored her. I wanted to be a dancer so much."

"What are you going to do?"

"Karl says I have to work as an escort at some agency he runs."

"Cupid's Angels?"

"Yes, that's the name. I've told him I won't do it and he can't make me."

"In that case, Suki, I think the best thing you can do is get as far away from Leeds as you can and do it straight away."

"But I don't want to leave. Why should I?"

"Remember what Kelly told you. Karl is a dangerous man. Believe me, you don't want to cross him."

As the two women got to the bottom of the stairs, Kelly came out of the club and made her way into the foyer. She smiled warmly at her sister.

"Well, how did your first shift in the exclusive VIP lounge go? Was it as much fun as you thought?"

"I'll leave you two to talk," Deloris said as she hurried towards the exit. "I have a taxi waiting."

Kelly linked her arm with her sister. "Is everything alright, love?"

"Can we go home, Kelly? I'm exhausted."

"Not yet. I have a surprise for you."

"I hate surprises."

Kelly smiled. "I don't think you'll hate this one."

62

Inspector Calvert sat across from several senior officers from the Major Incident Team in a meeting room at Holbeck Police Station. Chief Superintendent Ronan Trulove was chairing the meeting.

"This character, Oscar Wright, has managed to keep below the radar for the last five years," he said. "He has no convictions for fraud, nor for that matter for anything else. Are you absolutely sure, Calvert, that he's a key player? We have limited resources, remember. I don't want to be wasting my team's time and the public's money investigating this man on mere suspicion."

Calvert cleared his throat. "With respect, sir, Peter Sutcliffe had no convictions for murder but he went on to kill at least thirteen women."

"That's not quite the same thing, inspector, as well you know."

Calvert opened the file in front of him. "I requested a deep forensic search of Wright's business dealings. I'm still awaiting their findings."

"I'm aware several of his clients have suffered thefts throughout the country, but I see no evidence linking him or his company to any of them."

"Well, sir, things have moved on a little since you were submitted with the file."

"Oh? In what way?"

"It's true we couldn't point the finger at Wright Securities directly for the thefts. Apparently, the security systems they had installed became inoperative prior to the incidents, it was thought through the work of a hacker."

"Oscar Wright can't be held responsible for that though, surely?"

Calvert shrugged. "Earlier this week, along with a couple of our IT guys, I visited A W Morgan & Sons, a small jeweller over in Bradford. They had been clients of Wright Securities. Their company had been done over three years ago."

"What was the purpose of your visit?"

"I interviewed Albert Morgan about his business dealings with Wright Securities. He said Wrights had installed the alarms and provided security for his computers. Since the theft, Morgan ceased working with Wright Securities and moved his business to another company."

"Which of course was his prerogative."

"Yes, it was. But when our IT guys examined Morgan's computers, they found something extremely curious."

"What was that?"

"They're still testing it, of course, but it appears the device which they recovered is capable of relaying information back to Wright Securities."

"Information? What information?"

"Stock deliveries for one thing. Details of large shipments of gems, watches and gold, and what route they will be taking."

"Are you sure about this, Calvert?"

"Absolutely. After our discovery at Morgans, the team visited two of the other clients of Wright Securities who had been robbed. They checked their computers, looking for the same device."

"And did they find any?"

Calvert shook his head. "No, sir, they did not."

"In that case, I don't see how—"

"The thing is, Albert Morgan ceased business with Wright Securities as soon as the theft. He wouldn't allow them back on his premises blaming them for incompetence. This meant that the device in the computer could not be removed. The two companies we visited were still trading with Oscar Wright. They both told me Oscar had visited their premises shortly after the thefts to check and maintain their computers. I believe this is when the devices were removed so Wright Security's involvement could not be detected."

"That's quite a theory, inspector."

"Yes, sir. A theory I intend to prove once I get sight of the forensic accountant's report."

"Have you identified any of Oscar's associates? If you're right, he can't have carried out thefts of this magnitude on his own. He must have had help."

"I've requested Oscar Wright be put under twenty-four-hour observation. I'm still waiting for approval."

"Well, you've got it, starting today."

"Thank you, sir."

"What about the son, Miles? Do you think he's involved?"

"No doubt about it. Miles is the one who initially visits the client's premises to install the security equipment."

"In that case we'll put him under observation as well."

Trulove got to his feet. "I'll speak to forensics and see if I can hurry them up. If you're right, Calvert, I think we're on the verge of smashing one of the biggest organised crime units in the country."

63

"Where the hell have you been?" Oscar yelled down the phone at Patrick. "I've been trying to get hold of you all morning."

"I've been busy. What do you want?"

"I've had one of my clients on the phone. They said the police had been round examining their computer."

"What for, did they say?"

"No. Just that two geeks took it apart, then put it back together again."

"Why would they do that? Is there anything incriminating the police could find?"

"No. I took the device out soon after we did the job. There's nothing, but why are the police suspicious? What the fuck is going on?"

"Who was the client?"

"Rowley & Sons. They import Persian carpets."

"Oh, I remember them. We made quite a killing on that job."

"But what if—"

"Oscar, think for a minute. It's probably nothing to do with their security. The police are interested in the activities of Rowley's, that's all. They bring stuff in from the Middle East so they're bound to be of interest if you think about it."

"I... I don't know."

"Has any other client of yours had a visit from the cops?"

"No, not that I know, but I can't exactly ring round and ask them, can I?"

"Then sit tight and stop worrying."

"That's easy for you to say. Nobody can connect you. It's my neck on the line if anything goes wrong."

"Nothing's going to go wrong, so sit back and enjoy that nice comfy house of yours until we do the next job."

"I've been thinking about that. I want to quit after we do Millers. It's all getting too risky."

"Bollocks. We're all onto a good thing and I'm not ready to quit. Neither are your associates."

"That's where you're wrong. I was talking to Beauchamp yesterday. He's had enough too. The poor bloke's living on his nerves."

"What about your mate Laverick? Does he want to pack in as well?"

"I don't care whether he does or not. I'm not comfortable carrying on for much longer."

"You're forgetting about Maddox. His business is an oil well just waiting to be drilled."

"Maddox hasn't signed the contract yet. I think we should forget about him."

"Absolutely not. I have a personal feud with that bastard. I'm going to take him for everything he has, then I'm going to—"

"Going to what?"

"Never mind. Invite him over for dinner or something, then make sure to get his business. Okay?"

"I don't like it. Maddox is no fool. He'll—"

"Oscar, just do it."

Before Oscar could reply, Patrick had put down the receiver.

64

"Who was that on the phone?" Lisa asked as she busied herself filling the dishwasher.

"That," Karl answered, "was Oscar Wright. He's invited us for dinner at his house tonight."

"Who's Oscar Wright? I don't think I've met him."

Karl grinned. "He's a bloke touting for business."

"What did you say? Are you going?"

"I wouldn't miss it for the world." He sidled up to his wife. "Why don't you go into town this morning and buy yourself a new dress? I've heard Oscar's house is something special. You want to give a good impression."

"Well, I suppose I could do with a party frock," she said. "I only brought a few things with me from Australia."

Karl handed her a wad of cash. "Buy a blue dress. I like to see you in blue."

"Thank you," she said, putting the money into her purse. "By the way, I don't suppose you had chance to speak to Christina?"

"As a matter of fact I did speak with her, for what good it did. She's determined she's not going back to Matthew. Where is she by the way?"

"She rushed out of the house first thing. She said she was meeting a friend."

"What friend?"

Lisa shrugged. "She wouldn't say, but she was wearing makeup and her low-cut blouse, so it's probably a man."

"What man? Do you know?"

"I've no idea. I'm the last person she confides in."

"We have to get that girl to face her responsibilities. She can't be going around acting as if she were single."

Lisa sighed heavily. "I know that. I rang Matthew yesterday to try and make him see sense, but he was abrupt, in fact he was almost rude. It was obvious he didn't want to speak with me about the situation."

"In that case, I don't think there's anything we can do. Just let them get on with it."

"But Karl—"

"I'm sorry, Lisa, but I've washed my hands of the whole thing, and I think you should too."

......

Christina hurried down to the burger van parked on Millennium Square. The person she had come to meet was already there.

"Sorry I'm late," she said, kissing him lightly on the cheek. "My mother can be such a pain."

"Don't worry about it," he said smiling. "I've bought you a coffee. You do drink coffee, don't you?"

Christine began to giggle. "Of course I drink coffee. Mind you, I do prefer gin and an occasional vodka."

"It's a bit early for that," he said. "Now tell me, Chrissy, where do you want to go? There's not much happening in Leeds on a wet Wednesday in November, but we could always—"

"Let's go to yours" Christina said. "You did say your dad was away on business most of the day."

He grinned. "Well, if you're sure?"

"Of course I'm sure."

Christina reached out her hand, taking his. "Let's have a wonderful day getting to know each other, and sod everyone else."

"Okay, if that's what you want," he said. "West Top Manor here we come."

65

It was almost lunchtime when Luke got back to the hotel. He went straight to Patrick's room.

"I managed to get everything you asked for," he said, depositing two carrier bags on the couch."

"You remembered not to get everything from the same place?"

"Of course I did, stop worrying. I went to three different outlets." Luke tipped out the contents of the first carrier bag. "I got the tie-wraps from Hepworth's haberdashery, and the gaffer tape and pliers from The Tool Bar in Randolph Street." He picked up the second bag. "This lot came from the chemist on Briggate."

"That's great," Patrick said, examining the contents of the second bag. "You can take all these round to Amber House." He laughed harshly as he handed Luke the key. "I'll get the rest of the stuff this afternoon and we should be ready to go."

"How... how are you going to get them both?"

"Don't worry about that, just leave it to me. Just be ready when I get there tomorrow."

Luke shrugged. "Okay," he said. " It's almost one o'clock. Can we go to eat? I'm starving."

"Sure, I'm peckish myself."

"Do you want to eat in the hotel restaurant?"

"No, I don't think so. Not today."

"Why not? The grub's great here."

Patrick frowned. "It's probably my imagination," he said, "but that black guy working behind the bar… there's something about him I don't like. He makes me feel… he makes me feel uneasy somehow."

"You don't think he's onto us, do you?"

"No, of course not. I just get the feeling sometimes he's watching me."

"I can't say I've noticed him," Luke said as he headed for the door. "One bartender is pretty much the same as another as far as I'm concerned." Luke reached for his coat.

"Do you fancy that place on Boar Lane? I've heard the food's not bad."

"Sure, why not?"

"How long do you think it's going to take once we've done Millers Motors? I really don't feel safe hanging about here too long."

"Once Oscar has got Maddox's contract signed it shouldn't take long. He's seeing Maddox tonight so that should be done and dusted. The guys are on standby to hijack Millers delivery tomorrow night, and Laverick's got everything in place to move the vehicles on."

"Don't you think it's a bit too soon to do over Millers? They've only just signed their new contract."

"Why wait? Besides, Oscar's getting cold feet. Both him and Beauchamp are wanting out."

"What are we going to do? We can't carry on without them."

"No we can't can we? Maybe it's time to think about closing down operations."

"Does this mean you won't be doing Maddox after all?"

"It means nothing of the sort. We can be in and out of his accounts before he's finished smoking his cigar."

"What about the other business? Are we still going ahead with that?"

"Of course we are. I've booked that room at Amber House for a week, so there's plenty of time." He gave a raucous laugh. "Then it's back to the sunny shores of... well, does it matter?"

66

Alex was pouring himself a coffee from the cafetiere when Lisa arrived at his flat.

"Ah, just in time," he said, reaching into the cupboard and taking out another mug.

Lisa threw her coat onto the kitchen counter and plopped onto a chair. She sighed heavily.

"What's up, Mum?" Alex said, handing her a mug of coffee. "You look done in."

"Oh, it's your father. He's making a fuss about me going back to Australia. He wants me to stay here with him."

"Would that be so bad?"

"I can't stay with Karl. His lifestyle is... well it scares me to be honest."

"I thought once he got his beloved Emerald back up and running, he was going to settle for an easy life."

"Easy life? He doesn't know the meaning of the word." She sipped her coffee, a faraway look in her eyes. "A few days ago I found him huddled in a meeting with Danny and Lenny at the house. Simon and Paul were there too. It all looked suspicious to me. They're up to something. I know they are."

Alex shrugged. "He's not said anything to me. I'll have a word and see what I can find out what's going on, if you like."

"Would you? He might talk to you."

"I can try, but I have to tell you, I owe Dad a lot. He helped me get out of trouble when I was a suspect over Gina's murder, so he's not all bad."

"What do you mean? He only persuaded you to tell the truth about your whereabouts the night she died." She turned and put both her hands on Alex's shoulders. "There's nothing to be embarrassed about spending time in a gay bar. You do know that?"

"But that's just it, Mum. I wasn't in Bar Dalziel that night."

"What do you mean? Danny and Lenny said...?"

"They said what Dad told them to say."

Lisa's frowned. "If you weren't there, then where the hell were you? You didn't... Alex, tell me you had nothing to do with what happened to that girl."

"Of course I didn't hurt Gina. I was in love with her."

"Then where were you that night that you had to lie? This doesn't make sense."

"I couldn't tell Dad where I was that night because—"

Lisa jumped to her feet. "Because what? Where were you? Tell me the truth."

Alex lowered his head and inhaled deeply. "The night Gina Beauchamp was stabbed to death I was at Napoleons."

"Napoleons? What's that?"

"It's a casino in Leeds."

"But you promised you'd stay away from gambling after what happened last time. You gave me your word."

"I know I did, and I'm sorry but I can't help it. Nothing gives me the same buzz as when I'm in a casino. It's exhilarating. I feel... I feel alive." He took a sip of his coffee. "You should try working twelve-hour shifts in A&E day after day. You'd want some relief as well."

Lisa shook her head slowly. "How could you be so stupid? So weak?" She reached for her coat. "How much are you in debt this time? Don't expect your Dad to bail you out. As far as your gambling is concerned, he's washed his hands of you."

"I know that."

"So tell me, how much do you owe this Napoleons Casino?"

Alex smiled. "That's just it, I don't owe them anything. This last few months I've been on a winning streak."

"You've been winning? I don't believe it."

Alex opened a drawer in the kitchen unit and took out a bank statement. "See for yourself," he said, handing the document to his mother. "Not bad, eh?"

Lisa stared at the document in disbelief. "But there's over two hundred thousand pounds here."

"That's right. Enough for me to buy into a private medical practice like I always wanted to, but not in Canada like before. I thought maybe Australia. You could come with me and... well hopefully

Christina will get back with Matthew and we'll all be one big happy family."

"And what about Karl? Is there any room for him in your plans?"

"He can come if he wants, but Dad has his club. Running that, with all its dramas is what makes him happy. He's not bothered about you or me, and from what I've heard from Chris, things aren't going too well between them either."

"Matthew has served divorce papers on Christina. She's determined not to go back to Australia."

"Then let her stay here. Just you and me go, Mum. It'll be like the old days. Remember?"

Lisa patted Alex's arm. "Oh, Alex, you're such a dreamer." She leant over and kissed her son lightly on the cheek. "I can't stop you gambling," she said, "but promise me you won't get into the same situation you did before. I couldn't bear it."

Alex put his arm around Lisa's shoulders. "Don't worry, Mum. I've learnt my lesson. These days I only bet what I'm prepared to lose."

"Well, I hope you know what you're doing, son," she said walking slowly to the door.

"Do you have to go? My shift doesn't start until twelve today. I thought we could have a proper catchup."

"Sorry, Alex, I'm going into town to buy a dress for this evening."

"Oh? Going somewhere nice?"

"Karl's been invited to dinner by some bloke he's doing business with."

"Who is he? What sort of business?"

"His name is Oscar Wright. He runs a security firm. Surveillance cameras, that sort of thing. Karl thinks The Emerald's security system needs updating."

Alex scowled. "Is Oscar Wright related to Miles Wright by any chance?"

"I've no idea. Why do you want to know that?"

Alex shrugged. "Oh, no reason. Enjoy your dinner."

Lisa grinned. "I'll try, but knowing Karl, it's probably all going to be about business. I'll call round tomorrow and tell you all about it."

"'Bye Mum," Alex said as Lisa opened the door to leave. "I'll see you tomorrow."

"'Bye, Alex. Love you."

67

"Oh, Oscar, what a beautiful home you have," Lisa purred as she walked slowly around the elegant lounge that evening. "I've never seen anything quite like it."

Oscar beamed his pride. "It is rather special, isn't it? Would you like Clara to give you the grand tour before dinner?"

Lisa clasped her hands in excitement. "Yes, please," she said. "That would be wonderful."

Oscar pressed a button on the wall next to the marble fireplace and within seconds, the young woman who had greeted them at the door came into the room. Dressed in a black and white uniform, she stood in front of the lounge door.

"Ah, there you are, Clara," Oscar said. "Show Mrs Maddox around the house, will you?" He began to chuckle. "Make sure you don't reveal any of the skeletons, though."

"Yes, sir," Clara answered, a faint smile on her otherwise sombre face. She turned to Lisa. "If you'd care to follow me, madam," she said, standing to one side to let Lisa through the door and into the grand hallway.

"There, that's better," Oscar said, taking out a cigar from the box on the side table. "I can't talk business with women in the room." He walked over to

Karl carrying the cigar box. "Try one of these. They're from Havana."

"Very nice," Karl said, examining the cigar. "These are hard to get hold of. I know, I've tried."

"A friend of mine gets them," he said. "In fact I think you know him. Roger Laverick?"

"Yes, I know Roger."

Oscar began to chuckle. "I don't think there's much he can't forage. I'll have a word if you like and get you a couple of boxes."

Both men were seated in elegant brocade armchairs, a cut-glass decanter of malt whisky in front of them, together with four glasses.

"Fancy a drink before dinner?" Oscar said, picking up one of the glasses.

"I don't mind if I do."

From the grand hall, the grandfather clock began chiming eight o'clock. Oscar frowned. "I was expecting Miles to be joining us," he said. "I wonder where he's got to?"

Karl grinned. "If he's anything like my son, he'll be out on the town chasing girls."

Oscar leant forward and winked. "I think he took care of that this afternoon," he said. "Miles spent the day with your daughter. Christina, isn't it? She's a pretty girl."

Karl put down the whisky and puffed out his cheeks. "What do you mean, he spent the day with my daughter?"

"When I got back at five this afternoon, they were both engrossed with each other on that very couch," he nodded, indicating a large brocade chaise longue at the far side of the room. "They were both in a state of undress. What it's like to be young, eh, Karl?"

Karl jumped to his feet. "Christina is a married woman," he said. "Your son was out of order."

"Come on, Karl, chill out. It takes two to tango you know."

The lounge door opened and a smiling Lisa entered the room. "Oh, Karl, this house is simply wonderful. You must come and see." She said, her eyes shining with excitement. "There's an indoor swimming pool at the back and a small gym, and there's even a snooker room." She turned to Oscar. "Your home is simply fabulous Oscar. I'm so envious."

Karl grabbed Lisa by the arm. "Come on," he said as he roughly guided her towards the hallway. "We're leaving."

"But Karl, what's wrong? What's happened."

Karl turned sharply towards Oscar. "Forget about doing business with me," he said, "and tell that fucking son of yours if he comes anywhere near my daughter again, there'll be consequences."

Oscar got to his feet. "Karl, wait. We can work this out. I..."

But Karl and Lisa were already at the front door, Karl slamming it shut behind them.

......

"Are you going to tell me what that was all about?" Lisa said, as they drove along the motorway. "What's made you so angry?"

Karl's grip tightened on the steering wheel of his Mercedes as he held his foot on the accelerator. "I'll tell you what that was about," he said. "His son has seduced Christina, that's what happened." His jaw tightened and his eyes narrowed. "Miles took her to his house and... and took advantage of her."

"You mean they had sex?"

Karl began to shake with rage. "Of course they had sex. That bastard's not getting away with it. I'll—" Suddenly a white van coming towards them blared its horn and flashed its lights.

"Karl, for goodness sake calm down. You nearly caused an accident driving on the wrong side of the road."

Karl took a deep breath and reduced his speed.

"You'll need to speak with Christina," he said. "I'll deal with Miles."

"What exactly do you expect me to do? She's a grown woman. I doubt anyone could seduce our daughter unless she wanted to be seduced."

"What are you saying, that our daughter is a whore?"

Lisa shrugged. "She used to be."

Karl pulled into the layby. "How dare you," he spat. "That was years ago. She was alone with no support around her. That's all behind her now."

"What I'm saying is that Christina does exactly what Christina wants. She's always been headstrong, even as a child. If she's formed some kind of relationship with Miles Wright, I know she will have gone into it with her eyes wide open."

Karl inhaled deeply and leant back into his seat; his arms outstretched holding onto the steering wheel. He was silent for a few minutes, then he turned to face Lisa.

"Oscar Wright is a crook," he said at last. "His son is also a crook. They're involved in... well it doesn't matter. Let's just say that I'm aware of what they're up to."

"If you know that, then why the hell do you associate with him? You told me you were going to run a legitimate business. Nothing like before. Were you lying?"

"For fuck's sake, Lisa, don't be so naive. In my line of business, you have to seize every opportunity to—"

"To what? Tell me Karl, what exactly is your line of business these days? I thought you were running a poxy club for over-sexed wankers to come and watch young women flaunt themselves. Not very tasteful but definitely not illegal."

"I am legit. Ask Simon. Ask Paul."

"I wouldn't trust either of them to tell the truth. Whatever you're up to, I don't want any part of it. You're on your own. I'm leaving for Australia as soon as I can."

"You're not leaving me, Lisa. I won't allow it. You're my wife and you will stay by my side no matter what."

Lisa attempted to open the car door but it was locked. "Let me out," she screamed. "Let me out of here."

Karl turned on the ignition. "I'm going home," he said, "and you are coming with me."

68

After Karl left, Oscar picked up his phone and rang his son's number. There was no reply. He redialled with the same effect half a dozen times. "Where the fuck are you? "He hissed. "Answer the bloody phone."

After trying to contact Miles without success for the best part of an hour, Oscar rang Patrick.

"We have a problem," he said as soon as Patrick answered his call. "Maddox is not going to give me the business."

"Why not?"

"He changed his mind."

"Bollocks! Maddox knows a good deal when he sees it and what we put together was an extremely good deal, so why isn't he in?"

"It's... it's complicated."

"Complicated? What the fuck are you talking about? What's going on?"

"He... he got upset when he found out my son, Miles, was seeing his daughter. I'm sure I can straighten things out with Karl. It's just going to take a little more time."

"We don't have more time, Oscar. Where's Miles now?"

"I've no idea. He isn't answering his phone."

"Then find him. He's not going to screw this deal up because he couldn't keep his dick in his pants."

"I think we should abandon the plan to do Maddox over. I've never been comfortable with it and—"

"I don't give a shit what you think. We're going after him and that's an end to it. Now I suggest you get that randy little shit of yours found and get him to apologise to Maddox. No excuses, and make sure he doesn't go anywhere near the girl again."

"I'll try, but Miles is a grown man. I can't tell him who he can and can't fuck."

"This isn't up for discussion, Oscar. Find him. If you don't, I will."

……

The house was in darkness when Karl and Lisa got home.

"Christina must have gone to bed," Lisa said as she took off her coat and hung it on a hook in the hall. "I'll go up and see if she's alright."

Karl huffed. "Tell her to come down here now. I need to speak with her."

Lisa hurried up the stairs whilst Karl meandered into the lounge and poured himself a large whisky. Before he had time to drink it, Lisa hurried into the room carrying a slip of paper.

She handed the paper to Karl. "She's gone off with Miles. Christina has taken her clothes and gone. She says she won't go back to Australia and we can't make her."

Karl studied the note. "The stupid bitch," he muttered. "I'll get the lads onto this. They can't have got far."

......

"Well, how do you like Scotland?" Miles whispered as he drew Christina close.

"Darling, it's wonderful, just like you." She tiptoed and kissed him on the lips.

"We can stay here as long as you want," Miles said. "They'll never find us."

Christina began to giggle. "We can't stay here for ever, silly. What are we going to do for money?"

"Don't worry about that, darling. I have plenty." Miles opened his suitcase revealing dozens of rolls of twenty-pound notes.

Christina stared open-mouthed. "Where... I mean how...?"

"Pops and I have an extremely lucrative business going on," Miles said. "This is nothing to the stash we have in Geneva."

Christina frowned. "What exactly is your business, Miles? You can't make this amount of money through security cameras."

"Don't worry about it. All you need to know is I can take good care of you. I'll make sure you'll never go back to Australia." He kissed her lightly on the lips.

Christina picked up her phone. "Do you think I should ring and let mam and dad know I'm okay? I don't want them to be worried."

Miles reached out and took the phone from her. "No, Chris, I don't think that's a good idea. You need to ditch the phone so you can't be traced." He hurriedly took out the SIM card and bent it in two. "There, that's better. Now we're really alone. Alone and untraceable."

69

The three vehicle transporters drove in convoy through the night. Each vehicle carried four luxury cars, all bound for Millers Motors, an upmarket car showroom in Leeds. It was one-thirty. Rain lashed upon the windscreens and a howling wind made driving the heavy vehicles uncomfortable. The first driver indicated to his companions his intention to pull into the motorway stop. Soon all three transporters were lined up in a row in the area reserved for large vehicles.

The three drivers and their co-drivers got down from their cabs, relieved to be able to stretch their legs.

"We'd better be quick," Mike, the driver of the second vehicle said. "You know we're not supposed to stop when we're carrying this type of load."

"Oh, fuck 'em," Bernie said. "I want a piss and a warm drink. It's against health and safety to deny me that."

"Do you want me to stay and guard the load?" Alfie, a newly recruited driver's mate volunteered. "I don't mind."

"Don't be daft, lad," Bernie said, putting his arm around Alfie's shoulders. "Who'd be daft enough to try and pinch one of these vehicles?"

"But—"

"They're not like a car. You can't just get in and hotwire," Bernie said. "They have a code to get into the cab and to turn on the engine. A code that's changed every journey. Now come on and stop twittering."

All the men laughed as they made their way to the cafeteria with its inviting warm glowing lights and the tempting smell of frying bacon.

Two minutes after the drivers entered the café, a white transit van pulled up alongside the transporters and three men jumped out. Each man approached a vehicle, tapped in a code on the lock and within seconds gained entry into the cab. Tapping out the same code on the front panel of the dashboard, the vehicles roared into life and slowly headed towards the exit of the lorry park.

Suddenly the park was illuminated by flood lighting as a dozen uniformed police officers emerged from their unmarked vehicles and surrounded the transporters. The three drivers began kicking and punching at the officers as they were dragged unceremoniously from the driver's cab. A man who had been left in the white transit van, hurriedly took out his phone and dialled a number. "The cops are here," he managed to say before the van was entered by two officers and he was pulled from the van and placed under arrest.

Inspector Calvert walked towards the handcuffed men. "Gottcha," he said, a broad smile across his face. He turned to a police sergeant. "Get the crew out of the café. I want them down at the station as well."

……

"Fuck," Patrick roared after receiving the phone call. "The bastard police have nabbed the load."

Luke turned off the television and turned to Patrick. "What do you mean?"

"They were waiting at the lorry park when our blokes took the transporters."

"But how... how did they know? There's no way the cops could have known about it."

Patrick snorted. "It's obvious, isn't it? Somebody must have told them."

"But who? Apart from us, the only other person who know the details was Oscar and our blokes. I don't think any of them would have ratted."

Patrick was thoughtful for a moment. "Maybe not, but Oscar's son might."

"Miles? Why would he do that? He's in this up to his neck."

"Oscar said Miles is seeing that Maddox girl. Maybe he told her and... whoever it was, we can't hang about here any longer. Let's get our stuff together and go."

"But it's two o'clock in the morning. Where can we go?"

Patrick began pulling clothes from the wardrobe and putting them into his suitcase. "I know somewhere," he said, "now hurry up and get packed. We're leaving in ten minutes."

"Don't you think we should warn Oscar what's happened?"

"Fuck him. He'll find out soon enough."

"So what's the plan now? The Miller job has fallen through, so has Maddox. Maybe it's time to call it a day."

"Like hell it is. I have unfinished business."

Luke sighed. "We've made more money than we're ever going to need. I think we should leave well alone. We can ring Roger and—"

"And what? Run away like a whipped dog? I don't think so."

"But Patrick, we're fucked. Surely you can see that. I'm going back to—"

Patrick rushed at Luke, pushing him against the wall. "You're going nowhere until I tell you," he snarled. "Now get ready. We're leaving."

70

It was almost four o'clock in the morning. Inspector Calvert and Sergeant Burrows were in the police canteen having a cup of lukewarm coffee.

"Great result," Burrows said. "I wish we got more anonymous tips like that."

Calvert grinned. "It certainly leaves a breadcrumb trail right back to Oscar Wright."

"He's been arrested and taken over to Millgarth Police Station."

"I'll get over there and interview him later. I think I'll let him sweat for a bit first though."

Burrows grinned. "The IT team are wetting themselves going through his computer. They've managed to access dozens of cryptic files, thanks to the information supplied by the informer. I wonder who that was?"

Calvert shrugged. "Oscar was certainly a clever bastard. The IT bloke said he's never seen anything so sophisticated as the setup he had."

"Let's hope they can find where all the money has gone. There must be millions."

"I'm sure our lads will find it," Calvert said.

"I wish I had your confidence, sir."

Calvert got to his feet. "The four blokes we caught red-handed are saying nothing except demanding a solicitor. Let's hope the drivers are more forthcoming."

"They all claim to know nothing about it."

"Maybe they don't. This job seems too elaborately planned and executed to be left to the cooperation of a bent driver."

Both officers made their way to Interview Room One. Calvert took his seat at the metal table whilst Burrows sat to the side. "Bring the driver of the first vehicle in," Calvert said. "Let's see what he's got to say for himself."

Bernard Elkin was in his mid-forties, almost six foot tall with unruly ginger hair and a thick beard. Both arms were heavily tattooed, and he had several metal piercings threw his nose and ears. Scowling, he bounded into the room, flinging himself onto the plastic chair, his arms folded across his ample chest in a gesture of defiance.

"Now then, Bernard," said Calvert. "You don't mind if I call you Bernard, do you? You seem to have been dropped right in it, don't you?"

Bernard curled his lip but said nothing.

"I understand that it was your suggestion the transporters stopped at that particular café. Is that right?"

Bernard huffed. "I needed a piss," he said. "The next place was twenty miles away. What was I supposed to do? Besides, I always stop there when I'm taking motors from the docks up north."

"Why didn't you leave someone to watch over the vehicles? I understand Alfie Reid offered to do that but you said no."

Bernard banged his fist onto the table. "We were told it was impossible for anyone to get into the vehicles, let alone drive them away without knowing the code setting. There's no way some scrote could make off without that."

"When were you given the codes?"

"Just before we set off from the docks. Geoff Miller, he's the customer, telephoned me and gave me the codes. It was a different code every journey."

"So, none of you had a copy of the code once you left the dock?"

"That's right. They were in here." He pointed his finger at his forehead.

"In that case, explain to me how three men were able to gain entry into the cabs and drive the transporters away?"

Bernard shook his head. "I have no fucking idea. That must have come from Miller himself, not me." He leant forward, resting his elbows on the desk. "Look mate, I've been doing this job for nearly twenty years and never had any problem. Check my record if you don't believe me."

"But you can see how it looks, Bernard? You conveniently stopping where you did where a van load of villains just happened to be waiting?"

"I've done nothing wrong, and you can't prove I have. I'm not saying another word without my solicitor."

71

Patrick yawned as he began to wake up from a troubled sleep. It was six o'clock. He sat up in the bed and swung his legs down, pushing the red velvet cover to one side. He squinted in the gloom to see Luke asleep in the leather chair. Getting to his feet, he walked over to his companion and leaning over him, began shaking him by the shoulder.

"What time is it?" Luke said sleepily, stretching his arms.

"Time to get up," Patrick said. "We've got things to do."

Luke frowned. "No, Patrick. It's time we fucked off. We can't stay in this room. It's... it's weird."

"Stop moaning. It's just for a couple of days until we've finished our business."

"You're still going ahead with it then? You're mad. I say we leave, and we leave now."

"And I've told you, we're not going anywhere until I make Maddox suffer." Patrick walked towards the door. "Come on, I know a place where we can get something to eat, then we're going after the women."

Luke sighed and slowly shook his head as they locked the room and going down the staircase, entered the street.

......

It was seven o'clock when Lewis raced along the hotel corridor to Joe's room. He knocked briskly on the door. It was Sarah who opened it.

"Get Joe," Lewis said. "Get him now."

Joe came to the door. "What's going on, Lewis?"

"They've gone," Lewis said. "They left about two this morning."

The muscles in Joe's face tightened. "For fuck's sake, I thought you said he was being watched?"

"He was, by me and by you, but we both have to sleep. I couldn't exactly alert the night reception, could I?"

Joe sighed. "No, I suppose not. I don't suppose Patrick gave a forwarding address?"

"He told reception he was going to the Leeds/Bradford Airport. He was flying to the States."

"America? Have you checked with the airport?"

"Of course I have. There are no flights to America today."

Joe cupped his fist into his hand. "Where the hell is he, and what is he up to?"

"I think we should let Maddox know they're gone."

"Yeah, I suppose we'd better. Give me five minutes to get dressed and I'll go over to his house."

"Do you want me to come with you? Safety in numbers and all that."

Joe shook his head. "No, you stay here with Sarah and Charlotte, and for fuck's sake Lewis, don't let them out of your sight."

72

Karl was in the kitchen enjoying a hearty breakfast when Joe stormed into the house.

"Well?" Karl scowled. "What brings you here at this time in the morning, in fact what brings you to my house at all?"

"Patrick's gone," Joe said. "He packed up and left the hotel at two o'clock this morning."

Karl jumped to his feet. "I thought you were supposed to be watching him?"

"We couldn't keep an eye on him twenty-four hours a day. Something must have spooked him to make him take off like that."

"Do you have any idea where he went?"

Joe shook his head. "He hardly ever left the room. Neither of them did." Joe stepped closer to Karl. "What was he doing here in the first place?"

"How the fuck do I know?"

"Oh, I think you do know, Karl. Does it have anything to do with Charlotte?"

"I wouldn't think so."

"Then what?" Joe inhaled deeply. "I wish I hadn't listened to you in the first place," he said wagging his finger. "I should have told the cops as soon as I knew who he was. In fact, I think I'll do that now. There's CCTV images of him at the hotel. It shouldn't be too hard for them to find him." He turned to leave.

"No, we don't want the cops involved."

"Then tell me what's going on."

Karl sighed and sank back into his chair. "Alright, I'll tell you what I know, but it stays between us."

Frowning, Joe perched on the breakfast bar stool, his arms folded across his chest. "Well," he said. "I'm waiting."

Karl proceeded to outline what he had found out from Spud about Oscar Wright's activities on the computer.

"So you're planning on taking all the cash they've all squirrelled abroad? That's quite a plan. You say this Oscar Wright he's the ringleader?"

Karl shrugged. "I can't work out whether he is or if it's Patrick."

"So what's your plan? How are you going to stop him? I presume you are going to stop him?"

Karl smirked. "I already have," he said. "The gang attempted to take three transporters full of high-end motors last night. Unfortunately for them the cops were waiting."

Joe raised an eyebrow. "You ratted on him?"

"I did what I had to. The vehicles were of no use to me."

"Then why did you do it? I wouldn't have taken you for a grass."

"Oscar was planning on doing me over once he got his claws into my business. The bastard deserves all that's coming to him."

"So that's why Patrick fucked off?"

"Probably. There's no point in him staying here. He can't operate without Oscar supplying him with information."

The kitchen door opened and Lisa entered the room. She gave Joe an icy stare as she glided to the counter and poured herself a coffee.

"Good morning, Lisa," Joe said. "It's good to see you again. You're looking well."

Lisa merely huffed her contempt.

Undeterred, Joe continued. "I hear you're a grandma now. Congratulations."

Lisa banged her coffee mug on the counter. "Yes I am, and I'd probably have another grandchild by now if you hadn't stolen Alex's wife."

Karl reached out and grabbed Lisa's arm. "That's enough," he said. "That's over and done with. It's time to move on."

Lisa flung back her head, her nostrils flared. "I'll never forgive that man for stealing Sarah. It was a wicked thing to do." Picking up her coffee cup she hurried towards the hall. "I'll take this upstairs," she said, "then I'm going to see Alex. We have things to discuss." She slammed the kitchen door behind her as she made her way up the stairs.

"Bloody women," Karl scoffed. "Can't live with them and can't live without them."

Joe got to his feet. "I'll go back to the hotel. You never know, they night turn up again."

"Hey, Joe."

Joe turned. "Yeah?"

"It's good to have you back on board, mate. I've missed you."

Joe scowled. "Fuck you," he muttered as he barrelled through the main door, slamming it behind him.

73

"Chris, let's spend the day in bed today," Miles said, pulling the duvet up to his neck. "The weather's lousy and—"

"Darling we can't do that. You know we can't."

"Why not?" He began to nuzzle her neck as he gently pushed her hair to the side.

"Well, for one thing you have a job to go to. Your dad's not going to be too pleased at you bunking off, is he?"

"I don't care. I want to be with you."

Christina began to giggle. "You do realise Karl's going to break your legs when we get back. He'll probably break mine too."

Miles pulled Christina close to him. "I mean it, Chris. I don't want to go back. I want to be with you far away from both of them."

Christina propped herself onto her elbows. "I want to be with you, Miles, but I'm not running away. It wouldn't be right."

"Why not?"

"Well, Mum would worry herself sick for one thing. She still thinks of me and Alex as children."

"We can let her know you're alright in a couple of days, but right now I want us to be alone and get to know each other."

Christina grinned. "Oh, I think I've got to know all about you this last few days," she said.

"Chris, I'm serious. Let's go to The Grampians. A friend of mine owns a little cottage up there. I can give him a ring. He'll rent it to me, I know he will. Nobody will ever find us there."

Lisa frowned. "The Grampians? They're mountains, aren't they? I don't want to climb a mountain, not in those shoes," she said, pointing to her black patent stilettos at the other side of the room.

"Don't be silly, you won't have to climb a mountain. I promise." He picked up his phone and dialled a number. "I'll ring him now."

……

Paul arrived at Karl's house just after ten that morning as Karl was returning the phone to its cradle.

"That was Spud," he said, a wide grin on his face. "That girl's a little diamond."

"Oh? What's she done now?"

He began to chuckle. "Let's just say Oscar Wright's going to have the shock of his life when he sees his bank balance."

Paul raised an eyebrow. "You don't mean she's—"

"That's exactly what I do mean. Every single penny."

"That's great. I don't suppose she can do the same to Patrick?"

"She's working on that, but we have a problem. The Irish bastard has disappeared from the hotel."

"I thought Joe was supposed to be watching him?"

Karl shrugged. "He was, but now he isn't. Patrick left the hotel in the early hours this morning."

"He must have heard about the consignment going tits up."

"Knowing what a cunning bastard he is, you can bet he'll have a Plan B."

"What about Laverick? Have the cops got onto him yet?"

"I've no idea. I tried ringing him a couple of times this morning, but it's gone to answerphone."

"Laverick's slippery. He'll have an escape route ready; you can bet on that."

"Jeramiah's bound to have been nicked. That's going to upset our little blackmailer chum, isn't it?"

"Debbie? She hasn't said a word to me about her association with Oscar. Every time I mention anything to do with her work she changes the subject."

"That girl's dangerous. You need to dump her."

Paul scowled. "But you were telling me to keep her onside. Make your mind up."

"I don't think there's anything she can tell us about the operation that we don't already know. Get rid of her. The sooner the better."

Paul shrugged. "Okay. All good things come to an end; I suppose."

74

Detective Inspector Calvert, accompanied by Detective Sergeant Burrows arrived at Millgarth Police station at nine-thirty that morning. They were shown to an interview room and within a few minutes, Oscar Wright was escorted into the room by two officers.

Oscar took his place at the metal table, staring defiantly at Calvert.

"May I remind you, you are still under caution," Calvert said. "For the benefit of the tape, can you please give your full name."

Oscar snorted. "You know my name."

"Mr Wright, I need you to confirm your full name."

"Oscar Reginald Wright," he said. "Is that better?"

"Thank you. Also present are myself, Detective Inspector George Calvert and Detective Sergeant Kate Burrows." He turned to Oscar. "I understand you do not want a solicitor present. Is that correct?"

Oscar scowled. "I don't need a solicitor. I've done nothing wrong."

Calvert leant forward. "Early this morning, an attempt was made to steal three transporters from a roadside café. Each one of those transporters was carrying several extremely expensive motor vehicles."

"What's that got to do with me?"

"The company who own those motor vehicles is Miller Motors. I believe they are clients of yours. Is that correct?"

"I've supplied them with surveillance equipment if that's what you mean."

"Whilst providing this equipment, you also had access to their computers. Is that also correct?"

"I had to have access. The whole thing is interconnected."

"Oscar, our IT department are examining your computers as we speak. They've already come up with material which can only be described as... well, incriminating shall we say."

The colour visibly drained from Oscar's cheeks. "I don't believe you. All of my computers are protected. There's no way you can gain access."

"Really? Do the names Roger Laverick and Jeramiah Beauchamp mean anything to you?"

"I know them, yes. Jeramiah is my solicitor."

"And Laverick? How do you know him?"

Oscar began to fidget uncomfortably. "I was introduced to him by Beauchamp."

"According to my information, Beauchamp is complicit in moving your ill-gotten gains to offshore accounts. Is that correct?"

"My finances are none of your damned business," Oscar retorted.

"I also understand that Laverick is the one who disposes of whatever it is you've stolen."

Beads of sweat appeared on Oscar's brow and his breathing became erratic. "You're talking out of your arse," he said. "I've never done business with Laverick."

Calvert opened a buff-coloured folder. "It's this feller I'm really interested," he said, pushing a photograph towards him. "What can you tell me about him?"

Oscar glanced at the picture and sniffed. "Never seen him before."

"Probably not. This was taken before his face surgery. He looks a bit different these days."

Oscar's hands began to tremble.

"His name is Patrick Flynn. Are you sure you haven't met him?"

"I've told you, no."

"According to the information gleaned from your computer, I believe that you know this man very well. Very well indeed."

Oscar stared down at the floor, twisting his fingers in front of him.

"What do you have to say to that, Oscar?"

Oscar took a deep breath. "I think I will have a solicitor after all," he said.

75

It was ten o'clock when Lisa strode into the kitchen. Karl was reading the Yorkshire Post.

"Going somewhere?" he asked, not looking up from his newspaper.

"I've told you; I'm going round to see Alex. It's his day off today so I thought we could have lunch and do some shopping later."

Karl slowly shook his head and tutted. "You indulge that boy, you always have."

"He's my son... our son. He's had a terrible time with that Gina Beauchamp business. I just want to give him moral support. It's a pity you can't do the same."

Karl lowered his newspaper. "What the hell do you think I've been doing? If it wasn't for me, Calvert would have him locked up and thrown away the key."

Lisa walked into the hall. "I'm not arguing with you, Karl," she said, opening the outer door. "Oh damn, it's raining again." She walked back into the kitchen. "Do you have an umbrella I can use? I didn't bring one with me."

"Why don't you take a taxi?"

"I would, but I need to make a couple of calls first. It's going to be easier to walk. Alex's flat isn't far."

Karl snorted. "There's one in the hall cupboard. You can take that."

Lisa opened the cupboard and took out the umbrella. She scowled. "Don't you have another one? This has 'The Emerald Club' blazoned all over it."

Karl shrugged. "It was used for the club promotion. Take it or leave it. That's all there is."

Lisa sighed as she ventured outside; opening the umbrella.

76

It was midday. Karl slammed the phone down in his office at The Emerald as Paul and Simon arrived.

"Anything wrong, boss?" Paul asked. "You've a face like a slapped arse."

"It's that girl Suki. She didn't turn up for work yesterday."

Simon frowned. "Oh, that surprises me. She told me how much she was enjoying working at the club."

Karl huffed. "I decided she would do better working at Cupids Angels. She was supposed to start work there last night."

Simon shrugged. "Maybe Suki changed her mind. It's a big step going from poll dancing to escorting."

Karl banged his fist on his desk. "Damn it, she'll do as she's told. I want you to go round to her flat and bring her here to me."

"You can't make her do that sort of work if she doesn't want to."

The veins in Karl's neck began to pulsate as the colour rose in his face. "Don't argue with me if you want to keep your job. Get round there and bring the stupid bitch here. Fetch her sister Kelly as well. She didn't turn up at the club either."

"Alright, Karl. I'll see what I can do, but if she doesn't want to come, I'm not going to make her."

Karl leant back into his chair. "As if I hadn't enough on my plate without having to deal with temperamental tarts. What the fuck's happening to the world? There was a time when these girls would fight tooth and claw to get on my books."

Paul perched on the arm of the couch. "Stop worrying. I visited Cupids Angels a couple of days ago and Julia says business is booming on all ten sites."

Karl huffed. "That's something I suppose."

"Julia says they're getting requests from overseas clients to provide girls to attend events in Europe. There's a big business convention in Brussels next month. The guy organising it, a bloke called Manuel, has asked if we can send six girls over."

Karl frowned. "Why? Don't they have tarts of their own?"

"According to him, French and Italian men prefer English women."

"We could try it out I suppose. I'll leave it with you to make the arrangements with Manuel."

"Sure thing. This could prove to be extremely profitable."

Karl shrugged. "We'll see. By the way..." The phone on Karl's desk gave its shrill ring. Looking at the screen, Karl could see it was his son. "Yes, Alex, what is it? I'm a bit busy at the moment.... What?... Lisa left the house a couple of hours ago. She's probably trying on some frocks somewhere... Have you tried her phone?... Let me know as soon as she turns up."

Karl slammed the phone back into its cradle.

"Is everything alright, boss?"

"That bloody woman. She was supposed to be seeing Alex this morning. She hasn't arrived, and she's turned her phone off."

"You don't think she's gone to the airport, do you? She keeps threatening to leave."

Karl reached into his desk drawer and pulled out Lisa's passport. "She won't get far without this," he said.

"Did she set off by taxi?"

"No. She wanted to walk. She said she had a couple of calls to make first."

"Did she say where she was calling?"

"I didn't ask. I assumed she was shopping. Lisa likes to shop."

Paul got to his feet. "I'll retrace her route," he said. "I'll find her. Don't worry."

"Thanks, Paul."

Karl took the accounts ledger from the safe and for the next half hour began studying the figures. A wry smile crept across his face as he saw the amount of profit The Emerald was making. He was about to pour himself a drink when Simon burst into the office.

"I've been to Kelly's flat," he said, breathlessly. "There's no sign of her or Suki of Kelly."

"Are you saying they've fucked off?"

Simon shrugged. "Pete, the bloke in the next flat said they left together yesterday morning carrying a load of suitcases. He assumed they were going on holiday."

"In December?"

"They were with a big bloke."

"I don't suppose this Pete knew who the big bloke was?"

"Yeah. Pete said he's the owner of the gym he uses. His name's James Moore."

"Is Moore a pimp?"

"Not as far as I know. He owns a few businesses, gyms, health clubs and stuff like that, but he spends a lot of time at his dojo."

"What the fuck's a dojo?"

Simon grinned. "A dojo is where you go to practice martial arts. It seems James Moore is quite an expert in that field."

"Is he now? Where is this dojo?"

"Shadwell."

"Well, maybe we'll pay James Moore a visit at Shadwell."

"We'll need to take some muscle with us, Karl. This karate stuff can be pretty lethal."

Karl huffed. "So can a boot in the goolies."

Karl's phone rang again. It was Paul. Karl listened intently to what Paul was saying, the colour draining from his face. "I'll be right there," he said. His hand was trembling slightly as he put the receiver back on its cradle.

"What's happened? You look like you've seen a ghost."

Karl rushed to the door. "Lisa's missing."

77

Karl arrived at Alex's flat in less than five minutes, a journey that would usually take nearer fifteen. Alex and Paul were in the kitchen.

"What's happened?"

"I retraced her steps on the route she would have taken," Paul said. "It seems she'd stopped at the travel agents up the road and bought a ticket for Australia."

Karl scowled. "She's already bought an open ticket, not that I'll let her use it."

"The ticket she bought was for Alex."

"Why would your mother buy you a ticket for Australia?"

"Because I was going with her," Alex said, pulling away from his father. "We were both going to start a new life out there."

"How far is the travel agent from here?"

Paul shrugged. "Five, maybe six hundred yards. When she left, she took the shortcut through the alleyway."

"How do you know that?"

"Because I found this in the alley," Paul said, picking up an umbrella from the kitchen counter. "This is one that was used for the promotion when we opened The Emerald isn't it? I take it Lisa was carrying this when she left the house?"

Karl nodded. "I found this as well," Paul said, handing Karl a black leather court shoe. "Is this Lisa's?"

Karl stared at the shoe. "It could be," he said. "She has so many shoes, I can't be certain."

"Mum was wearing those shoes the last time I saw her," Alex said, tears trickling down his face. "What's happened to her, Dad? Who's got Mum?"

Karl's fingers curled into fists as his eyes narrowed. "It can only be one person," Karl said quietly. He turned to Paul. "Get the lads together. All of them. We have to find her."

Alex picked up his mobile. "No, we must ring the police. They can find her." Karl reached out and grabbed the phone.

"No cops," he said. "I'll deal with it my way."

Paul huffed. "Where do you suggest we start looking? She could be held anywhere."

"We'll be hearing from that bastard, I know we will, and when we do—"

Alex rushed forward, pushing Karl in the chest. "Is this because of you?" he screamed. "Is someone hurting Mum because of you?"

"Calm down, son. This isn't helping."

Alex began sobbing. "Mum never hurt anyone," he spluttered between his sobs. "You have to find her, Dad. Promise you'll find her."

"I promise," Karl said. "Now I have to sort some things out. You stay here in case… in case your mother rings. Okay?"

Alex nodded. “Just find my Mum.”

Karl stormed out of the apartment, Paul by his side.

78

Lenny, Danny and four of the doormen were waiting in Karl's office when he returned.

"Right, you all know what has happened," Karl said as he handed out photographs of Luke and Patrick's new identity. "We must find them. I'm certain these bastards have Lisa."

Paul frowned. "Do you think this is because of the money you nicked from Oscar?"

"Unlikely. They won't know the money has gone for a couple of days yet. No, I think there's something much more sinister going on here."

"What about Spud? Can't she help?" Paul said.

"I'll give her a ring, but I'm not hopeful. Until I hear from them, all we can do for now is get out on the street and ask questions."

"What about Joe?" Paul asked. "Should I let him know what's happened?"

"Absolutely not. It's through that bastard's carelessness that Patrick is out there somewhere."

"But surely another pair of eyes?"

"I said no. Now get out there all of you and find my wife."

....

The room was cold and gloomy. Semi-conscious and fully clothed, Lisa was spread-eagled on the bed, hands and ankles firmly fastened with leather straps.

"That was easier than I thought," Luke said, placing gaffer tape over her eyes and mouth. "That chloroform worked like a dream."

Patrick grinned. "It's what was used to get girls into the vans back in the good old days. They didn't have time to scream or make a fuss. It's a pity his daughter wasn't with her though. We'll have to save her for another time."

Luke stared at Lisa. "Not a bad looking bird for her age, is she? I wouldn't mind giving her one."

Patrick frowned. "There'll be time for that, but first we're going to make Maddox sweat."

"How long before we... before we get rid of her? The longer we stay here the more dangerous it becomes."

"Stop fretting, Luke. We'll send the first pictures to Maddox about midnight. He'll have had plenty of whisky by then. His mind will be working overtime."

"Okay, but I need to eat. I haven't had anything all day."

"There's a pizza place down the road. Get me one as well."

"Any pizza in particular?"

"I don't mind, as long as there's no pepperoni or pineapple on it."

"Okay. I won't be long. Should I… should I fetch her something?"

Patrick raised an eyebrow. "What do you think?"

Luke raised his hand. "Fine. Nothing to eat for the lady."

79

It was almost midnight before Paul arrived at The Emerald. He went straight to Karl's office. Karl was behind his desk, cigar in hand, a large glass of whisky by his side.

"Well?" he demanded as soon as Paul entered the room. "Have you heard anything?"

Paul was shocked at how pale Karl looked. His eyes were sunken, and his hands had a slight tremor.

"Not much," he said, plonking himself into a chair. "A rough sleeper claims to have seen a woman being bundled into a van by two men this morning, but the guy was off his head on drugs."

"Where did this happen?"

"At the entrance to the alley where we found the umbrella and shoe."

"Did he give a description of the men?"

"Nah, I doubt he could describe himself. The poor bastard was out of it."

Karl gulped at the whisky. "Just a thought but… do you think they have Christina as well?"

"I thought she'd fucked off with Miles Wright?"

Karl shrugged. "So did I, but what if she didn't? What if these bastards have my daughter as well as Lisa?"

"There's nothing we can do until they contact you. I've got the lads ready to go at a moment's notice."

Karl drained his glass and was about to pour himself another whisky when his mobile phone, which was on his desk, gave out its shrill ring. He grabbed it, noting it was a withheld number. As soon as he pressed the green button to accept the call, an image appeared on the screen. It was Lisa, spreadeagled on a bed with tape over her eyes and mouth Sitting on the bed brandishing a six-inch blade knife, was a man wearing a novelty mask. He ran the knife lightly across Lisa's throat several times before lowering it and running it across her breasts.

Lisa was wearing a blue silk blouse and black trousers. The man carefully pierced the blouse with the knife and began to rip it into shreds revealing her white bra. Next, he began meticulously ripping at the trousers with the knife, one leg at a time, until they fell away from her. The man was silent whilst he was doing this. It was only when he had finished, did he turn to face the camera. "Soon, Maddox," he whispered. "Soon," Then the screen went blank.

Karl stared at the blank screen, his whole body shaking with rage. His hands clenched into fists as he gave a low guttural roar. "I'll kill the bastard. When I get my hands on that Irish bastard, I'll..." Sweat began running down the back of his neck and his breathing became erratic.

"Steady on, Karl," Paul said. "You'll be having another heart attack."

"Did you see what that bastard is doing to Lisa? What he's threatening to do to her? How can any man stay calm?"

Paul poured whisky into Karl's empty glass, before getting himself a drink.

"At least we know one thing," he said. "It doesn't look like he's got Christina."

......

Luke put his phone back in his pocket. "What I would give to have seen Maddox's face," he sneered. "I bet he's shitting himself right now."

Patrick gave a raucous laugh. "We'll give it half an hour, then we'll send him more. Something a little more... a little more personal next time." He flung himself into the chair. "Is there any whisky left?" he said. "Making a movie is thirsty work."

80

Karl paced nervously around his office muttering obscenities whilst Paul slowly sipped his whisky. He was in a pensive mood. It was some five minutes before he spoke.

"Karl, I have an idea. What's the name of that bloke who used to come to The Emerald a few years back. He only had one eye?"

"Eh?"

"You remember. He got sent down for organising bare knuckle fights?"

Karl frowned. "How the fuck do I know? What do you want to know about him for anyway? I don't think bare knuckle fighting is going to help find Lisa."

"I'll give Danny a ring. He'll know who I mean." Paul took out his mobile and made a call. When he finished, he turned to Karl. "His name's Tommy Woodall," Paul said triumphantly. "He lives in Chapeltown."

"Paul, what the fuck are you jabbering about? Some mad Irish bastard has kidnapped my wife and all you can talk about is some one-eyed crook who likes to watch bare knuckle fights."

"Ah, but that's not all Tommy is in to," Paul said, walking towards the door. "These days he orchestrates most of the pawn movies circulating around Leeds."

Karl frowned. "Are you saying that this Tommy Woodall has got Lisa?"

"No, but I think he will know where she is."

"How will he know that?"

"That room where Lisa is being held, I've seen it before. In fact, I've seen it quite a few times."

Karl looked perplexed.

"Occasionally I... well, I spend the evening watching the odd pawn film. I'm certain that Lisa is in the same room where most of these films are made."

"And you think this Tommy bloke will know where the room is?"

"I'm certain he will. Danny has given me an address for him so I'll go there straight away."

"I'll come with you," Karl said.

Paul frowned. "I think it's best you stay here. Flynn might ring the landline."

Karl huffed as he flung himself onto the couch. "You will find her, won't you? Lisa is... Lisa is everything to me." Tears began to stream down Karl's cheeks as he began to cry unashamedly.

Paul bounded down the staircase, two steps at a time. "Try not to worry, boss. I'll ring as soon as I find anything out."

......

"Time for a little more fun," Patrick said, putting on his mask. "Get Maddox on the phone."

Karl picked up his mobile on the second ring. He stared at the screen, hardly daring to breathe. Lisa was blindfolded and spread-eagled on the bed, just as she had been in the first video. Patrick was leaning over her, knife in hand. He cut her bra in the centre and it fell back, revealing her bare breasts. Holding the knife in his right hand, he cupped her right breast with his left hand and squeezed hard. Then he leant over and placed the point of the knife directly onto her nipple. Karl could hear Lisa's muffled cries through the taped gag she was wearing. Patrick then did the same to her left breast, making Lisa squirm in pain. He got up from the bed and was out of camera shot. He returned a few seconds later with two metal nipple clamps. He attached one to each nipple. Karl watched helpless as Lisa thrashed about in pain. Patrick turned to camera. "What does it feel like watching me playing with your wife's tits?" He laughed harshly. "Keep watching, Karl. Episode three is coming right up."

Luke turned off the camera phone and leered at Lisa as she squirmed in pain on the bed. "I'm going to take her pants off," he said. "I want to fuck her."

Patrick put his hand on Luke's shoulder. "Be patient. You can do whatever you want with her but I want Karl to see you do it."

Luke huffed. "How long will that be? My balls are about to explode."

Patrick laughed. "In that case, mate, you'd better go to the loo and have a wank."

81

Paul banged on the yellow-painted door of 17 Sharpe Street in Chapeltown. It was a rundown mid-terrace house with dingy net curtains hanging at the sash window. It wasn't until his third knock that a light came on in the front bedroom. A few minutes later, bolts were being drawn back and yale locks turned before the door was opened a couple of inches, protected by a door-chain.

A middle-aged woman, wearing a pink chiffon dressing gown, stood in the gap. Her straggly bleached hair was down to her shoulders and her face bore traces of makeup from the previous day. "Do you know what fucking time it is?" she snarled. "Who are you and what do you want?"

"I'm looking for Tommy Woodall. Is he here?"

"Who wants to know?"

"I do. It's urgent I speak with him."

"What's he done? You're not the filth are you? My Tommy's done nothing; do you hear?"

"Where is he?"

"Tommy don't live here no more. Not since he took up with that tart, Dorothy."

"If he doesn't live here, where does he live?"

"With her. He has done for three weeks, but he'll be back. He always comes back after his little adventures."

"Where can I find him and Dorothy? Do you know?"

"They're at that caravan site by the canal, if the police haven't moved them on again."

Paul turned and raced back to his car. He could hear bolts being drawn and locks being turned, making 17 Sharpe Street a safe haven once more.

......

Paul arrived at his destination just before two o'clock that morning. Half a dozen caravans were scattered across a small area of grass at the side of the Leeds Liverpool canal on the outskirts of the city. All of the caravans were in darkness. A couple of the vans had dogs tethered close by, but even a stranger's presence in the camp did not arouse their interest at such an unearthly hour.

Paul got out of his car and began to walk slowly around the camp looking for some indication which one was home to Tommy Woodall. When he got to the last van, a blue and yellow Hobby caravan, he noticed a stack of girlie magazines on the back window ledge. He took a deep breath and knocked sharply on the door. It took several minutes before it was opened.

The door opened, "Yeah?" asked the scantily dressed young woman with flame-red hair, as she rubbed her eyes from sleep. "What do you want?"

Paul smiled. "I'm looking for Tommy Woodall," he said. "I was told he was here with you."

The woman scowled. "Who told you that, his missus?"

"I need to speak to Tommy. It's urgent."

Still scowling, the woman stepped back into the van. "Wake up, love," she said. "There's someone to see you."

It had been five years since Paul had last seen Tommy. He was shocked at the transformation. Tommy's face was thin and gaunt with his bony torso protruded through his vest. His skin had an unhealthy pallor. Tommy wore his usual black eyepatch over his left eye.

"Who are you?" he said, scratching his head. "What's so urgent that it couldn't wait until morning?" He squinted at Paul. "Don't I know you? I've seen you somewhere before. Are you in one of my films?" Dorothy joined Tommy at the door, resting her elbow on his shoulder.

Paul shook his head. "No, I'm afraid not."

Tommy sighed. "Pity," he said. "I'm always looking for handsome studs. Isn't that right, Dorothy?"

Dorothy giggled. "Maybe I should audition him. Is that alright with you, Tommy?"

"I'm not here to audition for anything," Paul snapped. "Tommy, I need your help."

"What's up?"

"I need to know where you make your pawn movies."

Tommy scowled. "Why should I tell you that? Are you trying to muscle in?"

"No, of course I'm not, but a woman is being tortured in a room that you use in your films and it's being live screened. I have to find that room."

"Tortured you say? Is that part of the film?"

"No it isn't. It's for real. The man responsible will kill her if I don't find her first."

Tommy ran his tongue over his lips. "Put the kettle on, love," he said. He turned to Paul. "You'd better come in mate."

Paul followed Tommy into the caravan.

"I don't have much time," Paul said. "Tell me where the room is."

Tommy shrugged. "I use half a dozen locations around the city. Can you be more specific where this is happening? Can you describe what you saw?"

"There was a four-poster bed dressed in red velvet," Paul said. "I've seen that in a couple of your films."

"I'm sure you have. I use similar props in all of my films. Was there anything else?"

"The walls were painted white if that helps."

Tommy shook his head. "For fuck's sake it could be anywhere. There are rooms like that all over the city."

"Where exactly? Give me the address of all of them."

Tommy shrugged. "There's one place in Chapeltown that's used a lot, but I think some Chinese are using it this week."

"Chinese?"

"Oh yes. The Chinese like a bit of hanky-panky, just like the rest of us."

"What about the others? Where are they?"

"I use a big house in Beeston. Olivia, one of my top pawn stars lives there. She rents the house out when she's working away."

"Is she working away at the moment?"

"I've no idea. I can give her a ring and find out if you like."

"If you could, Tommy, I'd be grateful."

Tommy took out his mobile and rang a number. It was answered on the sixth ring. "Olivia, is that you love? It's Tommy here.... Sorry to bother you so early. I wanted to check if your house is being used by anyone at the moment.... Oh, by you? What are you up to?... Oh, you naughty girl. Have fun. Nighty night." Smirking, he turned to Paul. "You won't believe what Olivia's doing at this very moment."

"I really don't give a fuck. I take it her house is a no-no?"

"It certainly is. Now then, let me see. You could try the place behind the Merrion Centre."

"What sort of place is that?"

"Well, if I was a betting man, I would say that that is your best bet. A penthouse apartment with panoramic views of the city. It looks a real picture at night."

"This place has a four-poster and red drapes?"

"I've told you, they all do. Punters like to see that sort of thing. I've been in this business long enough to know that." He began to chuckle.

"Is there anywhere else you think a woman could be held captive?"

Tommy shrugged. "There's half a dozen rat holes where someone could be doing this." He walked over to his bureau and took out a small notebook. "There are two flats in Morley ran by a pimp called Alfie. Then there's a flat in Pudsey. Raymond, a bloke in his sixties lives there. He rents out his back room once or twice a month to top up his pension." Tommy began to snigger "A proper dirty little bastard is Raymond. He tries to hump the girl at the end of the movie. He thinks it's a perk."

"Anywhere else?" Paul asked. "Somewhere more… more secluded?"

"Let me think," Tommy said. "I suppose there's Amber House. It used to be an office block but it's been closed for a couple of years, a sign of the times I suppose. It's due for demolition next year."

"Where is this Amber House?"

"It's at Balby Quay by the canal. Richard, the caretaker makes a bit of extra cash by renting out one room on the top floor for porn videos. I've made a few films there, but to be honest, it's a bit of a shithole. I haven't used Amber House for the last couple of months."

"Thanks for your help," Paul said rushing to the door.

"Well good luck. I hope you find the bastard and that the girl's alright."

But Paul was already at his car, turning on the ignition.

82

Karl sat motionless, staring at the phone on his desk, willing it to ring but dreading it at the same time. He repeatedly clasped and unclasped his hands as he tried unsuccessfully to stop shaking. His office door flung open and Alex bounded into the room.

"What's happened to Mum?" he demanded, rushing towards Karl and placing his hands firmly on the edge of the desk. "Have you heard from her?"

"Alex, go home, I haven't time for this. I'll let you know when—"

"Something's happened to her. I know it has."

Before Karl could respond, his mobile rang. It was Paul. He quickly relayed to Karl what he had gleaned from Tommy Woodall.

"I'm on my way to the address behind the Merrion Centre," Paul said. "If there's no joy, I'll go over to Morley and check out the two flats there. I'll take Danny and Lenny with me."

"I'll go to Pudsey with Simon," Karl said.

"But I thought—"

"You thought what? That I'm going to sit on my arse and do nothing? If those bastards want a fight, I'll give them a fight they'll never forget."

"What about the next video?"

"I've decided I'm not playing their game, not anymore. The next time they send one through I'm going to hang up. That'll really fuck their plans, won't it?"

"Don't you think that's a dangerous ploy? What if—"

"They're getting their kicks out of making me squirm. Well guess what? I'm not squirming. Not anymore. From now on I'm on the attack."

"Okay boss, but I hope you know what you're doing."

Karl put down the phone. He opened a drawer in his desk and removing a knife, placed it in the inside pocket of his jacket.

"What the hell was that about? Who's trying to make you squirm? Tell me, Dad. I have a right to know."

Karl curled his lip. "Some bastards are holding your mother captive. They're threatening to kill her."

Alex gasped. "Who are these people, and why Mum? She wouldn't hurt a fly."

"To get at me, of course. Now if you want to help, stop yapping and come with me. We don't have much time. We'll pick Simon up on the way."

……

Paul and his two companions arrived at the impressive tower block behind the Merrion Centre which Tommy Woodall had identified as a possible venue. Not waiting for the lift, they raced up the four flights of stairs. Paul hammered on the door of the penthouse. The door was opened a few minutes later by a man in his thirties, dressed only in boxer shorts.

"Who are you?" he said, rubbing the sleep from his eyes, "and what the fuck do you want?"

Paul pushed past him, followed by Danny and Lenny.

"I'll check the rooms," Paul said, dashing to a door to his right.

The man rushed over the table and picked up his phone. "Get the fuck out of my house," he yelled, "or I'm calling the police."

Lenny strode over to him and grabbing the phone from his hand, roughly pushed him onto the couch. "We're looking for someone," he said. "If she's not here we'll be gone. No harm done. If she is… "

"No sign," Paul said after checking all three rooms. "Let's go."

"Sorry to have bothered you," Lenny said, handing the man his phone. "Nice place by the way." He laughed coarsely as he followed Paul and Danny down the stairs and out into the street.

"Where now?" Danny said, as their car sped away into the night along the A650.

"Morley. According to Tommy, there are two flats used for filming."

Lenny tutted, "And I thought Morley was so respectable. It just goes to show."

83

Karl's Mercedes pulled up outside the address supplied by Paul. Simon was in the front seat and Alex sat in the back.

Simon scowled disapprovingly. "Is this it? It doesn't look... well it doesn't look like it's the sort of place where porn happens, does it?"

Karl studied the building, an end-of-terrace two up, two down stone-clad house, with dark-brown plastic window frames and a purple door. The house was in darkness. He turned to Alex. "Stay in the car," he instructed.

"But Dad..."

"Do as I say. Stay in the car. I don't want you going in there."

Karl and Simon strode over to the house. Karl banged on the door. Silence. He banged again. This time a light came on in the front bedroom and the curtain was pulled slightly to the side and someone could be seen peering out. Karl looked up at the window as he banged on the door once more.

It was several minutes before the front door was unbolted and an elderly man wearing blue pyjamas came into view. He squinted at the three men standing on his doorstep.

"Can I help you?" he said.

Karl stepped past him into the small hallway.

"You must be Raymond?"

"Yes, that's right, but who are you and what do you want with me? You're not the police, are you?"

"Why would you think we're the police? What have you been up to, Raymond?"

"The room is only used once or twice a month," Raymond said, wringing his hands nervously. "It's just a bit of pin-money, that's all."

"Show me this room."

"It's through here." Raymond opened a door off the hall and turned on the light. It was a small room with gold-flocked wallpaper and a grey carpet. In the centre was a four-poster bed, draped in red silk with red silk bedding.

Karl scanned the room. "When was this last used?"

"Two days ago. Leroy, he's a regular, brought three girls."

Simon grinned. "As a matter of interest, how much did Leroy pay for using the room?"

"Two hundred."

"For an hour?"

"Nah, for the day. It's not much but it helps prop up my pension."

Karl strode towards the hall. "Come on, this isn't helping to find Lisa, is it?"

Karl was behind the wheel when his mobile rang. It was Paul. He listened intently as Paul told him both flats in Morley had drawn a blank. Karl sighed. "Okay. You take the lads and have a poke around in

Leeds. See what you can find. I'll go with Simon and Alex over to Amber House at Balby Quay."

Two minutes later his mobile rang again. This time it was Joe's number that appeared on the screen.

"Sorry, Joe. Can't talk right now. I've some urgent business to attend to."

"Okay, but just to let you know I've had the feelers out looking for Patrick. No joy I'm afraid."

"That bastard has grabbed Lisa. He's holding her somewhere and… Joe? Joe, are you there?" The phone went dead.

84

"Time to have more fun, I think," Patrick said as he put on his novelty mask and strode over to the bed. "Ring him," Patrick ordered. "It's time to bring this to an end."

"You're not really going to kill her though, are you Patrick?"

"What do you think?"

"I... I don't think I can do this. Fucking with Karl's head is one thing, but killing his wife... Why don't we just leave her here? I think Maddox got the message."

Patrick strode over to Luke and, still holding the knife, pushed him back against the wall. "I've told you what's going to happen. Are you going to help me or not?" He held the knife to Luke's throat.

Luke nodded weakly.

"Good. Now ring Maddox and let's start filming."

Luke sighed as he dialled Karl's number.

Karl's mobile gave out its shrill ring. Glancing at the screen, he saw the number was withheld. He pressed the green button accepting the call and the image of Lisa, prostrate, with her breasts bare, wearing only her panties, appeared on the screen. Patrick, still wearing his novelty mask, was sitting on the side of the bed. He began running the blade up and down the inside of her thighs before placing the point of the blade directly between her legs. Karl immediately switched off his mobile.

"He's hung up," Luke said. "The bastard has hung up."

The veins in Patrick's neck began to pulsate as sweat ran down his face. "Ring him back," he screamed. "He must witness what's going to happen."

Luke redialled. The call was rejected. His hands began to shake. "For fuck's sake, Patrick, just leave her. Let's get out of here whilst we still can."

Patrick ripped off his mask and threw it across the room. "If that's the way Maddox wants to play..." He bent down and picked up a plastic bag off the floor "This is Karl's fault," he whispered as he roughly placed the bag over Lisa's head. "He's to blame for this."

......

Amber House was in darkness when Karl's vehicle pulled up outside. Alex was first out of the car. Karl and Simon rushed to the door but it was locked.

"There's a broken window over there," Simon said. "We can get in that way."

All three men climbed through the broken window and raced up the stairs to the top floor. Karl and Simon turned on their torches and scanned their surroundings. It was a labyrinth of passages whose walls were covered in graffiti. It had doors on both sides, some hanging off their hinges.

"You two check down there," Karl said. "I'll go this way."

Karl made his way along the corridor, checking each of the empty rooms. He had reached the last room. Through the gloom he could see the silhouette of a man leaning over a four-poster bed cradling someone in his arms. Removing the knife from his jacket, he rushed towards the bed. He stopped abruptly.

"Joe? What the...?"

Joe gently lay Lisa back onto the bed, covering her nakedness with his coat. "I got here too late," he whispered. "She's gone, Karl. Lisa is dead."

Karl walked tentatively towards the bed. He saw the gaffer tape had been removed from her eyes and mouth and her wrists and ankles had been untied.

Karl stared at the body of his dead wife. "How... how did she die? What did those bastards do to her?"

Joe picked up the plastic bag from the floor. "This had been placed over her head. They suffocated her."

Karl pulled back the coat covering her body. He gasped as he saw there were dozens of stab wounds across her breasts and stomach, as well as her genitals and thighs.

"I think that was done after she died," Joe said. "There isn't much blood."

Karl reeled back in shock, steadying himself against the wall. He gently took Lisa's hand in his.

"I've called the cops." Joe said. "Do you want to be here when they come?"

"I'm not going anywhere."

Simon came rushing into the room. "There's nothing up there," he said. "I—"

"Get Alex out of here," he yelled. "He mustn't see his mother like this."

Alex approached the room. "You mustn't go in there, Alex," Simon said, steering him away from the open door. "Your mother is dead. There's nothing you can do for her."

"I'm a doctor, for fuck's sake. Let me see here. Maybe I can..."

Simon put his hand gently on Alex's shoulder. "I'll take you home. That's the best thing to do." He turned to Joe. "Stay with him. The cops shouldn't be long."

Joe nodded. He turned to Karl. "Come and sit over here mate," he said, attempting to steer him to the chair. Karl pushed him away.

"I'm not leaving her," he said, tears streamed down his face. He lifted her hand to his lips and gently kissed it. "I'll get the bastards, Lisa," he whispered. "I'll get the bastards. I give you my word."

85

Three days after Lisa's body had been found, Detective Inspector Calvert was sitting across from Karl in an interview room in Holbeck Police Station. Present in the room was Detective Sergeant Kate Burrows.

"I'm sorry about what happened to your wife," Calvert said. "You should have told the police straight away. Maybe… maybe we could have found her before..."

"I doubt it."

"It's a pity you and Joe Stevens messed with the crime scene. You do know you shouldn't touch anything, don't you?"

"We just gave her some dignity. She deserved that."

Calvert studied the document in front of him. "I understand from your statement you claim to know who was responsible for Lisa's death?"

"Patrick Flynn killed her," Karl said. "How many times do I have to tell you that?"

"But if he was wearing a mask like you claim when he sent you the videos, how can you be sure?"

"I'd know that Irish bastard anywhere." Karl got to his feet. "Flynn killed Lisa. If you can't get that into your thick skull, I'll deal with this myself."

"Sit down, Maddox," Calvert said firmly. "Tell me what you know about Patrick Flynn."

Karl flung himself back into the chair. "Flynn was involved with sex trafficking before he went into hiding. There are warrants for his arrest all over Europe, but surely this is all a matter of public record?"

"I understand Patrick had connections with Oscar Wright."

"I've no idea."

"You do know Oscar, don't you?"

Karl scowled. "He quoted for some surveillance equipment for the club but I didn't give him the job."

"Would it surprise you to know that Oscar was involved in illegal activities?"

"I wouldn't know. I hardly knew the man."

"What about Jeramiah Beauchamp? You're familiar with him?"

"You know I am. Jeramiah is my solicitor."

"And Roger Laverick?"

"Roger resold me The Emerald Club, but what the fuck has any of this got to do with my wife being murdered?"

Calvert shrugged. "We believe these men worked together in a criminal syndicate, and you know all of them."

"So what? I know lots of people."

"You're saying it's a mere coincidence? The thing is, Maddox, I don't like coincidences. To me it smells of conspiracy."

"You read too many books. Now, are we done? I have a funeral to arrange."

Christina was at the house when Karl returned from the police station. She ran to her father and flung her arms around his neck. "Dad, I've only just heard." She began to sob uncontrollably. "Why Mum? Who would do such a wicked thing?"

Karl guided her to the couch and sat next to her, holding her hand. "It was Patrick Flynn," he said.

"What? I... I thought he was hiding abroad somewhere. What's he doing in Leeds?"

"It's a long story, Chris."

"I should have been here. If I had been with Mum—"

"If you'd been here, Patrick would have taken you too. It's a good job you weren't."

"Do you think the police will catch him?"

"No I don't, but I will. One way or another."

Christina walked over to the drinks cabinet. "Fancy a whisky?" she asked as she began to pour a drink. "I know I do." She poured two large whiskies and brought them over to the couch. "What are you planning to do, Dad?" she asked, handing a glass to Karl.

Karl kissed her lightly on the top of her head. "I've got a few ideas," he said, "but these things take time. Time and planning."

"You will be careful, won't you? I couldn't bear it if anything happened to you too."

"Don't worry. I know what I'm doing."

Christina took a sip of her drink. "Did Alex tell you he's planning to go to Australia? Apparently Mum bought him a ticket."

"So I heard. Do you think he'll go?"

Christina shrugged. "He seemed determined when I spoke to him this morning."

"Well, let's hope it works out." Karl sipped his whisky. "And what about you, Chris? What are your plans?"

"I'm not going back to Matthew, I do know that. But apart from that, I'm not certain."

"What about Miles? I thought you two were close?"

Christina shrugged. "He's alright I suppose. He's been arrested, did you know? The police raided the cottage we were in in Scotland. It seems they'd been following him, It was really frightening, them bursting through the door like that. I think it's something to do with fraud."

"If you take my advice, which you never seem to do these days, you'll stay well away from that family."

Christina tutted. "I thought it was too good to be true, living in such a lovely house as West Top Manor. It's a pity though. I think I would have made a perfect lady of the manor." She smiled weakly. "What do you think, Dad?"

Karl got to his feet. "I think you're best out of it. Now, I'd better get over to The Emerald. We'll be opening up tonight."

"Already? I thought you'd close down for a week at least."

"The show must go on, Chris. The show must go on."

86

Inspector Calvert was sitting in a specially convened meeting of senior officers at Millgarth Police station. Detective Chief Superintendent Trulove was chairing the meeting.

"Two murders in as many weeks, Calvert," Trulove said. "Do you think they're connected, Inspector."

Frowning, Calvert shook his head. "No, sir. I don't."

"Really? Tell me about this Patrick Flynn character. I hear he's been identified in this Oscar Wright business."

"Yes, sir. An anonymous tip claims that Patrick and his gang are responsible for the thefts up and down the country based on information supplied by Oscar Wright's dodgy software. As a result of the information, we arrested four people attempting to steal a consignment of high-end motor vehicles. They are in custody now, but so far none of them have said a single word."

"And this anonymous tip also mentioned the distributor? The bloke that arranges to get the booty out of the country?"

"Roger Laverick."

"Have you arrested him?"

"No, sir. Not yet, but we will. I'm sure we will."

"Well let's hope so. You say Maddox is certain that Flynn killed his wife?"

"Yes, sir. He's provided photographs of Flynn's new identity." Calvert handed Trulove the photograph. "It seems he had cosmetic surgery performed in South America."

Trulove studied the photograph. "How did Maddox know about that I wonder?"

Calvert shrugged. "He seems to know a lot of what goes on. It's a pity he's bent. He'd have made a good copper."

"You don't think Maddox had any involvement in this operation?"

"There's no evidence to suggest he was. What we do know is there was bad blood between Maddox and Flynn going back a couple of years."

"So, you think Lisa Maddox was taken by Flynn to get back at Karl?"

"Yes, sir."

Trulove huffed. "It seems a bit far-fetched to me. What about the Beauchamp murder? Have you established a motive why someone would stab that young woman to death in her own home?"

"No, sir, we've drawn a complete blank on that. Gina Beauchamp didn't seem to have any enemies. The two young men she was involved with were interviewed, but both have alibi's for the time she was killed."

Trulove banged his fist on the table. "So you're no closer to finding the culprit now than you were the day the body was found. Is that what you're saying?"

"I have reason to believe that the murderer did enter the building that night. A couple of residents confirm that someone did enter as they were leaving. That would have been close to midnight. Unfortunately they were unable to give a description."

"And there were no fingerprints or DNA in the apartment?"

"No, sir. Either the culprit was lucky or he knew the ropes. There's no way of knowing."

"Well keep at it, Calvert. It doesn't look good when a solicitor is murdered in the city."

"Yes, sir."

"What about Jeramiah Beauchamp? Any luck in finding him?"

"He hasn't been to the office for a few days and his colleagues can't make contact, but we'll find him. He can't have gone far."

"Well make sure you do. This doesn't put the Force in a good light, Calvert."

"No, sir."

87

Karl was in his office when his phone rang. It was Danny.

"What's up, Danny?" he asked, "have you found anything?... When?... Keep your eyes peeled, mate. I'm on my way."

He dashed downstairs into the club. Simon was standing by the bar talking to the bartender.

"Si," Karl yelled. "Where's Paul?"

Simon walked over to Karl. "He's gone home. He wasn't feeling too good. I think what happened to Lisa has upset him more than he cares to admit."

Karl took out his phone and dialled Paul's number. The call went to voicemail.

Simon looked perplexed. "Anything I can do?"

"I need to get down to Felixstowe," Karl said. "Danny thinks Flynn is at the docks."

"I'll come with you. I'll round up a couple of the lads and—"

"There's no time for that. I have to go now." He took out his mobile. "I'll ring Joe. He'll want to be there."

Twenty minutes later, Karl's Mercedes was racing down the A63 towards Felixstowe. Inside were Karl, Simon, Joe and Lewis Cameron.

"Is your man sure it was Flynn he saw?" Lewis asked.

"Danny didn't see Flynn, but he did see Beauchamp scurrying along the dockside."

"Beauchamp? What the hell's he doing with Flynn?"

"Long story," Karl said, "but right now, Jeramiah Beauchamp is running for his life."

Joe frowned. "You say Laverick has arranged everything?"

Karl nodded. "That's what he does. He has more contacts at the docks than you've had hot dinners."

Lewis laced his fingers and took a deep breath. "Don't you think we should… I mean shouldn't we let the police know? After all, these men are dangerous."

"What the fuck are you doing here, Lewis?" Karl snarled. "If you want to get out I can stop the car now and you can walk home. That bastard killed my wife and I'm going to kill him."

"How… how did you know he'd be at Felixstowe?" Lewis asked.

Karl raised an eyebrow. "Maybe I'm psychic," he said, "or maybe I have an informant."

"An informant? Who?"

"Never mind. Felixstowe is freight only. I know from personal experience that there are fewer people about the dock to ask questions. Once he's in one of the containers he's on his way."

"But how—"

"For fuck's sake, Lewis, give it a rest. It's a long journey so try and get some kip."

"I'll take over driving at the next services," Joe said. "You look done in, Karl."

"Yeah, that would help. I haven't slept since… since I found Lisa."

88

Exhausted, Paul arrived at his flat at ten o'clock that evening. He was in the shower when the doorbell rang. Reaching out for his bathrobe, he walked along the hallway and opened the door. Deborah Wallace was standing in the corridor.

"Hi, Paul," she said, pushing past him. "Aren't you going to invite me in?"

Paul scowled. "What do you want? I thought we'd agreed to call this to a halt the other night?"

Debbie threw herself onto the couch. "But why? I don't understand. What did I do that was so wrong?"

"I don't have time for this. My mate's wife has been killed and I have things to attend to."

"I heard about that. It's terrible. How is Karl?"

"How do you think he is?"

"Does he know who's responsible?"

"That's none of your business."

"Did you know my boss has done a runner? The police are out looking for him."

"So I heard. Now, will you please go? I have things to do."

"I'm not going anywhere until you tell me what's the matter. I thought things were good between us. Is there someone else? Are you screwing another woman?"

"No, I'm not seeing anyone else. I just... I just don't want to see you anymore. Now, will you please leave?"

"But Paul, we were good together. You know we were."

Paul reached out and grabbed Debbie's arm, forcing her to her feet. "Leave now," he said. "I won't tell you again."

"Please, let's talk. I'm sure we can work things out."

"I don't think so. I know all about you blackmailing Oscar," Paul said.

"What?"

"You really are something. So sweet on the surface but underneath you're rotten to the core."

"You don't understand. Oscar was into stuff that was illegal. Him and Beauchamp."

"So you thought you'd have a slice of the cake too?"

"Why not? Do you know how much a legal secretary earns? Believe me, it's not much. Why shouldn't I have a share?"

Paul sneered. "You disgust me."

Debbie threw back her head. "You sound like that snooty bitch, Gina. She called me a parasite when I told her what I wanted. Can you believe it?"

"You are a parasite," he said, grabbing her arm and roughly steering her towards the door. "Now, get the fuck out of here before I call the police."

Paul reached over her to release the yale as Debbie turned sharply and thrust the knife she had been carrying deep into his chest, causing Paul to stagger backwards. He collapsed onto the floor. Debbie leant over him, knife in hand.

"I didn't want to hurt you, Paul. Truly I didn't. I was hoping you and I could... well, it doesn't look like that's going to happen now, does it?"

Paul moaned in pain as blood poured from the wound. "Get help, Deb," he pleaded. "Get help."

She crouched down next to him. "Tell me, how did you know about the blackmail?" Did Oscar tell you?"

"Deb, please. I..."

"I listened to the recordings. That's how I knew Gina kept records he didn't want anyone to see. Gina didn't leave the files in the office but took them back to her flat with her."

She poked the semi-conscious Paul with her foot. "Are you listening to this? I need you to know what happened."

Paul whimpered softly but lay still.

"I had a copy made of her apartment key. It wasn't difficult. She was always sending me back to her apartment to fetch stuff so one day I visited Timpson's on the high street. Then, one lunchtime I went to her place to see if I could find the files. I made a bit of a mess in the study so she knew someone had been there." Debbie walked over to the window and looked out onto the street. "It looks like we're in for more rain," she said. She strode over to the drinks cabinet and poured herself a vodka before returning to stand over Paul.

"Where was I?" she said. "Oh yes, that's when Miles put cameras all over her apartment. That really pissed me off. It meant I couldn't route around anymore."

Paul's breathing became shallow. "You... you killed Gina? But why?"

Debbie shrugged. "I stood outside her place in the freezing cold for hours that night. I'd seen Alex come charging out, then later a couple opened the door to leave and I pushed past them into the foyer. There was no-one about and I went straight up to her apartment."

She scowled at the unconscious Paul and roughly shook him by the shoulders. "Are you listening to this? You wanted to know why she was stabbed, well now I'm telling you."

Debbie stood up, took a sip of the vodka and began slowly pacing around the room. "Gina was halfway through a glass of wine when I arrived. The look on her face when she saw me standing in her lounge was priceless." She began to chuckle. "She screamed at me to get out and there was a bit of a scuffle, but to be honest, I think Gina had had more than one glass of wine that night. She didn't put up much of a fight."

Debbie walked over to the couch and sank into the cushions. "I told her I knew what she was up to and if she wanted me to keep quiet, it was going to cost her. Can you guess what she did then, Paul? She laughed. That's right. She laughed in my face and told me to fuck off."

Debbie got to her feet and sashayed over to where Paul was lying on the floor. She crouched down by his side once more. "I hadn't intended to kill her. You must believe that. After all, she was going to be the golden goose. But she became abusive, calling me horrible names. She said I was fired, the stupid cow. How dare she say that to me? Nobody rejects me, nobody. Not her and not you."

Debbie reached out and placed the back of her hand on Paul's forehead. "Oh, you do feel clammy," she said. "I really think you should see a doctor."

Paul gave a low guttural groan. His eyes flickered for a brief second as life finally drained from his body.

89

Karl pulled up at the side of the dock. Several MSC container ships were moored in a line. Taking out his phone, he rang Lenny.

"I see you," Danny said. "You need to be at the other end of the line. I saw Beauchamp going into there about two hours ago. The ship's bound for Holland."

"Thanks, mate. I'll see you soon,"

"Don't worry, Karl. Everything's ready."

Karl turned on the ignition and began to move slowly forward towards the ship marked 'MMX.' He hadn't gone more than fifty yards when two security guards blocked his path.

"No unauthorised personnel beyond this point," said the younger of the two men. "You must turn around now."

The second man was short and plump with black curly hair, wearing steel-framed spectacles. "What are you doing here?" he said.

Karl got out of the vehicle and approached the second man. "I'm looking for my friends," he said. "Roger Laverick said—"

"Oh, Laverick? You're a friend of Roger?"

"He said to meet him here, but the traffic… well, I don't need to tell you."

The man nodded his understanding as he walked over to the Mercedes. "How many of you?

Roger didn't say there would be anyone else doing the crossing."

"Well, I didn't know if I'd be able to make it," Karl said. "Cops were everywhere."

"It's going to cost more. You do know that?"

"No problem, mate," he said, as going to the boot of the car he took out two iron bars. He handed one to Joe, keeping one for himself. He took out a wad of cash from his pocket and handed it to the security guard. "There are two of us travelling. I'm sure you can squeeze us in."

Snatching the money, the guard looked around him nervously.

"Why the iron bars?"

Karl winked. "Security, mate. I don't want any nosy copper over in Holland getting close."

The man grinned. "Don't worry. Laverick's got it off to a fine tea. There'll be no trouble, but you'll have to be quick. The ship sails in fifteen minutes."

......

Inside the blue and black painted container it was cold and dusty. Dozens of wooden crates were piled high at the back. Jeremiah Beauchamp sat on the floor in one corner clutching his laptop. His head was bowed.

"Cheer up, Beauchamp," Patrick said. "It won't be long now before you're lounging in the sun with all that lovely money." He laughed coarsely.

Luke walked over to Beauchamp and squatted down in front of him. “Have you decided where you’re going once we land?”

Beauchamp lifted his head. “I’d like to go to Spain. Costa-del-Sol has beautiful weather all year round.”

Luke huffed. “Sure it does. That’s why half the criminals in the world go there. It’s also the first place the police will go looking.”

Beauchamp huffed. “I... I wouldn’t know. I’ve never been on the run before.”

“Take my advice,” Luke said. “Find a country which doesn’t have an extradition treaty with the UK. It’s the only way to stay safe.”

Sitting on the floor and stretching out his legs, Roger Laverick lit a cigarette.

Patrick rushed towards him, snatching the cigarette from his hand and stamping on it. “For fuck’s sake, put that out.”

Laverick got to his feet standing menacingly in front of Patrick. “Who the hell do you think you are?” he said, poking him in the chest. “If I want to smoke, I’ll smoke. It’s nothing to do with you.”

Patrick pushed Laverick back against the container wall and raised his fist. “It’s dusty enough in here,” he snarled, “without that shit filling the air.”

Laverick writhed free of his grasp. “Don’t you forget who’s getting you out of here,” he said, moving to the opposite end of the vessel. “If it wasn’t for me, you’d have the cops up your arse.” He laughed coarsely. "Even that new mug of yours can't save you now, Patrick. They know exactly what you look like."

Luke stood up. "What I don't understand is how the cops know about your new identity. Who told them?"

"It's obvious, isn't it?"

"Is it?"

"It must have been Oscar, or that son of his, but they won't get away with it."

Beauchamp raised an eyebrow. "What… what do you mean?"

A malicious grin crept over Patrick's face. "That fancy house of his, the one he's so proud of, it'll be a mound of ashes by tomorrow morning."

Beauchamp slowly shook his head. "You're wrong about Oscar. He wouldn't do that."

"Of course he did," Patrick said. "Who else could it have been?"

"What about Maddox? Maybe he found out and—"

"Maddox didn't have a clue I was back in England, let alone what I looked like." He laughed coarsely. "He knows now though."

Beauchamp raised an eyebrow. "What… what do you mean by that? How does he know?"

"Well, let's just say I made the acquaintance of his missus."

Luke smirked. "And very tasty she was too."

Beauchamp gasped. "Oh God. You didn't hurt her, did you? Please say you didn't hurt her."

Luke came over and steered Beauchamp over to the corner of the vessel. "Sit down," he said. "What's done is done."

"I don't like this," Beauchamp said. "I don't like this one little bit." He rushed over to the container door. "Let me out. I've changed my mind. I don't want to go abroad. I'll take my chances with the law."

Patrick grabbed him by the arms and spun him round. "You're going nowhere," he snarled, "not until you sort the money out."

"I can do that anywhere."

"You'll do it in our presence. Now, let's all sit down and be quiet. We'll be on our way any minute."

90

The engines began to fire up.

"Here we go," Luke said. "Next stop Rotterdam."

Suddenly the door of the container slid open and Karl and Joe rushed into the vessel, each brandishing an iron bar. Luke was first to his feet and charged towards them, fists flaying. "What the..."

Joe sidestepped and brought the iron bar crashing down onto his shoulder. Luke screamed in pain as he collapsed onto the floor. Joe continued to wield the metal bar down on Luke's body as he struggled unsuccessfully to get to his feet.

At the same time, Patrick sprinted towards Karl, screaming obscenities. Karl dodged to the side before bringing his iron bar down on Patrick's neck, causing him to fall to his knees struggling for breath. Karl reigned more blows about his head and body until Patrick lay prostrate on the floor of the container, barely conscious.

Laverick and Beauchamp huddled together at the far side of the vessel. Beauchamp was visibly shaking with terror.

Laverick tentatively took a step forward. "Karl, mate," he said, "there's no need for this. I had nothing to do with what those two were up to. They were working on their own. You've got to believe me."

Legs planted apart; Karl held the iron bar firmly in his hand. "Why should I believe you? My wife is dead, murdered, and I think you were complicit."

"No, no, that's not true. I knew nothing about what they were up to until a few minutes ago."

"That's right," Beauchamp said. "I never hurt anyone. I'm not a violent man. You know that Karl."

Karl scowled. "And what about you, Laverick? Are you a violent man?"

"I'm a fixer, you know that. I arrange stuff, that's all."

"Like getting stolen goods out of the country?"

"Yeah, that's right. People too. I helped you. Remember?"

Karl was silent for a moment. "That's right, you did. That's why I'm not going to kill you."

"You mean I can go?"

"That's not what I said."

Karl sat on one of the boxes, his hands clasped. "You're going to finish your journey to Holland, but the police will be waiting for you when you get there." He turned to Beauchamp. "You too, Jeramiah," he said. "A long prison sentence for both of you I would imagine."

"But Karl, we have money. Lots of money. We can give you a large share. You'll be made for life."

"You can have my share," Beauchamp said. "All of it."

Karl smirked. "Oh, I know I can. In fact every penny you all squirrelled away is now safely in my accounts."

Laverick scowled. "What do you mean? You can't have done that. It's impossible."

"But I have. Everybody's cash has gone. Even Oscar's."

"Karl, we'd better hurry up," Joe said. "They're starting to come round."

Karl turned to Laverick. "Both of you sit over there. When the police come you say nothing about them," indicating Patrick and Luke, "or about me and Joe being here. Understand?"

"What... what are you going to do with them?" Beauchamp asked.

"Nothing that concerns you."

Karl held the semi-conscious Patrick beneath the arms and dragged him through the open door. Joe did the same with Luke. The narrow deck was deserted as they held their foe against the ship's rail.

"Wake up, Patrick," Karl said, slapping his face. "Time to go for a swim."

Patrick's eyes flickered open. Realising what was about to happen, he began violently thrashing about to break free from Karl's hold, but the pain from his broken shoulder was overwhelming. He opened his mouth to speak, but Karl brought back his fist and punched him in the mouth.

"This is for Lisa," Karl hissed.

"Let's get this over," Paul said. "I think we're far enough out now."

Karl looked down at the black water of the North Sea. He leant Patrick over the rail, then kicked his feet from underneath him. The splash as he hit the water could barely be heard against the noise of the ship's engine. Karl watched as Patrick's head bobbed above the water for a few seconds before being swallowed up by the sea.

Joe laughed as he pushed Luke over the rail. "That's a good end to bad rubbish," he said. "We'd better hurry up and get ready. Danny will be here any moment." Both men ran along the deck to a small unit containing life jackets. They quickly donned one each, just as a small boat pulled up alongside the ship.

"Hurry up," Danny shouted. "Jump."

Karl and Joe climbed over the rail and jumped into the black icy water. Danny leant over the side of the boat and hauled them both on board.

"I'm fucking freezing," Karl said through chattering teeth.

Danny grinned. "Don't be such a wuss. There's a couple of blankets over there, and I brought a bottle of whisky. I thought you might need it."

Joe reached out for the blankets, handing one to Karl. "Well, that's that," he said. "Job well done I think."

Karl reached out his hand. "Thanks Joe. I couldn't have done it without you, mate."

Joe shook Karl's hand. "I keep telling you, I'm not your mate. Not anymore."

Karl shrugged. "Suit yourself," he said, putting the whisky bottle to his lips. "It's a pity Paul couldn't join us. He'll be gutted when he hears what he's missed."

91

Detective Inspector Calvert and Sergeant Burrows were in the interview room sat across from Deborah Walsh. Also present was Amanda Bruce, the duty solicitor.

"Let me get this straight, Ms Walsh," Calvert said.

"Debbie, please."

"Very well, Debbie. Are you confessing to being responsible for Gina Beauchamp's death as well as that of Paul Borowicz? Remember you are still under caution."

Deborah flung her head back. "Of course I killed them. How many more times?"

"But why? I don't understand why you would do that."

"They both pissed me off, that's why. Nobody says no to me," she said. "Nobody." She crossed her arms across her chest and stared intensely at Calvert. "Now, that's all I have to say. I did it and I'm not sorry."

……

Calvert and Burrows were in the canteen later that afternoon having a late lunch.

"Do you think she's mad?" Burrows asked. "Killing two people for no real reason. Then just walking into the station like that and confessing. I think she's mad."

"That will be for the court to decide," Calvert said. "She's been charged with double murder."

"It's been a pretty good week for clear-ups, boss. Oscar and Miles Wright, Jeramiah Beauchamp and Roger Laverick all in custody, as well as a double murderer. I wouldn't be surprised if there isn't a commendation coming your way."

Calvert huffed. "It's a pity Patrick Flynn and his mate got away. There was no sign of them when the ship docked in Rotterdam."

Calvert sighed. "Patrick was a slippery bastard by all accounts. They'll probably be abroad somewhere. Let's hope they stay there."

"How did Oscar take the news about his house burning down?"

"I think going ballistic would be an understatement. It's a pity though. It would probably have been seized as proceeds of crime. When our IT blokes finally tracked down his overseas accounts, and that of the others, there wasn't a single penny."

"Where do you think all the money went?"

Calvert shrugged. "Who knows? Maybe there's a member of the gang we don't know about and they moved it."

"Maybe," Burrows said. "Oh by the way, sir, you'll never guess what James has done."

"James?"

"My friend, James Moore."

"Do tell."

"He's getting married. He met a girl at The Emerald a couple of weeks ago, and they're got married as soon as they can. Isn't that great?"

Calvert grinned. "He's marrying a stripper that he met just two weeks ago? I always said he wasn't very bright. I rest my case."

92

It was the day after the funeral of Lisa and Paul. Karl was in a melancholy mood, drinking his way down the whisky bottle in his office at The Emerald. Simon was sat across the desk.

"What's the next move, boss?" he asked. "Will The Emerald's doors ever open again?"

Karl sank back into his chair. "I don't give a fuck about the club," he said. "Everybody's gone. Lisa, Paul, even Alex is going to Australia next week."

"I'm still here," Simon said, "and there's Christina. She wants to help."

Tears welled in Karl's eyes as he reached for a cigar. "Thanks, Si, but—"

The office door burst opened and Joe Stevens entered the room. "I need a word," he said, "in private."

Simon got to his feet, nodded a greeting to Joe and strode over to the door. "I'll be downstairs, boss," he said, closing the door.

Karl looked up. "I didn't get the chance to thank you properly the other night for helping me get rid of those two lowlifes," he said. "You did a great job. It was like old times." He smiled weakly. "Joe, this is difficult for me, but I need to apologise for what I did to you. I shouldn't have doubted your loyalty. I'm sorry."

"Sorry? You stabbed me. You tried to kill me. If it hadn't been for that paramedic in the pub that night I'd be dead."

"Well you're not. I'm sorry for what I did, so now can we please move on?"

"That's what I've come to see you about," he said. "Moving on."

"Eh?"

"I want us to go into partnership. An equal partnership. Everything cut right down the middle."

"You want half The Emerald?"

"That's right. Half The Emerald and half the cash you took from Oscar and his mates."

Karl huffed. "You've got to be kidding."

"You can't run this place on your own. You know you can't."

"I've got Simon."

"Simon's great at managing day-to-day stuff, but you know the situation, Karl. There's too many firms wanting to take over the business. You won't be safe on your own."

"So what exactly are you proposing?"

"I'll take over security, the same as Paul did, but I'll have a more active role to play in the club itself. Who knows? We could start looking at a second club in the future and build up the business again."

"Why the sudden change of heart?"

Joe shrugged. "Maybe I enjoyed the other night on the boat more than I should. I miss the action."

"What does Sarah think to you working with me again? She can't be happy."

"Don't worry about Sarah. She'll do as I ask."

"And Charlotte?"

"She's getting married and moving to the Caribbean with Lewis. I doubt I'll see much of her."

Karl drummed his fingers on the desk. "You'll help with organising the escort agency? I've got big plans for moving forward."

Joe nodded. "Sure. I've done it before."

"This time it's going to be bigger and better. Are you up for that?"

"We're wasting time," Joe said. "Get the contract drawn up, money transferred to my account, and we can start right away."

Karl slowly stroked his chin. "This is all happening quickly," he said. "Maybe we should step back and—"

Joe got to his feet. "If you're stalling you can forget it. I want this deal done today or I'm out."

"Okay, slow down. I'm erring on the side of caution, that's all."

"The question is simple, Karl. Do you want me as a partner or not?"

Karl inhaled, then got to his feet, arm outstretched. "Welcome on board, partner. Welcome to The Emerald."

Paul frowned. "I think we should look at changing the name of the club. If we're going to have a new business, we need a new name."

"What do you suggest?"

"How about The Pheonix?"

Karl grinned, "Rising from the ashes?"

"Exactly."

Karl poured two whiskies and handed one to Joe. “Or perhaps The Emerald Pheonix?”

“The Emerald Pheonix it is,” Joe said, raising his glass.

About the Author

Eva Carmichael followed her dream to live by the sea when, along with her husband and miniature schnauzer, she moved from the heart of West Yorkshire to live in Redcar in 2016.

Eva comes from a legal background, working first as a shorthand typist for the West Yorkshire Police and then as a Special Constable. More recently, Eva worked as a legal PA in Leeds.

Although she has always enjoyed writing fiction, it wasn't until she came to live in Redcar that Eva took her writing seriously. She became a member of the U3A in Saltburn and joined the novel writing group in Guisborough, where she was encouraged to pursue her dream of writing a crime novel.

Eva's first crime novel, 'Bad Blood Rising' was published towards the end of 2019, and she has had a book published every year since.

In 2024, Eva was delighted to have her own website, giving readers a flavour of her work.

www.evacarmichaelauthor.com

EVA CARMICHAEL'S BOOKS

BAD BLOOD RISING

A NORTHERN CITY… MONEY… GIRS… CRIME… MURDER… AND BAD MEN. AN EXCITING ROMP THROUGH THE CRIMINAL UNDERWORLD…

When a young prostitute is murdered by her pimp, Karl Maddox, he thinks the terrible secret she had threatened to expose is buried with her.

But when the murdered prostitute's daughter arrives in Leeds eighteen years later, she is seeking answers.

Slowly but surely, Karl's life as the wealthy, powerful kingpin of his clubland empire begins to unravel as loyalty is replaced by treachery, and friendship is replaced by hatred.

Is Karl about to find out that no secret can remain buried forever?

AN EXCITING ROMP THROUGH THE CRIMINAL UNDERWORLD

……

MORE BAD BLOOD

MORE MURDER... MORE GIRLS... MORE BAD MEN

A thrilling gritty novel which delves into the seedy underbelly of the sex trade in the North of England.

Karl Maddox is content with his lot as kingpin of the sex industry. His beautiful, estranged wife is now back in his life, along with his son and daughter. However, when one of his escorts dies after stealing a briefcase from a client, Karl finds himself caught up in the sinister and dangerous world of sex trafficking.

When danger knocks directly on his door, Karl needs every ounce of his ingenuity to keep those close to him safe. However, the real danger is much closer than he realises. A danger which threatens everything he holds dear.

A THRILLING, GRITTY NOVEL WHICH DELVES INTO THE SEEDY UNDERBELLY OF THE SEX TRADE IN THE NORTH OF ENGLAND

....

LET THERE BE BLOOD

BETRAYAL… VIOLENCE… BAD MEN

Filled with drama, violence and betrayal, life has never given Karl Maddox an easy ride, but with several attempts made on his life, things move to a new and frightening level.

The pressure builds when Karl learns an investigation is being undertaken into events in his past – events he thought had been buried forever.

With his back to the wall, Karl is at his most dangerous as he begins to retaliate in the only way he knows how.

THE SEX INDUSTRY CAN BE A DANGEROUS PLACE, ESPECIALLY WHEN YOU DON'T KNOW YOUR ENEMY

……

A TWISTED MIND

When a young girl goes missing from a crowded each, Detective Inspector Andy Bainbridge of Cleveland Police, is put in charge of the case. Despite endless enquiries, no trace of the child is found, and it is assumed she has been swept out to sea.

Sixteen years later, when a number of young women go missing from the same resort, Bainbridge is horrified to realise that their disappearance, and that of the young girl years earlier, are connected.

Bainbridge comes up against the worst type of evil – the pure evil of a twisted mind.

....

FRENZY

Newly promoted, Inspector Jack Mason arrives in Redcar with his beautiful young wife, Annika, to take up his role with the Cleveland Police, under the supervision of Detective Chief Superintendent Andy Bainbridge.

Mason is soon dealing with his first ever murder, that of an elderly man, savagely beaten, soon to be followed by a second murder. The injuries to both victims are so similar they convince the police the same killer is responsible. With no witnesses to the attacks, and little forensic evidence, Bainbridge suspects the person responsible for both murders is a local villain. But a third body, viciously stabbed and mutilated, leads Bainbridge to conclude a second killer is at large.

A killer more violent and more dangerous than anyone he has come across in his long and distinguished career. As Bainbridge and Mason's investigations continue, more chilling facts come to light, as both men come face-to-face with their frenzied adversary.

....

MADDOX

When Karl Maddox eventually returns to England, he hopes his past dramas are behind him and he can enjoy a comfortable life. But as always, trouble follows Karl like night follows day. He soon becomes embroiled in an audacious and illegal scheme to make money, which takes every ounce of his cunning and ingenuity to survive.

Karl soon finds himself playing 'cat and mouse' with an adversary from his past and is convinced he has the upper hand. However, he underestimates how wicked and contriving his enemy can be with catastrophic consequences.

Seeking revenge, Karl is at his most dangerous as he pursues his enemies with deadly consequences.

....

Printed in Great Britain
by Amazon

46827043R00195